KRIS KENWAY

Kris Kenway's work has appeared in *The Face*, *Dazed & Confused*, and the *Time Out Book of New Writing*. Born in Bristol in 1972, he spent several years working in the film industry in London, before moving to Los Angeles to study screenwriting at UCLA. His previous novel, the critically acclaimed *Too Small for Basketball*, is also published by Sceptre.

www.kriskenway.com

KRIS KENWAY

Bliss Street

SCEPTRE

Copyright © 2003 by Kris Kenway

First published in Great Britain in 2003 by Hodder and Stoughton
A division of Hodder Headline

A Sceptre paperback

10 9 8 7 6 5 4 3 2 1

A CIP catalogue record for this title is
available from the British Library.

ISBN 0 340 79274 4

Typeset in Sabon by
Palimpsest Book Production Limited,
Polmont, Stirlingshire

Printed and bound in Great Britain by
Mackays of Chatham Ltd, Chatham, Kent

Hodder and Stoughton
A division of Hodder Headline
338 Euston Road
London NW1 3BH

For Suha

01

'Happy 2000' was written in fairy lights above the door. The little bulbs fizzed in the rain and James looked at them suspiciously, wondering whether they were about to explode. His suit was damp, and the drizzle was seeping through to his skin. He ran a hand through his tangled hair and decided he would look more professional in glasses. He double-checked he had the right name: Mr S. Connelly – another emergency to which James had been dispatched like an SAS man, armed with a string of Nokias and accessories. He knocked on the door.

'Sell him everything,' James quietly repeated to himself while he waited for an answer. '*Everything*.'

The door flew open to reveal a stocky, middle-aged man who thrust out his hand and declared, 'I'm Simon Connelly.'

'James Hamlyn.'

They shook hands as James quickly analysed his new customer's clothes: jeans, open-neck shirt, Timberland boots. Older man trying to be young. Mid to late forties. Probably likes Sheryl Crow. Wants to be a cool dad. He was giving himself away so easily.

'Thanks so much for coming over – do you always work on holidays?' Connelly asked, beckoning for James to enter the house. As James followed him inside, he worked out their age difference, probably twenty years, and adjusted his pitch accordingly.

'Not normally,' he replied. 'But I got your message and I know how frustrating it can be.' *Make the customer know you feel their pain.*

'We had a little office problem.'

'What happened?' James asked.

'A temp decided to help himself to four of my reps' phones.'

'Oh dear.' James arranged his face in a way that suggested his dog had just died.

'I called the police.'

'Good idea.'

'They weren't that interested.'

'That's disgusting.' James's dog had died, *then* someone had stolen the body.

'I thought so.'

'So . . . you need to reload,' James said, clicking his tongue twice so Connelly could almost visualise the gun. As they made their way through the hall, James continued to throw images of jungle warfare at him, and he swallowed them, quickly crowning himself as the commander-in-chief of his office. *Make him feel he is important.*

The Christmas decorations in the living room looked a little tired. As they entered, a young girl, perhaps sixteen years old, slipped out, squeezing past them. She wore a tight T-shirt with 'babe' written over her chest in silver sequins.

'My daughter, Samantha,' Connelly explained as they watched her jump into a waiting car full of equally young

Friday-nighters dressed in Camden Market clothes. James clocked it: daughters need phones too. He would get to that in a moment.

Ten minutes and one glass of brandy later, Connelly had bought new handsets for his entire staff.

'It's like giving them a bonus,' James explained, pretending to wrap up the day's business, before adding, 'So, your daughter is off to a party? That's nice.'

'Her friend is having a *do*.' Connelly wobbled his head when he said 'do', as if it was something he didn't understand.

'A lot of parents feel safer when they know their kids have a way of getting in touch,' James said. This was it. The *line*. James managed to conceal the disgust that rose within him as he said this; he was becoming very good at not showing how much he hated his job, how much he hated himself for being so damn good at selling. That morning his boss had said, 'You were born to do this,' before announcing that – as their most productive employee – he was being sent to the Dubai Shopping Festival. As if the compliment hadn't hurt James enough, he was sick of being sent abroad every month, standing in malls, in hotel conference centres, pretending he was in his late forties and that he really cared about mobile phones; pretending he had never had other ambitions and, above all, pretending that his earlier, happier life as a successful director of music videos had been only an illusion. For each sale to be successful, he had to forget it all over again. It felt like chewing lemons, then having to swallow them, only to be force-fed even more the next day.

Connelly paused, absorbing James's comment, but then shot back with, 'Oh, she has a phone card.'

James had expected a retort like this. Connelly was putting up a wall, but James knew he could break through it. 'Good idea,' he said.

'There's *no* need for a sixteen-year-old to have a mobile.' Connelly laughed to make his position clear.

'You are so right,' James agreed. 'And so open minded.' Connelly liked that. James continued, 'It's great to let kids just do what they like, isn't it? A phone card is perfect. All she has to do is walk to a phone box. I mean, they're on most streets, aren't they? You see them everywhere in Soho. She can just zip straight into one of those and make that call. Some of them are even lit up at night, aren't they? When it's dark outside.'

'Yes.' Connelly sounded hesitant.

'She can just pop off down the road by herself and give you a call to say everything is okay.' James added some weight to 'herself', but not too much. Just enough to set it apart from the rest of the sentence.

'Er . . .'

'That's the thing with teenagers, they're so independent, aren't they?' There were times, when he was in full sales-man mode, when James didn't recognise his own voice; he didn't recognise his accent or even the clothes he found himself wearing. Music had always been the love of his life, but now his head, tormented night and day by ring tones, was empty of beautiful sounds and rhythms. He pulled himself together; he would finish this job with Connelly and go home and let something from Cuba ease out of his new Mission speakers and soothe his eardrums.

'Teenagers *are* independent,' Connelly agreed.

'And you don't want to cramp their style.'

'You know what they're like at that age.'

James could sense the tide turning. 'Of course, with a text message, she'd only have to write "I'm okay" or "Back at ten".'

'Usually ten-thirty at weekends,' Connelly corrected.

'That's the beauty of it. It's all your choice, isn't it? You decide the time and the terms, but you always know you have that all-important . . . I don't want to say *lifeline*, but you know what I mean.'

Connelly nodded sombrely as James continued, deliberately softening his voice so that the other man would have to lean towards him.

'I remember when I was a kid and I decided to camp outside in the garden. I had a walkie-talkie with a long cord that went into the house. It was this old thing, a toy walkie-talkie, but I could just beep if I was scared. At *night*. When I was *alone*. I know it gave me a lot of comfort, although of course kids of all ages are too proud to admit that, aren't they?' James laughed, paused for two beats, then said, 'How old is Samantha?'

Connelly looked as if he might cry.

An hour later, the deal complete, James leaned against his car, resting his head in his arms on the roof. He was breathing hard, and he felt as if he was going to be sick. A shiver went through his body, and there was an unpleasant taste in his mouth. He was reacting this way more and more often.

Fran wasn't there when he got home, so he slumped in a chair and looked at his ticket to Dubai. Eventually, he pulled himself up to check the brand-new hi-tech answering machine that he had bought that week, to see if she had left a message saying she was going to be late. No messages. James hated these machines.

The history of the new answering machine was the recent history of his relationship with Fran. A year earlier, on the actual day he was fired from his directing job – and that was fired *on* the film set, *in front of everyone* – he had headed straight home. When Fran didn't ask why he was back so early, he said simply, 'I just lost my job.' To which she replied, without missing a beat, 'Our answering machine is broken.' The answering machine then stayed in that state for twelve months, a full year in which James learned to sell Nokias and Ericssons, phoned video production companies who wouldn't touch him, and watched his old career disappear. Neither James nor Fran cared enough to fix it. During this year-of-no-answerphone, James worked sixteen hours a day and drove over a thousand miles a week to claw his way back to solvency. And when he finally got there and reached the goal he had set himself, he felt more empty than when he had started. After paying rent and tax, he spent most of what was left of his salesman-of-the-year bonus on a new answering machine. That was two days ago, and when Fran had first seen it, she had said, 'Oh, do you like that colour?'

Neither of them had yet learned to work it.

Fran burst through the door, shaking the rain off her coat. Her hair was in a ponytail, and a few thin strands had come loose. Although he thought she looked sexy with raindrops running down her face, their journey interrupted by her heart-shaped lips, James suddenly felt the need to stand up to formally greet her. She had always used to sit in his lap and tell him about her day; today she just smiled a greeting.

'Did you call?' James asked.

'No, I didn't. Why?'

'It's just because the answering machine is . . . I can't work it and I wondered . . . never mind.'

'I had a drink with Sarah. She's having a birthday thing first week in February.'

'I'm going to Dubai then.'

'Why?'

'For the scuba diving.'

'What?'

'What do you mean "why"? The same reason I go everywhere.'

'Haven't you just come back from there?'

'No, that was . . . somewhere else.' James realised that he couldn't even distinguish between countries now.

'Can't you change it?' Fran couldn't mask the irritation in her voice.

'Not if I want to keep my job.'

Fran disappeared into the bathroom, and James could hear the shower start up. He couldn't comprehend her attitude. He was working so hard, doing all that travelling for *them*; he wanted her to understand. He wandered into the bathroom, watching her behind the distressed fake glass. He could just make out her outline. He thought how attractive Fran was, and how she seemed less so now that she wasn't affectionate towards him. He wondered whether she felt the same way about him. He had kept himself fit, going to the gym with people from his company; he hadn't had a haircut for a while, but Fran liked it slightly longer. There had been a couple of moments over the past few months when he'd had the chance to launch himself into affairs. He hadn't pursued them, but had still felt awful at the time for allowing the *idea* of them to make him feel better. Things had been different twelve months ago – James had been on a huge upswing, his career on a never-ending ascent, becoming *the* director of choice for new bands, and Fran had been his partner in everything. Their video collection was peppered with his triumphs and failures with various musicians, some established, others looking to break through, but all of them paying him, all of them making him believe he was doing something worthwhile.

James moved closer to the glass so he could watch Fran wash her hair. This action had mesmerised him when they had first got together. He tried to remember the last time he would have been able to jump in the shower with her, and for her to let out a pretend shriek before kissing him.

The shower door opened.

'What are you doing?' she asked accusingly, grabbing the towel for cover.

'I don't know,' James said to himself quietly, shutting the bathroom door behind him as he walked out.

When Fran emerged ten minutes later she said, 'You know I have that work thing tonight.'

As James drove them to the restaurant – the kind with cluttered walls and waiters in matador outfits – he looked over at her. She was preoccupied with reprogramming her mobile phone, a freebie he had wangled for her. Despite his expertise at reading people's facial tics and expressions for the sake of a sale, he was completely lost with Fran. He tried to work out whether she was punching at those numbers like a woman who was being unfaithful; he carefully followed the journey her bottle of water took to her lips and wondered whether that was the sipping action of a woman who kissed someone else's lips on the nights he worked late. But he was sure no one actually had affairs when their partners were working late. They had them when their partners were pregnant or had lost a parent or were about to move house.

James had been feeling anxious since their pre-Christmas holiday in France. They were both still smarting from it. Fran's friends would ask about it tonight, and the couple would put on a show and say how wonderful it had been, ignoring the haze that had set over their relationship, the stream of awkward moments, followed by lulls of silence. But Fran's eyes *had* lit up when James had surprised her with tickets to Paris, and he had hoped the trip would clear the haze. He had been sure that if they planned to do different things during the day they would meet up in the evening having missed each other. They would probably be the first couple to go to Paris and not walk around hand in hand, but so what? James thought. Relationships needed little shots of tonic after a long winter, and they would meet for dinner full of interesting experiences and anecdotes. On the first day – as James got lost in off-the-map areas of Paris in search of early Slick Rick records (rare, pre-jail vinyl) and Fran visited galleries (rare, pre-Cubist Picasso) – they were unified in only one thing: the resentment each felt at the other for being so unoffended by the idea of voluntary separation.

They spent the following day as a proper couple. Conversation was stilted, but hands were held. James's reaction to this was to make small talk, Fran's was to go silent. She also made sure she always had a book with her, reading at every opportunity, and so they sat in Parisian cafés, James watching people go by, Fran with her head in a novel. James tried to take her on at her own game, buying a book to counter her coldness towards him. He had no idea why he was buying novels in French since he managed to translate only every third or fourth sentence, but he was pleased with what he was *saying*, which was 'I would rather read a book I don't understand than talk to you'. At least, that was what he hoped it said. Maybe it said 'I'm so stupid I haven't even realised this book isn't written in English'. But the competition had started, and it continued at cafés by the Louvre, in Bastille, and in Montmartre. James would buy a thicker book, then the next day he would notice Fran with an even thicker one. This unspoken competition finished when, on their last day, Fran brought out Vikram Seth's *A Suitable Boy* while they waited for their train at the Gare du Nord and finally won the competition, signalling that, on the scale of troubled relationships, theirs was not a novella of 'maybe we can work at it' but a great multi-generational epic of 'we need help'.

On the train back to Waterloo James watched Fran doze off in the seat next to him, her head resting gently on his shoulder. For a few seconds, as France rushed past the window, it had given him some hope.

The beeping of Fran's phone was starting to annoy James. He turned up the CD player to try to drown it out. Fran shot him a look.

'What?' James demanded.

'This has games on it.' She often didn't bother to answer questions that didn't interest her.

'What's the matter?'

'Nothing. I just said you can play games on this phone.'

'Fran.'

'What?'

'You're in a weird mood.'

'I just hate the start of a new year,' she said.

'Me too.'

'Why are you wearing a suit? You never used to wear suits when we went out. This is a casual thing tonight.'

James shrugged. Fran sighed, and looked like she was about to say something else. Instead she leaned over, touched James's leg with her open palm.

'I love you,' James said. His voice sounded different, empty.

'You don't need to keep saying it.'

'Why're you being like this?'

'Like what?'

James tried to think of a way to tell her she was brittle, but couldn't construct a sentence that would avoid causing offence. Pulling away from a red light, he took a right and started rummaging in the glove compartment for a different CD. He was in second and accelerating as he searched through the junk. The revs increased until the car was at the point where lack of an immediate gear change risked engine explosion. James pushed the clutch down, waiting for Fran to put it in third. She always changed gear for him. But not this time. He looked up from the glove compartment to see her still frowning at her mobile phone as if it had insulted her. She caught him out of the corner of her eye.

'What?'

'Think you could change gear?'

When Fran didn't do anything, James gave up on his search. '*Jesus*,' he said. By this time, fumbling for the gear stick, he was in the middle of the road. Fran let out a scream as she saw the large Mercedes coming straight towards them. James swerved hard, knocking the wing mirror off a parked car, but avoiding the Mercedes. He slammed the brakes on and came to a screeching halt.

'*Shit*,' James said. 'You okay?'

'No, I'm not okay. What the fuck were you doing?'

'What is it with Mercedes? Do they own the road or something?' James said, twisting around and looking out of the back window. The Merc was long gone.

'You could have got us killed,' Fran said, with icy calm. James preferred her when she was shouting.

'Whose side are you on?'

'Just watch where you're going.'

'Watch where *I'm* going? Are you incapable of changing gear for me?'

Fran let out a long sigh. 'Let's just get to the restaurant.'

James nodded. He drove for a couple of minutes then said, 'I didn't mean to frighten you.'

'It's okay,' she replied with such precision he could get no hint of meaning from it.

They arrived at the party late. As they entered, James said, 'Why do we only go out with your successful friends?'

'Why do you always call them my successful friends?'

James shrugged.

'Well, you never see your video mates any more,' she said, as they merged with the group who, even in the way they held their drinks, seemed to mock James. He watched the roaming drinks girl with shot glasses attached to her belt as she met the alcohol requirements of the drunk, swaying men who clung to the walls like moss.

They had been seated at their table for at least one course when James turned to his left to have a conversation. The person to his left was Fran.

'I think we're in a hole,' he whispered.

'We don't have to stay long.'

'No, I don't mean tonight. I mean us.'

'I can't hear you,' Fran said, as a chart hit started pumping out of the large speakers attached to the ceiling. To James's right was one of Fran's work colleagues. He couldn't remember her name so he commented on the variety of colours in her cocktail.

'Are you still doing those videos?' she said, turning slightly to face him. 'I saw one of yours on MTV the other day.'

'Not so much any more,' James replied. He knew he was wincing.

'Oh, really? What are you doing now?'

'Business. Sales. I'm in sales.'

'Of what?'

'Communications.'

'That's . . . interesting.'

'Yeah,' James said. 'I get to travel a lot. Greece *and* Mexico back in November.'

'Do you get to see the countries at all?'

'I've developed a way of dealing with it,' James said, frowning to show seriousness. 'You can make almost every place the same if you plan well and put in the effort. You can go there and back without touching the sides.'

Fran drifted from her conversation about tech stocks and tuned into what was being said behind her. She continued to smile at the person she was talking to, and made the occasional comment about the Nasdaq, but her entire focus was on listening to this stranger, behind her. She felt the shock that comes when you watch a person you know change into someone completely different. She had to look round to check that it really *was* James speaking. It was. He was even talking in an unfamiliar accent, using expressions that were not Jamesisms, but the words of some jaded figure she didn't know.

'You know you can get a massage on some flights now?' James said to the cocktail girl, who was losing interest fast.

Fran, now struggling to maintain her smile, also tuned out and returned to her stock price conversation.

Later, when the plates had been cleared but the drinks were still coming, James looked over at Fran. She was wearing the pendant he had bought for her birthday two months ago. The first night she had worn it, one of the pendant's tiny stones had been lost outside the flat. He remembered how the two of them had spent the evening searching for something but never finding it. The difference now, James realised, was that neither of them was even bothering to look. Around the table, success dressed in casual clothes continued to chat happily. James's suit was itchy and uncomfortable. He finished his drink then left the restaurant by himself, withdrawing from the group unnoticed.

02

Maya's eyebrows were naturally arched in such a suggestive way that her mother used to brush them down when she was a child. It wasn't *decent*. Now in her twenties, Maya Hayek didn't light up a room when she entered, she detonated it. She was aware of her beauty, but never understood the obsession it caused. And not just among men. Women, it seemed – those women with eligible sons, that is – also lost their minds when they saw her. The hundred-metre future-mother-in-law dash took place at least once a week. Maya could be walking down the street quite happily when she would hear a woman shouting. She would turn around to see a middle-aged lady running after her, panting, yelling, and verging on an asthma attack. When the woman reached Maya, she would grab her hand, check for a ring, then announce that she *must* meet her son. *It was meant to be.*

'You will live like a queen,' the mother-suitor would say. And all Maya was doing was going out to buy a Coke. She was getting better at outrunning these women. But who could blame them? Finding a woman like that for their darling sons. They would boast to Maya about their precious boy's grade point average, which buildings he owned, which buildings *she* could soon own.

Then Maya would break free, and continue down the street alone.

Maya held a cup of coffee, an Amin Maalouf paperback, a cigarette and the steering wheel as she drove. She was like Devi, the beautiful multi-armed Hindu goddess, and the cockpit of her dusty old two-door was a whirlwind that never stopped. The juggling act wasn't interrupted by her constant commentary on other people's driving; she sighed '*Ya Allah*' when someone cut in front of her, or waved her hands, directing traffic, '*Yalla, yalla!* Let's go!', from inside her car at Beirut's four-way anarchy-sections. All this while singing backing vocals to Khaled on the radio. She would get through a whole chapter of her book, four cigarettes, one cup of coffee and three calls on her mobile phone on the journey to work and back. If anyone told her that reading while driving was dangerous, she replied as a Beirut taxi-driver would when told to wear a seat belt: 'Twenty years' war!' followed by a shrug. Taxi-drivers used the same argument for not stopping at red lights; it was only a few years ago that stopping on red gave a sniper a good shot.

Maya had something else in common with the taxi-drivers – she often worked at more than one job. Her last one had ended because her boss had licked her neck while she was typing. When she hadn't come in the next day he had phoned and yelled at her, saying she risked being fired. He didn't mention the incident. On the other end of the scale from the neck-lickers were the 'I am like your brother' co-workers who only wanted to help. They wanted to help a lot less when they realised she wasn't going to sleep with them. Maya knew that weird office politics went on everywhere, but she longed to be somewhere where there were laws against neck-licking; where she could go to work and people would understand she was there to *work*, not to find a husband. In an envelope on her passenger seat was her route out: an application to study for an MBA. She had downloaded it from a university website that morning and would fill it in later. But every time she worked on an application for a US or European college it was completed half-heartedly, because she was always ninety per cent short of what she needed for her fees. She could never decide whether it would be worse to be rejected outright or to be accepted but not have the money to go.

Maya swerved around a motorist who was reversing the wrong way up a one-way street, finished her coffee, crumpled the tiny plastic cup, and pulled up to her house in Ashrafieh. The exterior had the faded glamour that characterised many of the Florence-style villas of east Beirut, its centrepiece a once-grand balcony, just waiting for Vivien Leigh to stand on it and weep.

'*Shu*, Maya. What time do you call this? It's not *decent*,' Mrs Hayek scolded her daughter.

'*Khalas*, Mama,' Maya said dismissively as she flew through the door and into her room.

Mrs Hayek changed her line of attack. 'I was worried, they were bombing!'

'I wasn't hanging out at any power stations, don't worry,' Maya shouted from her room. She switched on her computer and checked her e-mail, her nightly ritual before poring over her company's numbers and trying to find a way to cut overheads.

To: MayaHayek@qserv.net
From: Maroun@mfaasolutions.com

Dear Mayoush,

I want to say thanks for the dinner what we had last time. On the other hand, I have to say I never met someone I felt is so close to the heart as you. Shame that you had to left so early. Ma'lesh, once I forgot also a cousin's weddings (lol). Maybe next time I return back we can had dinner another time. Sorry, I want to write for you in Arabic, but my computer has not this option.

Personal Best Regards,

Maroun F. Abu Abdullah

NB. Tell to your mother and father that I say hello very much.

Maya deleted the message instantly and forgot it just as quickly. She'd had dinner with Maroun months ago. He worked in engineering, one of the Big Three: medicine, engineering, law. He *was* very eligible. Maya switched over to her Office program and started work.

Maya's mother had been through a tough afternoon. Mrs Jihad, her next-door neighbour, was revelling in her own daughter's recent engagement. And she wasn't just engaged to anyone, but to a rich Lebanese lawyer! From a good family! Mrs Hayek tried not to grind her teeth when she spoke to Mrs Jihad; she managed to maintain her natural elegance in almost all areas of her life, apart from where her daughter and her plump neighbour were concerned.

For her part, Mrs Jihad envied Mrs Hayek, a beautiful woman who didn't cheat on her husband even though he wasn't even in the country! What made her so special? It was almost, she reflected angrily, as if Mrs Hayek thought she was better than her!

Mrs Jihad had arrived in the early afternoon with a tray of coffee and the bowl in which Mrs Hayek had given her some *mujadra* – a rice and lentil dish – the week before. The bowl had been courteously refilled and returned with one of Mrs Jihad's home-made specials. Mrs Hayek thanked her, and then asked whether she had enjoyed the *mujadra*.

'It was so good it stayed in the fridge for a week,' Mrs Jihad replied, then tempered her line with 'We were fighting over it'.

Mrs Hayek didn't respond.

'I'll only stay a minute,' Mrs Jihad added, picking up a picture of Maya from the mantelpiece. 'She is so pretty, and she's finished her education. She's not missing anything. We hope to see her married soon.'

'God willing,' Mrs Hayek replied. It was part brush-off, part silent prayer that Maya would settle down. Mrs Hayek still held an enviable success rate – her other daughters, Maya being the youngest of the three, had both married and moved away, one to Canada, the other to the Gulf. But as she heard the words *she's not missing anything* come from Mrs Jihad's mouth, she was reminded of an advert for cheese which was playing non-stop on television. An interfering aunt corners her nephew while they eat lunch, asking him why he isn't married. After all, she says, he isn't missing anything.

'Would you like some cheese?' Mrs Hayek asked, then realised her mind had wandered.

Mrs Jihad wasn't interested in cheese. She was weighing up more important things. 'Maya *is* attractive, but it's not good to be big headed.'

'Well, she doesn't have to marry the first man who shows some interest,' Mrs Hayek countered, pointedly looking at the picture of Mrs Jihad's newly engaged daughter which had been brought over with the coffee.

'*Haram*, it's not good for a girl to be single. Maybe the problem is she doesn't fix herself?' Mrs Jihad offered, noting Maya's subtle, minimalist approach to make-up. Mrs Jihad favoured, particularly on a single girl, thick waves of blue eyeshadow, *ktir* eyeliner, and a dark contour line that traced the edge of the lipstick, making the mouth look enormous.

Maya had natural looks, so even without airbrushed make-up people talked more, *suspected* more. If she was attractive there was no reason for her not to be married. Unless she was 'loose'. And what was wrong with the family? they asked. Couldn't they keep her under control?

'She's not home yet?' Mrs Jihad asked, her voice rising. She had been sitting there for hours.

'Oh, I think I heard your husband come back,' Mrs Hayek said, ignoring the question.

'You're so open minded. So *brave* not to worry. I'm such a worrier, I'd never let my daughter go out, but that's my problem.' Mrs Jihad sighed.

'I heard she's out *quite* a lot.'

'She goes to the library on Friday and Saturday nights. That is all.' Mrs Jihad nodded as if to seal her sentence as an irrefutable fact.

'Which library?' Mrs Hayek switched from defence to offence.

'The one in Jounieh.'

'There is no library in Jounieh. Just nightclubs.' Mrs Hayek could taste victory now, however small.

The whole street was engaged in this cold war of information transfer and double-crossing. They were secret agents keeping each other up to date with who was doing what wrong, while never knowing when they themselves might be under surveillance. The myriad affairs that simmered beneath the surface, the little lies that people told one another, and all the joys and faults that made up the lives of men and women all over the world were kept nicely under wraps. Keep up appearances was the unwritten rule. Keep up with the Jihads.

Mrs Hayek felt a double responsibility for her daughter, because her husband Najib spent so much time away from home. Maya's father was a doctor. Not just any doctor, he was a cardiologist working on revolutionary treatments for coronary heart disease. The obsession with doctors in Lebanon had caused a surplus, a doctor mountain, and many of them were forced to go to the Gulf to find work. There was no one to mend the roads in Lebanon, but there were plenty of people who could do a triple bypass. The only doctors who stayed and grew rich in Lebanon were plastic surgeons.

Najib Hayek worked in Abu Dhabi, and continually threatened to move the whole family out there. Mrs Hayek resisted – she had retired from fashion designing, but now ran a boutique that she didn't want to give up. And besides, all her family were in Lebanon. While this impasse remained, Najib communicated daily with her via telephone, and she kept him updated on the quest to find their last daughter a husband. Mrs Hayek knew her husband would have liked at least one boy, and now she wished his prayer had been answered: worrying about three daughters had been a life's work already.

'Maya is quite a lot older than my daughter, isn't she?' Mrs Jihad said.

'She's *two months* older.'

As Mrs Jihad launched into a new monologue, Mrs Hayek heard a beautiful sound. But even the low grumble of Mr Jihad's car as he pulled up outside didn't stop his wife from continuing her story of how she had beaten Catch 14 – a name she had learned only that morning from a neighbour but now repeated constantly – to her first choice of wedding venue. The million-selling group – four haircuts from somewhere in Ireland – would have to find somewhere else to play.

But it really *was* Mr Jihad this time, and Mrs Hayek could see him through the window as he climbed out of his car. Perhaps wifely duties would finally take her neighbour away, she hoped. Mrs Jihad calmly noted her husband's arrival, opened the Hayeks' front door and screamed at her Sri Lankan maid. 'Dilki! Whisky for sir. *Yalla!*'

Mr Jihad, after a long day at work, would be served his evening tipple by the maid. Dilki never mixed the whisky properly, but she hadn't been with them for very long and she would learn. The last maid had run away, so this time Mrs Jihad had been sure to take out insurance. Insuring maids against escape was as easy as finding a second-hand car or renting an apartment, and Mrs Jihad had located a suitable company from the back page of the newspaper.

Mrs Jihad closed the door and turned back to Mrs Hayek, who had taken the time-out to think about her trump card, but then decided not to play it yet. She had arranged for a suitor to arrive on Saturday, and she was so excited about it she had kept it a secret from Maya, who would only come up with an excuse to be out.

Two more coffees later, Mrs Jihad finally returned to her house to find her husband asleep in his favourite chair, and Dilki clearing up. The sound of dish-washing woke Mr Jihad up.

'How are you, *habibte*? Did you have a good day?' he asked, bleary eyed.

'So tiring,' Mrs Jihad simpered. 'I've been so busy.'

'My heart. You should take it easy, let Dilki do the work.'

'No, *habibi*, I must struggle on.'

'How is the new kitchen?'

'The designer came over today.' Mrs Jihad perked up. 'He thinks it will be a *long* job.'

'Don't worry,' Mr Jihad said, leaning forward and

watching Dilki wash the floor. 'You will have your per-fect kitchen.' He hoped this would mean his wife might finally start cooking for him. He was bored with Sri Lankan food and was starting to dream about *hummus* and *fattoosh* salad.

Dilki listened in to the conversation from the half-finished kitchen, and wondered whether Mr Jihad knew *why* it was taking so long to finish the remodelling job. Mrs Jihad had made the early and incorrect assumption that Dilki was stupid. 'The *Sirilankieh*, she doesn't understand anything, they have small brains, you know,' Mrs Jihad would tell anyone who asked. For Dilki's part, the only thing she *didn't* understand was why Mrs Jihad said and did anything she liked around her, presuming her maid, like a very young child, was unable to comprehend anything of the world around her. But Dilki knew it all; she knew that Mrs Jihad's conferences with the designer were becoming more and more frequent, and were based mostly in the bedroom.

Maya came out of her room and made herself a cup of coffee in the kitchen, putting the papers from her car down on the table.

'What are these?' Mrs Hayek asked.

'Been speaking to the serpent next door?' Maya said, looking at the photograph of Mrs Jihad's daughter that she had left behind. Every house on the street, all of east Beirut, now owned a commemorative picture of Mrs Jihad's daughter. If Mrs Jihad knew Maya was planning on leaving, on going abroad to study, she wouldn't sleep for a week from excitement. What would happen to her outside Lebanon? What terrible habits would she pick up? How would anyone want to marry her then? That kind of gossip would keep Mrs Jihad going for years. It would probably prolong her life.

'Don't be rude. What are these papers?' Mrs Hayek demanded.

'Nothing.'

'Are you applying for college again?'

'Don't start.'

'You already have a degree.'

'I want another one.'

'Why? *Why* do you make life difficult for yourself? You have such a pretty face.'

Maya considered this sentence for a minute, but she was unable to find a reply that satisfied her. She sipped her coffee, and eventually said, 'An MBA lasts longer than a pretty face.'

Everything in Maya's life would be better if she were married. Mrs Hayek was convinced of this. She had lost count of how many lovely men she had brought round to the house. Maya had not lost count, and suitor number twenty-four dutifully arrived for lunch on Saturday, armed with his parents. He was in his late thirties, owned two houses in Toronto, and was a respected businessman. He came from a good family which owned five buildings in Beirut.

Suitor Twenty-four sat with his father and mother on the couch as Mrs Hayek ran around the house in a fluster. She had cooked everything she knew how to cook. All at once. She and Maya would be eating left-overs for the next two weeks. The dining-room table was full of *mezze*: swirls of *hummus* with olive oil and chickpeas resting on top of the paste, *tabouleh* salad for which Mrs Hayek had spent hours chopping up parsley that morning. After the main course, a rice dish with nuts, they would have *baklava* for pudding, with its sugary syrup that melted in the mouth.

Maya looked at Suitor Twenty-four and wondered why a nearly forty-year-old man needed his mother to find him a bride. She knew the answer; she just didn't find it particularly attractive in a grown man. His mother had met Mrs Hayek at a wedding and they had quickly realised they had common interests. Now the hero was back from Canada, it was a perfect occasion for them to meet.

Maya excused herself and followed her mother into the kitchen.

'He's nice, isn't he?' Mrs Hayek was brimming with excitement.

'He's a foot shorter than me and owns a biscuit factory. What do I have in common with him?'

'*Ma'lesh*, who cares?' Mrs Hayek sang, still gripped by the euphoria.

When lunch was finished, and Suitor Twenty-four's elderly father had come to the reluctant conclusion that Maya hadn't been sufficiently enthusiastic, he pulled Mrs Hayek to one side. 'I know what the problem is,' he whispered. 'But please, tell her, we can sign something over to her before marriage.' He paused for a moment, so Mrs Hayek could take in this sweetener. 'To show good intentions,' he added. The 'something' turned out to be a building worth over ten million dollars. No matter how many times Maya saw this ritual, and she had seen it many, *many* times, she was always impressed by what great business it was. She had watched many of her friends become involved in similar transactions while looking for a husband – it didn't seem to matter what religion they were. It could have been videotaped and shown in a workshop on how to conduct business over lunch. *How to Get What You Want, Part 1.*

'You will live like a queen,' Twenty-four's mother announced in Maya's direction. Mrs Hayek looked completely won over – perhaps *she* wanted to marry him, or maybe it was the thought of all those biscuits. Either way, he was a Lebanese man who had made it in North America. That would stick a cork in Mrs Jihad's mouth for good.

'You don't like Canada? It is not a frightening place if you are with a man,' Twenty-four's mother soothed.

'I want to go to America,' Maya replied.

One by one, smiles shot around the room, building like a Mexican wave; if she would go to America, their smiles seemed to reason, then *surely* she would happily move to Canada.

'But to study,' Maya added. The smiles drooped.

'This is just silliness, she'll grow out of it,' Twenty-four's father whispered loudly to Mrs Hayek.

Suitor Twenty-four went back to Toronto without his bride, but he would return to Lebanon to continue his search soon. He certainly couldn't marry a Western girl. God knows she wouldn't be wife material! He hadn't got around to telling his Canadian girlfriend this just yet, and telling his parents about his Canadian girlfriend had just slipped his mind. The only thing that was certain was that a Western girl would just be trouble: for a start she wouldn't be a virgin – a good girl, a family girl. He presumed, as everyone would, that Maya fitted that description. Maya knew all about the requirements for good girls, and although only she knew she wasn't the angel she was being touted as, she played the game to perfection when she had to. No one suspected a thing. If she had been interested in Suitor Twenty-four and it came out that she'd had a boyfriend, the potential in-laws would probably turn a blind eye if it meant acquiring a beautiful Lebanese bride. But she wasn't interested, and he went back to his biscuit factory.

When Maya came back from work the following night, her mother was hovering around again. Maya just wanted to finish some work she had brought home then go to bed, but this time she didn't make it to her bedroom.

'Maya, we have guests this weekend.' Mrs Hayek sang the words in a weak attempt to take the sting out of them.

'I'm busy this weekend.'

'Maya! You'll give me heart disease if you keep on like this! Do you want your mother on medication? Your father is never here.'

'Well, he's in Abu Dhabi, it's not like he's in the pub.'

'You know what I mean! I have all this work to do.' Mrs Hayek quickly moved some dishes around as if to demonstrate.

'You mean finding me a husband.'

'Maya, dear. Why don't you fix yourself,' she said,

closely examining her daughter's face. 'How will you attract a man wearing no lipstick?' Mrs Hayek knew that *attracting* suitors was never any trouble for Maya, it was getting Maya to meet them that was so difficult, but she found that, after yet another long afternoon of Mrs Jihad, the words of her interfering neighbour had infected her and started coming out of her own mouth.

Maya shrugged, then opened the fridge and fished around until she found a pot of *labneh* and started making herself something to eat. She needed energy if this was going to continue. Mrs Hayek watched as Maya casually made herself a sandwich, adding slices of cucumber to the soft cheese, before rolling the flat bread around it and taking a bite. When she had finished her first mouthful, she said with some satisfaction, 'Apparently Roman prostitutes wore lipstick to show they would perform oral sex.'

Mrs Hayek's eyes widened. 'You see! This is what happens when you read! I don't know what to do with you!'

'Don't do anything!' Maya shouted back.

'You'll drive me back to Dr Karami, I swear. He understands. I will be on anti-depressants until you find a husband.'

For once, Maya didn't reply. Suddenly the room was filled with silence, a miasma that Maya was supposed to disperse with her retort. Even her mother looked shocked, an actor watching her co-star forget her next line. She waited for someone to prompt her daughter back into action, but now Maya was close to giving up and giving in. Every day it was Bollywood in their kitchen. All the melodrama, but none of the singing.

03

'I think you can drink in Dubai if you're not a Paki,' Michael said, leaning over James with mini-bar breath. Institutionalised racism was always being referred to in all the newspapers, but they never mentioned generalised racism: from Morocco to Bangladesh, over five thousand miles, one slur fitted all for Michael. James kept his eyes closed, hoping his fellow salesman would go away, but he could feel him staring. When James opened his eyes he was horrified to find Michael actually sitting in the free seat next to him, slurping down a miniature bottle of gin.

'This bloke I met at check-in said that his hotel is really cool. Maybe we should go there instead. What do you think?' Michael had been told he would accompany James on the trip only two days before and he was going to make the most of it.

'I don't think it's a good idea.'

'He said we could share a minibus to the hotel with him.'

'Okay, listen to me, Michael. Here is how it works: business class out and back. Only take a taxi with air-conditioning on arrival – it's worth the wait if there isn't one there straight away. No minibuses, no special offers and no good ideas. Stay at a Hilton or a Marriott. If someone recommends a great local hotel, avoid it. Don't be fooled. You don't know what you're getting and that's when it gets dangerous. I have dinner and two sleeping pills at ten p.m. and I'll be awake and free from jet lag the next morning – I'll have the chicken, please.' James glanced up at the flight attendant as she prepared to pass him his dinner.

'If you do all that you won't have any fun.'

'I'm not here for fun. I'm here to get it over with as soon as possible,' James said.

'Get what over with? This trip?'

'Just . . . everything.' James looked at his food, then back at Michael. 'I'm going to sleep. I'll see you there.'

James closed his eyes.

'Shopping Festival?' James obviously wasn't going to get any peace – it was the price he paid for having a free seat next to him. But it wasn't Michael's voice this time, so he decided it was safe to open his eyes. The owner of the voice was in his late thirties, and his young son was sitting on his lap.

'Phones.' James waved a brochure at him.

'Adel.'

'James.'

'You don't like it?'

'What, my name?'

'Phones.'

'No. No, I don't like it.'

Adel was from Egypt, and had been educated in Britain. His son slept peacefully on his lap and Adel soon dozed as well, the perfect person to have sitting next to you on an aircraft. James flicked to the promotional channel which showed off the wonders of the Gulf countries with a mixture of stallions, eagles, hi-tech hotels and jet skis. When he over-shot the music channel he paused for a moment – he could barely stand watching videos these days – but decided to flick back. The video playing showed a singer sitting in the back of a taxi; as it drove along the shot didn't change, but the people in the taxi did, fading in and out of each other – a woman with her child, an elderly couple kissing, a woman on her own, her head in her hands – always coming back to the singer. He sang in Arabic, occasionally switching into French, in a richly textured voice that effortlessly conveyed emotion to James in a way that made dictionaries and translations redundant. He found himself missing his old job.

'He's from Africa, like me,' Adel said, opening one eye. He had his headphones on, although they were bent at a strange angle because he had being leaning on them. His screen was set to the same station.

'He's Egyptian?'

'Algerian. He says . . .' Adel listened for a moment, working out the translation. '. . . *it's the night that is taking me farther from you, it's the night that's stronger than me.*'

An hour later James was still glued to the screen. Adel had slept for a while but was woken up by the flight attendants serving drinks in the cabin. He started watching James watching the videos.

'Are you okay?' Adel asked.

'Yeah,' James said, snapping out of it.

'Do you sing?'

'Me? No. Do you?'

'I play *al-Oud*.' Adel thought for a moment. 'The lute,' he translated.

'I'm not musical. I used to make these kinds of things.' James pointed to the monitor.

'But you prefer selling phones?'

'No, I don't prefer it.'

One year earlier, at around five in the morning, James was typing a message into his mobile phone. He pressed 'send' and one came whistling back almost immediately. *It's tooooo early. Luv u*, wrote Fran. She always replied to his pre-dawn text messages with good nature. James had woken up as usual at 3 a.m. Fran had reached a hand over to him, which he kissed then placed carefully back by her side, like a gun going back into its holster. She had smiled in her half-sleep. Now he was away from her and on the set, he tried to visualise her alone in bed without his body next to hers, but he could only see their bodies together.

James walked over to Kitty, who was standing by herself. Kitty had what it took to be a pop sensation in James's mind, and he was a good judge. She wasn't the first teenage fledgling star he had introduced to the world on celluloid. Or video, in her low-budget case. He knew she was going to get there, and she was going to get there as fast as possible with Bobby Del Pico. Del Pico, whose real name was Robert Daniel Pickford, wore a baseball cap pulled low, his greying hair sticking out of the sides like wings. When he had arrived that morning, he had informed

James that he was 'packin''. Why he might need a gun for a video shoot was beyond James, but he was too tired to question it. Despite his raspy east London voice, Del Pico didn't look threatening enough to pack a lunch. What he *could* do was make or break careers with one phone call. Del Pico had been James's chief employer since he had climbed the ranks to big-name acts, and had hand-picked him to direct Kitty's debut. Despite his shortcomings as a human being, Del Pico was undoubtedly a good producer. James accepted the job and dreamed that soon he would be in LA directing videos that looked as though they had been made in a kind of sunshine only several million dollars could create; videos that had been polished and buffed until you could see your face in them, until you found yourself buying a record that you never even knew you liked.

All around James, crew members were packing up equipment ready to move to the next location. It was still barely light. James had already completed the opening shot: Kitty walking through Chinatown at dawn, the lights on the pagoda twinkling against the red brick, a mysterious figure sauntering away from the camera who turns, reveals her face, and *bam*! It's Kitty's introduction to the world. James had leapt into the air when Pete, his cinematographer, had given him the *we've nailed it* look. The crew laughed at James jumping around, at his manic energy, but it spurred them on. They fed off it. The only hiccup had been a lorry driver refusing to get his truck out of shot. The assistant director had told him he could be in the video if he moved it ten feet, so the driver obliged, the AD positioning him well out of shot, assuring him he would be heavy rotation on MTV by the end of the week.

James watched Kitty shiver. She stood by a small white van with its hatch door up; large metal containers with tea and coffee were arranged on the counter along with spilt milk and boulders of solidified sugar. The van looked as if it had been used as a getaway vehicle in another life – its panels were dented, scraped and battered. James caught his reflection in the van's wing mirror. On shooting days his routine was: hit alarm button, get out of bed, avoid mirror. His hair told that story, styled by a pillow on one side only. But there was something satisfying about going to work looking like an *Ill Communication*-era Beastie Boy, baggy and trainered and full of energy. James's eyes were always on duty, and they sparkled with ideas and life.

The man serving the tea was unshaven with *Van drivers do it on the North Circular* written on his baseball cap. He asked Kitty whether she wanted anything else. She shook her head and pulled her thick coat tightly around herself, then caught James out of the corner of her eye, and marched off in the opposite direction.

When James caught up with her, she turned and remarked, 'Nice shoes,' as if he wasn't worthy of them.

'Oh, thanks,' he replied, not sure whether to be pleased.

'Vans?'

'Emerica.'

'Cool.'

'It's cold, isn't it?' James offered, trying to lift the conversation above one-word questions and answers.

'Well, that's January,' Kitty replied.

James tried something else. 'So, do you have a boy-friend?'

'Not interested.'

'Don't like boys?'

'I mean I'm not interested in going out with you,' she said.

'No, I'm not asking you out. I'm—'

'What?'

'I have a girlfriend,' James said.

'That's nice.'

'She used to work for a big multinational, but they stole millions of pounds.'

'She stole millions of pounds?'

'Her boss did. Now she works somewhere else.'

Kitty managed a little smile. 'I'm seeing this guy at the moment, but you know, it's hard when you're working so much.'

James nodded in agreement with the seventeen-year-old.

Kitty's voice softened to a whisper. 'Can you tell Bobby something?'

'Of course.'

'Tell him if he does one more of his "Oh, I didn't know you were changing" entrances into my trailer, I'm calling the police.'

'Wanna lift?' Del Pico hawked, his head hanging out of the window of his BMW.

'I'll walk,' James replied. He couldn't sit still long enough to get in a car, so he marched to the dance studio, reading his shot list and making notes as he went. A production runner approached him clutching handfuls of paper, a question on his lips. Before he could say anything James stopped him.

'Is that a coffee stain on my storyboards . . . ?' He took them out of the runner's hands. He had spent a week of nights drawing them up.

'Er . . . yeah,' the runner answered.

James sighed, grabbed the boards and strode into the studio, where he then spent a frustrating hour babysitting Kitty, trying to communicate what he wanted – or rather what Del Pico wanted and James *had* to deliver. Her response was mostly blank stares. Del Pico was already angry that they had dropped a shot that morning, but James had persuaded him it was better to go back later and get it, even if it entailed greater expense. Del Pico had let that one go grudgingly.

Kitty got into position. James crouched down to talk to her. 'You're looking down to sing the first line, then I want you to slowly open your eyes and look up at the camera. We get a nice movement on your eyelashes, you're looking *through* them.'

Blank.

James looked at Pete for help. Pete shrugged.

Del Pico butted in. 'Why doesn't she sing it lying on her back? She could wear that tight top and wiggle—'

James stopped Del Pico as he outlined imaginary female curves with his hands. 'We're fine.'

'What am I doing, then?' Kitty whined, flapping her arms in exasperation, like the wings of a contraption in *Wacky Races*.

'The lights are great on your face,' Pete said on auto-pilot. A few words from the man behind the camera always worked, and Kitty got into position. It made sense to James: people listened to cinematographers because they were experts in something. No one knew what a director did. And as for producers – their job description was even more vague, but James knew that it should *not* include harassing the new under-eighteen pop sensation.

'Playback!' the AD called, and Kitty's song boomed from the speakers. It sounded like Minnie Mouse trying to articulate love as Kitty, looking down, sang her first two lines. James willed her on: *Going well so far.* Then she perkily looked up at the camera as if someone had just offered her an ice cream.

'Shit!' James blurted out.

'Cut!' the AD said.

'What?' Kitty stood up.

'This is not working,' Del Pico stated, as if he were speaking at a conference. The crew huddled together.

'I don't want to relight. That shot is beautiful. You can get her to do it, James.' Pete looked at his friend hopefully.

James shook his head. 'She doesn't understand what I'm telling her.'

'What do you want to do?' the AD asked.

James thought for a moment. 'Okay, I've got an idea.'

They pulled themselves out of the huddle and put James's plan into motion.

'Action!'

When the soothing sounds of Astrud Gilberto came

out of the speakers, Del Pico screamed, 'What the hell is this?'

'It's to get her in the mood,' James explained. 'To get the sensuous thing you want. We still put the picture to her song in the end, it's just for the actual filming. I think it would be—'

'We're making a video for her song, not some flamenco band.'

'Actually she's a Brazilian solo—'

'Do it!'

Kitty's DAT was exchanged for Astrud's.

'Playback!'

'Action!'

The music started, and Kitty began to dance like a boxer warming up.

'Cut,' James said, his voice heavy with resignation. The music came to an abrupt halt, along with James's chance of capturing any graceful movements. Kitty scrunched her face up.

Del Pico was pissed off. 'What are you doing?'

'I have *sensuous* written on every script and storyboard for this shoot. I'm trying to give it to you,' James said.

Kitty pouted. 'I *am* sensuous.'

'Of course you are,' Del Pico soothed in baby talk. James felt the hairs on the back of his neck stand up; he didn't particularly like Kitty, but her comment about Del Pico's visits to her trailer now haunted him. For a split second James wished he was back at the start of his career, making videos for people who *liked* music, experimenting, laughing, getting paid in cash. But it hadn't paid the bills and now he wasn't in touch with that scene any more.

James glared at his boss in disgust, but Del Pico's back was already turned as he stalked over to the storyboards and started ripping them up. 'To hell with these,' Del Pico said, 'just shoot the fucking video. Dancing, dancing, singing, singing. What's so hard about that? You're a paid hand – just do the job. The record company wants low budget and low risk. Why are you turning this into something it isn't!'

'I'm low budget?' Kitty sniffed.

'No, I didn't mean it like that, darlin',' Del Pico honeyed. 'It's just we've got the record company coming down today, and we need something in the can.'

Del Pico's comment was still rebounding in James's head. 'I'm a *paid hand*? What does that make you? A *paid hand* doesn't get you that shot in Chinatown.'

'And you took twice as long as you should have.'

'I'm going as fast as I can!' James tried to calm himself down. 'We can still do something interesting and keep it simple. Less is more with these things.'

'No, more is more! Just do the damn shot and we can go home.'

James wished that Fran could be with him; he wished he was sitting with her, talking to her, lying next to her. She always helped him to calm down. All James saw in front of him now was a grotesque man, a monster who he shouldn't be working for, a man whose hand was always on Kitty, who used his power in the worst way. Del Pico's next words seemed to come out in slow motion.

'You do it or we find someone else.'

There was a long pause. 'Fuck you!' James shouted, then immediately wondered who had said that, as if he were only a witness, not a participant.

'That's it.' Del Pico whipped out his mobile phone and started dialling.

'You're just going to call some other director in, right, like that'll happen at eight a.m.'

'No. I was just booking lunch,' Del Pico said. 'I'll direct.'

A record company suit entered. 'How's it all going?' he asked nervously, measuring the tension.

Del Pico looked at James. 'Are you leaving?'

There was silence for a moment in the big room. Pete looked at James, who looked at Del Pico. Kitty had migrated to a corner and was twiddling her hair and drawing a moustache on Britney Spears in *Cool Teen* magazine. James walked to the huge doors and opened them, the wind from outside rushing into the studio. He sensed the pressure change; and then the free-fall of his career towards the earth. All the plans he had made for the future turned into sludge at his feet, a dark swamp that he would have to walk through for a long time, a swamp, he had the awful realisation, that might look a lot like an office, the kind of place he would have to navigate wearing a suit. His temper rose again and he felt the violence boiling inside him that came from falling at every hurdle whenever he tried to make something of himself and stick to his principles. As he watched his job dissolve in front of his eyes, he held on to the thought of Fran more strongly than ever.

He had to stop this; stop it from damaging everything in his life. He was terrified of becoming a part of nothing.

James looked at the record company suit. The suit looked confused, and James realised he had a chance: a chance to turn things around. He could apologise, he could say he was under a lot of stress. People forgave that kind of thing. It would all be part of his image as he took his career to the highest level, as he took his life to the next stage – buying a house, one day asking Fran to marry him, stopping *right now* the possibility of ever being lonely. He turned around in the doorway, and heard words come from his lips which he could not stop.

'There is nowhere left for us to go. Short of Kitty taking all her clothes off – and I'm sure that day will come – we have nothing else to do. Everything boils down to how many cleavage shots we can get . . . if we had an artist who could legally drink, and fall in love, and have their heart broken, and do all the things that make the songs we love . . .' James was getting off the point. 'Look, I don't appreciate being treated this way, seeing my work torn up, seeing it' – he looked at Kitty and imagined Del Pico all over her – 'treated badly . . .'

James let out a deep breath.

No one said anything.

Eventually, the record company suit said, 'Look, a lot of guys who Kitty dumps feel bad, but I think we've heard enough.'

'I'm the director!' James protested.

'Not any more.' Del Pico repositioned his baseball cap, symbolically moving the directing job over to him.

James turned and walked out. As soon as the doors shut behind him, everyone picked up where they had left off, as they might after any minor interruption. James couldn't believe it, standing out on the cold street, looking into the warm, well-lit studio.

'You'll be sorry when my career hits the big time,' he muttered, storming off and wondering whether a speech like that was really a good idea in a week when his rent was due. By the close of business that day, all of London knew that James had been fired.

'I think something is leaking,' Adel said, his voice an urgent whisper, one arm instinctively tightening around his sleeping son. James was slow to process the information. The music channel had changed to cartoons and no one had cleared away his uneaten meal. Adel leaned over him to look out of the cabin window, balancing himself with his elbow on James's chest. Adel's son didn't wake up, even though his father's movements threw him around like a lifeless puppet. The wing light flashed again for two beats, then there was darkness, allowing James only a brief glimpse.

'I'm not sure,' he said.

'I can *definitely* see something leaking,' Adel announced, louder this time, his words echoing around the cabin in a series of whispers – up and down one side of the aircraft, then jumping the aisle and racing up the opposite row as everyone shared what they had heard, and adding a little extra, just to keep the interest going.

'*Leaking*? Are you *sure*?' James gasped, Adel's elbow still lodged in his sternum, making it hard for him to breathe. He tried to remember whether the flight attendant had said the parachutes were under the seats or in the overhead compartments.

The little amber light was still illuminated. The fuel tank monitoring system was also showing a caution message on the main instrument panel. Captain Hamed checked the other fuel indicators on the overhead panel, then looked at the continuous prediction to see how much fuel would be remaining at each point on the route to Dubai. He then double-checked the prediction of how much would be left on arrival. This was the figure that troubled him. It had changed dramatically.

'Shall we tell the passengers?'

'No,' said Captain Hamed. 'Not yet.'

His co-pilot was on the radio. They were working at a speed Captain Hamed couldn't remember ever being simulated in flight school. He was doing six things at once, perfectly, efficiently, thinking clearly, as if the whole world had slowed down in order for him to try to save the lives of a group of salespeople heading to a mall in the desert. He watched all the monitors and silently wondered whether they were going to make it to any friendly runway, let alone Dubai. He had to move quickly and locate, then obtain clearance at, another airport. He ran through the different runways he hoped were within range, their length and direction, the local weather, calculating as fast as possible where he should try to land.

'The leak is coming from the left wing,' the co-pilot

confirmed, his tone well practised and ice cold. His calculations in the cockpit had suggested this, but he had sent an attendant along the cabin to try to subtly get a visual on its exact location.

There was silence in the cockpit for a long five seconds.

It was a clear night, with only occasional light turbulence. Captain Hamed looked at his co-pilot, the aircraft still set on course for Dubai, a place it no longer had enough fuel to reach. The two men held each other's stares, both hunting for clues in the other's eyes that would suggest fear, but both of them had been too well trained to give anything away.

The call came through.

There was a safe place for them to land – a city that, just hours before, had had its own share of airborne visitors: F-16s letting go of their bombs into the night sky.

'Now we'll tell them,' Captain Hamed said, picking up the radio and clearing his throat before pressing the intercom button. 'Ladies and gentlemen, this is your captain speaking. May I have your attention please. *Mesdames et messieurs, votre attention s'il vous plaît. Sayyidaati wa saadati . . .*'

One of the many left-over problems of colonialism was that air crises in the Middle East took a lot longer than elsewhere – people had to be told not to panic in several different languages, some indigenous, others left behind by long-gone rulers.

James gripped the seat rest until his knuckles turned white while the captain's calm voice on the PA reassured them that there was no need for alarm. In the darkness outside the window, he could now clearly see the vapour streaming from the trailing edge of the wing. Adel kept his hand on his sleeping son, looking up and down the aisle, his breathing shallow and fast.

'What can you see?' Adel asked, craning his neck.

'It's coming out fast,' James said, grappling under his seat for his shoes – he had taken them off earlier as he did on every flight, but he couldn't find them. The aircraft shuddered – it was unfair that there could still be turbulence during an emergency. Passengers in front of and behind James were standing up and talking to each other; firm friendships were being formed. *What have you heard?* Overhead lockers were being opened, mobile phones taken out. One woman started crying. Adel had a brief moment of calm, until he saw that his son had woken up and was starting to fidget nervously.

'Are you going to Dubai for work?' James asked, in an effort to restart the conversation and take his mind off the situation. The noise of the chatter in the cabin made it hard for them to hear each other.

Adel joined in willingly, leaning towards James. 'My wife is in Cairo, but I do a lot of business in London and the Gulf. I'm going to finalise some contracts in Dubai, and Hadi hasn't been there, so I thought I would take him.' His voice was full of guilt, as if he was somehow responsible for putting his son's life in danger.

'I'm sure they always have extra fuel on these aircraft,' James tried to reassure them both.

'God willing,' Adel said, twisting around in his seat and

waving at someone behind them. He turned back to James. 'Listen, my sister is about ten rows back and she looks very scared. Will you talk to Hadi while I'm gone?' He slipped out of his seat before James could answer. When he returned from consoling his sister, he found Hadi keeping James calm, showing off his precious Manchester United football cards.

The air brakes on the wings extended and the aircraft starting dragging through the thin cloud. James's popping ears told him the plane was losing altitude, although it was impossible to say how low they were – the black ocean below provided no reference. There was just darkness. Then land. Land that started abruptly, with no lead-in. Roads, cars, buildings and patches of sparkling lights. They were so low that they could see neon signs in Arabic on the shops. The city looked as if it were falling into the water. It was the beginning of the Middle East.

'Ladies and gentlemen, we will be landing in a few minutes.'

Captain Hamed spoke to the tower as the plane descended over the city, skimming rooftops that were wearing miles of laundry. The landing gear clanked down and locked into place. Worried Western salespeople looked out of the window, not knowing that this was the usual approach to Beirut airport. From the aircraft, they could see the coloured lights of the Ferris wheel on the Corniche road. Up in the cockpit, Captain Hamed wondered how many of the passengers sitting behind him would have imagined that one day Beirut would save their lives.

04

The Arabian Sands Trading Establishment of Beirut made deliveries. You called, left your order, they forgot it. You called again, they said they had never heard of you, you left your order again, they delivered it in three hours flat, even if you lived opposite. Abu Khalil and his family owned the mini-market. Abu Khalil spent most of his day stoned, and he had once sat at his checkout for an hour while one of the fridges in the back exploded and set on fire an entire rack of spices (ruining everything from cumin down to saffron). It was hard to know how many people actually worked for Arabian Sands. As with all shops, hairdressers', hardware stores, apartment blocks, there was the person who *did* the job (served you, cut your hair, found you a sink plug, gave you your apartment key), then four others: two to give their opinions on the person doing the job; two more to disagree with those opinions.

Hassan scanned the tall, glass-fronted fridges, looking for something to drink. He had said hello to Abu Khalil when he had walked in, but the owner looked to be asleep with his eyes open, cigarette in mouth. Hassan figured he must have been alive, though, as he was exhaling smoke out of his mouth in two streams – one either side of his dangling cigarette. At the back of the store, deep in the maze of fridges and giant cardboard boxes, Hassan paused for a second and rubbed his eyes.

'You've been gone for ten years,' he whispered to himself. It was a ritual he observed on this day every year – the anniversary forced him to think of Majed whether he liked it or not, and he would speak to the air in front of him and mark how long it had been.

Hassan opened the door of the blue Pepsi fridge in front of him. *Super sexy overdose, you know what is it!* was handwritten on the fridge door in thick green marker pen. He reread the home-made poster for the bright candy-coloured alcoholic drinks that was stuck on the outside of one fridge. Stacks of yellow Bacardi Breezers and pink vodka bottles glowed in the bright light. Hassan grabbed a can of Red Bull and a miniature of Smirnoff, catching his reflection in the glass door. People said he looked like Amr Diab, the Egyptian pop star, but Hassan didn't agree. He was far better looking and he knew it: muscular body, short dark hair, well-manicured sideboards and the kind of middle-distance stare that young American actors have been perfecting ever since Mickey Rourke. Every time that damn commercial with Amr Diab advertising Pepsi was shown on television, someone would make a comment about it to Hassan. If a director had been looking for a Stephen Dorff type to star in an Arabic movie, Hassan would have been the only choice. He wouldn't accept, of course. He was too cool for that kind of shit.

As he strutted to the counter, trying to retrace his steps around the half-opened boxes scattered all over the floor, he cracked open the Red Bull and took a long drink. He swallowed, then opened the vodka, before pouring it into the Red Bull can, mixing the two together. As he fished around for some change, he caught sight of his faithful BMW parked outside. He adored it. He knew its engine like he knew his own body; he could picture its colour in his dreams. He sometimes thought he knew what it was thinking. That car was his only love. Until the new Z8 convertible became available – Hassan was on the waiting list and was starting to get excited about finally owning a limited edition – then he would let this one rust. He paid Abu Khalil and left the shop. He didn't get a super sexy overdose, but he got a little buzz for his Saturday night.

The blue 425 poster glued to the wall outside the Arabian Sands store was scratched and peeling, almost a year old. Hassan glanced at it as he got into his car. Beirut wasn't just home for Hassan, it was all he knew, or at least all he *wanted* to know. It had been just a temporary measure when his parents had sent him as a teenager away from their village in the south, to live with his uncle Haj Ahmad in the capital. But it became permanent. His home for the last ten years had been the small, semi-private annexe connected to Haj Ahmad's two-storey apartment in west Beirut. The last decade of living in the city had been what had shaped him, not his brief childhood in a southern village, and he had no wish to return to that small ramshackle town where he was born, and where his parents and sisters still lived, struggling under twenty years of Israeli occupation.

Four-two-five. Hassan believed the world had forgotten about UN Resolution 425, requiring Israel to pull out from all areas of south Lebanon. He had chosen to forget it as well. But his country, his *city*, was still dotted with posters displaying those three numbers, which were faithfully glued to any available wall space every year. They caught him off guard – when he didn't want to see them they were everywhere he looked: shop signs, Pepsi banners, Marlboro adverts all merged into one haunting three-figure number.

Hassan turned the key in the ignition, the sound of the engine starting up pushed his memories into the background, and looked away from the poster that had nonetheless engraved itself on his mind. He was angry that he had let it have an effect on him; he rarely allowed himself to think about these things and he wasn't going to start on a Saturday night when there was a party to go to. There was nothing he could have done for his brother, and there was nothing he could do for his parents, rotting in a tiny house, stubbornly refusing to move to Beirut. They had an attachment to land that Hassan had never understood. Haj Ahmad had offered them incentives, places to stay and work, but Hassan's father would not budge. It was his land and he was going to suffer on it. Hassan's father was a carpenter; Haj Ahmad owned five restaurants and one hotel. Hassan had become Haj Ahmad's son, no longer his father's, growing up with the luxuries that his uncle's income afforded. Luxury had helped Hassan forget.

Haj Ahmad had recently started his first pizza restaurant, even though his personal taste was for the traditional Lebanese or French restaurant. Hassan sometimes wondered whether his uncle had simply come up with the idea of Welcome Pizza so he could give his own young son, Mahmoud, some holiday work making deliveries. Haj Ahmad was never there anyway – he was far too busy meeting and greeting Lebanese ministers at his hotel on the waterfront, or flying down to the Gulf to persuade rich Saudis to stay at his hotel during their Lebanese visits. (Haj Ahmad was no fool. He knew some of the rich Gulf Arabs liked to drink themselves stupid, so he always stressed the enormous bar in his hotel, the large wall around the perimeter and the discreet nature of the surroundings. It was not uncommon for him to come down to the pool area in the morning and see men from various dry states lying horizontal on the poolside, unconscious, still holding a bottle of vodka.)

Haj Ahmad was a businessman, he had worked hard for his wealth, but he was unfailingly generous with it when it came to his nephew. He had fuelled Hassan's bank account and paid for his education. And Hassan was not stupid: he could think faster in three languages than most people could in one, and had blazed through school, getting good grades and doing no work. It had been the same story at university. No one ever commented on Hassan's laziness, and no one ever said 'no' to him – at least none of his family did, because they all understood what had happened to his brother. Haj Ahmad could never bring himself to discipline his nephew in his youth, and now it was too late. He could only wait patiently and hope that Hassan would find his own way.

By the time he got back to his house, Hassan's super sexy cocktail had kicked in and he was feeling better. His little cousin Mahmoud had crept into his apartment and was sitting in the living room with some of Hassan's friends watching *Dexter's Lab* on television. Mahmoud was all gangly legs and a five-times-too-big Orlando Magic T-shirt. His hair was shaved to a grade four – just like all his friends' – and his giant digital watch had ten different games on it.

'Shouldn't you be doing pizza deliveries?' Hassan's voice was gruff. He wanted to get rid of him and tapped Mahmoud's leg with his foot to hurry him up.

'I'm *going*,' Mahmoud replied. The others hadn't really noticed him sitting there – he wasn't bothering anyone. The only non-Lebanese person in the room was Julien, a Frenchman in a Hawaiian shirt who was sucking on the long pipe connected to the *nargileh*, which stood three feet high, hot rocks glowing, its water bubbling as he inhaled. Julien, still slightly bewildered by Arab hospitality, had been staying at Hassan's house for the last five days, ever since they had met in a bar. Hassan had paid for everything and had insisted Julien stay with him until he could find somewhere to live. If Julien offered to pay for a meal or suggested moving to a hotel, Hassan would look at him as if he were insane. Julien had discovered that this behaviour wasn't just limited to Hassan – he had been invited to so many people's houses since he had arrived in Lebanon he couldn't keep track. But he hadn't yet grown used to the speed with which friendships formed. It didn't matter – he was now Hassan's friend, and the two of them cruised the city as if they had been doing it their whole lives.

The documentary Julien had been working on, which had brought him to Beirut, was now shelved indefinitely because of funding problems on the second day of filming. There always seemed to be funding problems, but these were serious enough to close the project down entirely. His first opportunity to make a film since leaving college in Paris had evaporated, and Julien realised that he would have to get used to introducing himself as an *assistant* cameraman for a little longer. His film-making partner had taken off as soon as the money had fallen through, but Julien hadn't left yet, although he wasn't sure why.

There was a deep, booming explosion. The lights went out.

'*Merde!*' Julien shouted. He had been taking a drag on the *nargileh* when the first bomb hit, and instinctively jumped away from the window holding on to the pipe. He tipped the whole thing over: metal pipe, molasses tobacco, stale water and two red-hot burning coals all crashed on to Hassan's Persian rug. As the glowing rocks landed they broke into tiny molten pieces, melting away the rug until they rested on the tiles underneath. It was too dark for Hassan to rescue it, and by the time he had found the metal pincers and lit a match, his carpet was pockmarked with little black circles.

'Why did I leave the *nargileh* in the hands of a Frenchman?' Hassan asked himself as he bent down to pick up the cinders.

'*Merde*,' Julien kept repeating, as he staggered to the window in the darkness to see what had exploded, kicking Hassan in the forehead by mistake.

'Mahmoud! Bring some matches,' Hassan yelled, putting two torches on their ends, so the spotlights shone on the ceiling. 'Julien, next party you can't smoke, okay? *Mahmoud! We need matches and candles,*' he shouted, but his cousin had long gone.

A minute later, the television and stereo came back to life as the power returned. Hassan flicked through the satellite news channels from around the world and listened to the almost instantaneous reports and commentary on Lebanon's burning power stations being broadcast in many different languages. Some called it an unprovoked attack, others called it retaliation. Hizbollah and the IDF, the Israeli Defence Force, needed each other in a perverse way, Hassan thought. Haj Ahmad said the occupation of the south was about water. There was lots of it in Lebanon, and during the war Hassan's wealthy uncle had drilled down into the ground, sunk his own well, and drawn fresh water every day.

'This is an escalation,' one reporter said.

'This is a *warning,*' Hassan said to the television. '*If we decide to retreat, don't try anything.*'

'They will never leave,' someone at the back of the room said. 'It's been twenty years.'

'I read that the Israelis *want* a pull-out. They are getting sick of their soldiers dying in the buffer zone,' Julien said in French.

'It's not a fucking buffer zone.' Hassan didn't shout; his voice was calm as he jumped languages. 'It's an occupied area of Lebanese soil. Okay?'

Julien gulped. 'Okay, Hassan.'

'Who gives a shit, man,' one of Hassan's Lebanese friends said, his American accent flawless.

'Why do you care?' another mumbled, opening another beer, and not expecting an answer.

'Why're you so upset tonight?' Julien asked. He had never heard Hassan even mention the south – he had always shown a total lack of interest in politics, just like his friends.

'It doesn't matter,' Hassan replied softly. He decided to leave the candles burning. Another power cut was sure to come any minute. He had felt the apartment shake when the bombs hit, even though they were some miles away from the power stations. He had grown used to watching and listening and reading about the back-and-forth exchanges across the border. They were nothing new, but Hassan believed, sitting in the candlelight, that the tectonic plates of Lebanese politics, resting uneasily since the end of the war, were about to shift again. And every time they shifted, people fell through the cracks.

He didn't want to think about it any more. This was Saturday night. Once the television news had run out of pictures of the power stations there was a breaking story about an emergency at the airport – the fire engines and ambulances were preparing for a precautionary landing.

'Welcome to Lebanon,' Hassan said to the television. He turned around and faced his friends, who were draped over various chairs and sofas. '*Shu?* Are we going out or what?'

'Is it safe?' Julien asked, standing up and putting on his coat. He suddenly felt nervous for the first time since his arrival. It was as if the country had decided to remind this Westerner exactly where he was.

'Of course it's safe,' Hassan scoffed. 'They're not going to bomb Bar Pacifico. *Yalla*, let's go.' He grabbed his Versace leather jacket, slung it on, checked his ruffled hair in the mirror, then raced out of the door. Soon he and Julien were in Hassan's BMW heading to east Beirut, to the parties and clubs and women that awaited them on rue Monot.

After a few minutes of blind panic, James felt a surge of quiet euphoria, the just-before-drowning kind. It was not shared by the rest of the passengers. He looked out over the city as the plane banked steeply, straining his eyes to make out the flashing lights of fire engines and ambulances on a distant runway. Adel had given up on conversation and was quietly repeating '*Bismillah al-Rahman al-Rahim* . . . *Bismillah al-Rahman al-Rahim*', while threading prayer beads through his hands. His son was busy comparing pictures of Ryan Giggs and David Beckham. About five rows up, a young woman was crouching in the aisle to get a view out of the window. James tried to lip-read what she was whispering to herself. He was sure it was the rosary, he could see her mouth form the words 'Hail Mary, full of grace . . .'

Near silence now fell over the cabin as its occupants rediscovered their faiths. Two of the three monotheistic religions were well represented, and from Seat 1A in first class right to the back, all kinds of prayers were being directed at Him. As if to provide balance among the one-God-dominated pleas for help, an Indian businessman was saying something to himself as he walked past James and Adel, frantically trying to get his mobile phone to work. James caught the man's words: '*Jai jala Ram, jai Ram*'. He was starting to feel that if the plane went down it was going to be his fault for being the only one not asking for a miracle, so he ran through the Lord's Prayer in his head twice – the first time he got lost in the middle – then returned to looking out of the window. All he could see below him was darkness as they passed the Beirut peninsula and flew back over the ocean again. James tried to recall everything he knew about Beirut and began to tense up accordingly, starting at his neck and working down through his body and into his legs. Historically, his memory was informing him, things hadn't worked out too well for Westerners arriving unannounced at Beirut airport.

The plane was in a holding pattern, in order to give the emergency services time to get into position on the ground. From the cockpit Captain Hamed thought he could see a burning power station in the distance, but perhaps it was his imagination. The gossip among the flight crew was that Israeli jets had been busy over Beirut that evening. He put it out of his mind and focused on his job. Captain Hamed was blessed with the kind of deep, smooth voice that inspired confidence in everyone and weak knees in the female flight attendants. When he said 'Let me assure you . . .', which was his favourite way of starting a sentence during any kind of conflict, the person being spoken to felt as if they were falling into a comfortable chair. It had been that voice which, back in the 1970s, had captured the heart of a Miss

Lebanon winner, and thirty years on Mrs Hamed still felt a twinge of excitement when her husband came home. She may have been given a crown and a title, but the highlight for her was being won over by a young trainee pilot. He had assured her that he would make her the happiest wife, and so far his promise had held.

The runway lights came into sight. Captain Hamed was given the all-clear for landing. He made one final turn and then started his approach.

Mahmoud wished he had been out on his bike when the strikes came. An F-16 fighter dropping bombs on a power station sounded as if the atmosphere were being ripped in two. He had experienced it many times before. Mahmoud had the fearlessness of a typical twelve-year-old, and as he sat on his bike, looking up at the Ferris wheel, he was disappointed that there were no more jet fighters to watch. If his father found out he was still out in the city he would be in big trouble. Haj Ahmad always told him to come straight home when he had finished his deliveries. But, Mahmoud reasoned, what could he do? First Hassan had chucked him out, and now he couldn't sleep. He was restless in bed – everything hurt. His mother said that he would never become a real man unless he suffered first, and his growing pains were making sure of that. Mahmoud failed to see the point of this sudden discomfort in his arms and legs, and didn't understand why he now slept so late he regularly missed lunch. He looked up and watched a passenger aircraft approach from the sea then shoot over head. He read aloud the serial number on the underside of the wing. The aircraft was leaking a thin trail of liquid from its wing. Mahmoud pretend-revved his handlebar grips like an accelerator, imagining what it would be like when he finally got a moped on his thirteenth birthday. Not long to wait now. Then he would be a real man. He spun his bicycle around and pedalled off, doing a wheelie off the kerb. The streets were dark as he cycled home.

The wheels were just a few feet above the runway, and with a steady hand Captain Hamed touched the plane down safely. When the aircraft came to a standstill, the passengers all exhaled at the same time.

'Ladies and gentlemen, welcome to Beirut International Airport.'

There was an instinctive rush off the aircraft as the engineers boarded, as though something awful could still happen. As the last of the passengers hurried down the steps to the runway, James still hadn't located his shoes. He asked a flight attendant to help him look, but the engineers wanted everyone off the aircraft, so James obeyed, navigating the steps in his socks.

The passengers were taken to a large room where an airline representative was waiting for them. She informed them that a new aircraft would be ready in four hours to take them on to Dubai. James spotted Michael at one end of the room, but he was fortunately too far away to hear him drunkenly describing to his new friends how he had stolen James's shoes and hidden them in the overhead lockers near the toilets. James sat by himself at the other end of the room, having lost Adel along with his footwear.

The announcement came three hours and fifty minutes later.

'Ladies and gentlemen, we're very sorry but another aircraft is not available at this time. We are taking you to a hotel for the night, and will keep you informed as to your connecting flight tomorrow. We are sorry for the inconvenience. Please fill out these compensation forms.'

James took his form and stuffed it in his pocket. A rep showed up with some old trainers for him which were too big, but he put them on anyway. Tired and still suffering from mild shock, he followed the group to Immigration. A man in front of him spoke to the cashier.

'*Visa touristique pour trois mois, s'il vous plaît.*' The man handed over thirty dollars and the cashier passed him two stamps under the glass. James caught only '*visa*' and '*touristique*' from the conversation, but he was fairly sure that it was what he wanted.

'*Le même?*' the cashier asked, as James approached the desk. James nodded, handing over some of his Dubai allowance and receiving his stamps. He then took them to the next booth where an immigration officer inspected his passport, pressed the stamps on to a wet sponge and stuck them in. He made a note of James's passport number, then hit the freshly added stamps with a metal device that could have branded a water buffalo. It thudded on the page and woke James from his trance.

James grabbed his bags then walked through a turnstile past another guard, unsure whether he had to show him anything.

The guard looked up at him from his chair. 'You are

welcome,' he said, waving James through. James thought he spotted Michael in a crowd of people by the door, but if it was him he disappeared instantly. Outside, a minibus was waiting. James got into the front seat next to the driver and looked through the dirty windscreen. In the distance the city lights twinkled and blurred in between patches of darkness. The driver glanced over at James.

'First time Lebanon?'

'Yeah.'

'You are welcome. Why you are in Lebanon?'

'Aeroplane ran out of fuel.'

People continued to file into the minibus until finally the driver shut the door and they left the airport terminal. He drove round a couple of sharp bends, past a few palm trees and a large painting of a mullah, dodged a crater-sized pothole, then slammed his foot on the accelerator as the road straightened out. James held on tightly as he watched cars flying down the highway to and from the airport.

'You see? Boom boom!' the driver explained as he careened around another pothole. 'Tonight. Boom boom.'

James didn't understand.

'Airport very quiet, no? No visitors, too much boom boom. Where do you go?' he enquired as he simultaneously lit a cigarette for himself and stuck the packet under James's nose.

'I'm going to Dubai tomorrow,' James said, waving the packet of cigarettes away.

'Shopping. Before we have very good shopping in Lebanon,' the driver said, indicating a row of buildings with no lights. 'This is why no more shopping.' He took his hands off the steering wheel, smacked them together. '*Finish*,' he said. 'Israeli planes – boom! – no power, no shopping. Always this when people want to come to Lebanon.'

The minibus rocketed through a tunnel, and as it exited the driver made a last-minute decision to take the right fork. They passed a church edged in strings of lights, a giant Christmas ornament.

'Armenian,' the driver explained, seeing James's curiosity. All James registered were the random shapes and shadows of a place he didn't know. He had broken one of his golden rules: he was not in an air-conditioned taxi. He had already left far too much to chance.

The bus pushed its way on to a main road as shops started appearing on both sides: bank after bank, cinemas, cafés, signs in French and Arabic. James found the French writing reassuringly familiar, for a moment able to pretend he had just arrived in Calais, before the Arabic names across the shopfronts shattered that illusion. The bus turned off down a small road, electricity wires hanging erratically across the street. At the bottom was an illuminated sign. The Lord Nelson Hotel was the end of their journey. The driver looked determined to smash into a white UN four-wheel-drive parked outside, but braked inches before colliding with its rear bumper. He then leapt out, flung the door of the minibus open, and proceeded to welcome them a second time. The passengers didn't appear to share his enthusiasm as they shuffled inside. It was very late. The desk clerk greeted the group and asked James if he was looking forward to his archaeological exploration of Lebanon. James was too tired to correct him.

'If you need anything, I am Kamal,' the desk clerk confided. James took his key and left reception, passing the hotel bar, where a group of people were sitting, eyes glued to the television screens and the flickering images of burning power stations.

James followed Kamal's directions up to the second floor. There was a comfortable, relaxed atmosphere to the hotel. He padded along the corridor and found his room, undressed and stretched out on the bed. It was relaxing to stare at something as boring as a ceiling, but he suddenly felt he wanted to speak to Fran, to tell her he was okay, that he missed her and that he wanted to be at home with her at that moment. But it was too late, so he decided to wait until the morning. He flicked on the television to distract himself from thinking about her and watched for a few minutes, until the TV suddenly went off and all the lights went out. It was too dark to fish out his sleeping tablets from his bag so he didn't even try. Counting the ever-increasing number of broken rules made him dozy, and he fell asleep to the sounds of the generator starting up below, giving power back to the building. And across Beirut – while its power stations burned – generators rumbled away, their mating calls echoing across the city. The geriatric generators which were used so often during the war still grudgingly went to work every day. By the time the TV and lights came back on, James was sound asleep. He couldn't be woken by the fluorescent bulbs shining above his head, or the eight continuous hours of Arabic music videos which fed into his subconscious until morning.

05

Haj Ahmad was balding, but the grey hair around his temples looked as if it had been subject to an expensive haircut. He had a young face, so young that it somehow cancelled out his hair colour. He wore long-sleeve shirts, with a sleeveless cardigan when it was cooler, and a well-cut pair of jeans. There were few people who looked as comfortable in themselves as Haj Ahmad. He didn't smoke, drink or eat bad food.

Hassan recognised the look on his uncle's face: he wasn't exactly angry, although it was obvious something was making him tense. It was different to the look he usually wore the day after air strikes, when he knew his business would inevitably be affected. His eyes always dimmed slightly before the subject of Hassan's brother was brought up, an early-warning signal to Hassan to start thinking of a reason to leave.

Haj Ahmad stood in the sitting room in Hassan's flat. Mahmoud sat on the floor, a few feet from the TV screen, watching intently, not interested in the conversation going on around him.

'Hassan, they would love you to visit,' Haj Ahmad said.

'I'm busy this week,' Hassan shot back.

'Your parents are very apprehensive at the moment. Their son should be with them.'

'I'm taking Mahmoud out for his birthday,' Hassan said.

Mahmoud looked up from the television excitedly, but as soon as he realised that Hassan was just using this as a diversion, he sighed and turned his attention back to the cartoons.

'*Ma'lesh*, you can do both,' Haj Ahmad suggested. When Hassan didn't answer, he continued, 'They are thinking about your brother . . . if Israel leaves the south . . .'

Hassan shrugged. 'If they leave then my parents live freely.'

'I'm talking about your brother. I'm talking about Majed.' Haj Ahmad paused for a moment. He knew mentioning Majed would take Hassan by surprise. It was the first time he had actually spoken about Hassan's brother in such a direct way – usually Majed's name was unmentionable.

Hassan played with the car keys in his hand. He found it annoying that in his own, seemingly passive way, his uncle was having an increasing influence on him. This influence was best displayed by what happened next: a reluctant Hassan found himself on the phone to his parents. He wasn't able to have any kind of conversation with them, but he didn't resent them, even though he knew their concern for his safety ten years ago had put a decade of different worlds between them.

While he spoke to his parents, Haj Ahmad took a seat on the couch in the living room. He didn't want to eavesdrop on his nephew, but he could hear that Hassan's conversation was peppered with long periods of him saying little. He wondered whether Hassan was listening or if there was just silence on the line.

'*Shu, Baba,* are you going to play Counterstrike today?' Haj Ahmad asked Mahmoud absent-mindedly, still watching Hassan.

Mahmoud didn't take his eyes away from the Power Puff Girls – although he would swear he hated them to anyone who asked – so he and his father talked while looking in opposite directions. 'If Hassan will take me.' He shrugged nonchalantly.

'What's the matter, *habibi*?'

There was a pause, then Mahmoud switched off the television and turned round to face his father, a look of confusion on his face. '*Baba*, what happened to Cousin Majed?'

'You know what happened.'

'You said he was gone but he would come back one day, *inshallah*.'

'And that is true.'

Mahmoud got up and sat next to his father on the sofa. 'Tell me what happened to him.'

'When you're older.'

'I *am* older.'

Haj Ahmad glanced around the apartment, hoping an answer would present itself, but his eyes found only an old *nargileh* which looked as if it had been in a battle, an empty packet of cigarettes, a not very well hidden can of beer and a Persian rug with a burn in it. He sighed.

'I want to know what *happened*,' Mahmoud pleaded. 'You always talk like I'm not here or I don't understand. Why does Hassan say Majed is dead?'

Haj Ahmad thought about how he could phrase it. He

had heard Hassan talking this way, trying to convince himself that Majed *was* dead. But Haj Ahmad was reluctant to confront him when he said these things, because Hassan was only half wrong.

'He is in prison,' he said eventually.

'Did he steal something?'

'No, he didn't steal anything.'

'Why can't we see him?' Mahmoud asked.

Haj Ahmad smiled at his boy's resilience to bad news; already he was looking for a way to make the best of it. 'No one can see Majed.'

Now Haj Ahmad found himself hoping Hassan would finish his phone call and come back in and disrupt the conversation, giving him a chance to escape. 'The prison that he is being held in is . . . we can't go to it,' he said.

'It's not in Lebanon?'

Haj Ahmad again paused while his son looked up at him. He was nearly a teenager, but he still possessed the precious quality of believing that his father knew all the answers.

'It is in Lebanon. But it is not.' Haj Ahmad spoke slowly, picking his words with care.

'Where is he?' Mahmoud asked.

'It is called Khiam.'

Mahmoud looked stonily at his father, his face then contorting into the expression boys adopt when they're determined not to cry. The look told Haj Ahmad that his son had heard of this prison, that he knew about it and now his young mind was doing millions of calculations as to the destiny of his cousin. He wondered whether Mahmoud would now work out all the things the family had kept from him because of his age: that Majed had been taken as a teenager, not much older than Mahmoud, thrown in the boot of a car, then driven to the hilltop detention centre where he remained, ten years later, without trial.

'Majed is a resistance fighter?' Mahmoud managed to get it out in one go. It made Haj Ahmad think back to his nephew growing up, and how unlike a fighter he had been.

'Majed was caught in the net. Maybe he went to school with people who were connected, maybe they were his friends . . . I don't know, but he was not in the resistance.'

Haj Ahmad knew that this simple fact made no difference at all – many of the detainees in Khiam were personally involved with Hizbollah, but some just had family members who were connected, and a few, including most of the female detainees, had no political associations at all. None of them even had prisoner-of-war status.

Mahmoud was listening intently, nodding while his father told him this, occasionally asking him to stop and repeat words he didn't understand.

Haj Ahmad didn't want to talk any more; it was too difficult. When he got up and left the room, Mahmoud tagged along behind him. They walked past Hassan, still in the middle of a stony silence on the phone, then crossed into Haj Ahmad's part of the house.

'Do you want anything?' Haj Ahmad asked, looking through the cupboards of food. He often called his son from the car, from the office, from the restaurant and asked him whether he wanted anything. *Baddak shi?* His wife did the same. It wasn't a question designed to provoke an answer, it was a question that just let him know his parents were thinking about him.

'No.' Mahmoud brushed the question aside. 'If he is in the prison in the south, then who do we speak to about it?'

Haj Ahmad took a seat at the kitchen table and started peeling an apple. 'There is no one we can talk to about it,' he replied, his face tightening in frustration. Khiam detention centre was run by a Lebanese militia who had grandly titled themselves the South Lebanon Army, but as far as Haj Ahmad was concerned it was common knowledge, although Israel often denied it, that the SLA was Israel's client militia, and Khiam was an extension of that: a very effective way for the Israeli army to keep control in the area it occupied. How could Israel say it had nothing to do with the prison, he argued endlessly, when it occupied the area, when a group of Israeli lawyers were trying to have it shut down? But it was Lebanese, *traitors*, as Haj Ahmad called them, who ran the place day to day.

'Why is he still there?'

'Mahmoud, *habibi*. When you want a new wheel for your bicycle, what do I say?'

'Clean your car for a week.'

'Exactly. Majed is a bargaining chip: sometimes the prisoners are exchanged for things the other side wants.'

So far Mahmoud hadn't asked about their living conditions, and although Haj Ahmad had decided to tell him the truth, there were some things that he didn't need to know. Anyway, how could he describe a place he had only heard rumours about, mixed with the odd line from a Red Cross report, all those tiny fragments that had

translated into horrifying pictures in his mind: the tiny
solitary confinement cell – one pace wide, two paces long
– that prisoners lived in when they were first interred.
How could he appreciate what Majed had felt: *gratitude*
that he hadn't been put in twenty-four-hour confinement,
in a brown metal box that a man could fit into only if
he crouched, like shutting a human being inside a deadly
cupboard; or what he had seen: the dirty yellow walls and
thin corridors harshly lit by naked light bulbs, or the room
he shared with ten other men, their boxy little bunk beds
all in a row, no natural light able to find its way in.

'If they hurt him, it will only be worse for them,' Haj
Ahmad mused to himself, as if to reassure them both
that there was some order, some justice that they could
count on.

'Will you *get* them if they hurt him, *Baba*?' Mahmoud
asked.

'I won't get them, but they will be judged. One day.'

Hassan walked into the kitchen and took a drink from
the fridge, his face sombre, his eyes fixed on the ground.

'You spoke for a long time,' Haj Ahmad stated quietly.

Hassan looked at Mahmoud, then at Haj Ahmad, wondering whether he could speak about Majed with the boy
in the room. Haj Ahmad nodded in the direction of his son,
signalling to Hassan that it was okay, they could now talk
freely in front of him.

'They've convinced themselves the prison will collapse
if there's a pull-out,' Hassan said, sitting down. 'They
watch the news every Sunday after the Israeli cabinet
meetings to find out what was being said. They're driving

themselves crazy. They hear these rumours the Lebanese government doesn't want a pull-out, that it's happy to forget the south.'

No one said anything for a moment. Mahmoud's eyes went from his father to his cousin and back again.

'Will you go and see them?' Haj Ahmad asked.

'Not yet.'

Only forty miles away, but in a separate universe, Majed was standing in the prison yard, having his first precious minutes of exercise in ten days. His first day was still a crisp memory, even if all the days since had melted into one. First stop had been the interrogation room, bigger than any of the other rooms in the prison, and not far from the women's section; then it was electrical torture – an old military telephone with a wind-up handle to create electricity attached to the fingers and genitals – and sleep deprivation, until delirium set in and the prisoner started giving information, even if they simply made it up to avoid more pain. Then there was the Pole – a tall metal reinforced girder that stood vertically against the blue sky for prisoners to be strapped to and doused in cold water.

Standing in the yard, Majed could see the blue UN flag that hung in the breeze, not far from the prison. He often wondered whether the UN men heard the screams. But they were there only to observe the border. He could just make out the lookout post, a small cube on stilts with the sun reflecting on the windows. He could catch only reflections and shadows, no human shape at all. Razor wire spun in curled webs across all the walls, blocking his view. The air was cold, but the naked sun baked the ground and stung his eyes.

There were purple spots on the ceiling. Eventually the spots faded as James's eyes grew accustomed to the bright light. The radio sang, '*Radio One. Weather check*,' before the DJ gave the day's highs and lows. '*Radio One. Travel newwwsss.*' James was lying on his back, very still, tuning his ears into the radio. He knew those phrases: they were from the 1980s, they were BBC Radio 1 jingles from the Live Aid decade. He had woken up in 1983 and any moment Mike Read was going to start his breakfast show and James was going to get up and get ready for school. His mind reached desperately for some kind of explanation. He looked at the bedside table. It wasn't his. It wasn't his bed. It *was* his travel radio, though, and it had faithfully clicked on the tuner to wake him up. Would he go downstairs and find both parents sitting at the table with his brother? Would he then search around his room for his Super-8 camera so he could film the school football match?

'Can you shout LEBANON!!' the DJ yelled, considerably narrowing down the chances of it being Mike Read.

The caller obliged. 'Lebanon!' she shouted back, and won a prize. Propping himself up on one elbow, James reached for the water by his bed, and took a sip. He coughed and tried to unstick his tongue from the roof of his mouth. He ran a hand over his face. His skin was tight and uncomfortable. He looked around the room. Although the curtains were drawn, and the lights were on, he knew that it was daylight outside. The sound of the radio was fusing with the TV, which was happily blaring way, a woman singing her heart out in Arabic, while the camera pushed into close-ups of her heavily applied eye make-up. She found herself in a series of increasingly perilous situations, as a man, in a series of increasingly expensive cars, repeatedly came to her rescue. He watched a little more, remembering how Fran had been furious when he had modified their satellite dish in London to receive Brazilian MTV. His modification was successful, although he had dislodged several tiles while standing on the roof, and they were never able to receive the weather channel again.

James summoned the energy to get out of bed and stagger over to switch off the TV. The events of the night before started coming back to him, all in the wrong order. Adel and his son, no shoes, Heathrow, Michael and his drinking theories on Dubai. James cursed himself for breaking all of his rules in one night. He had even taken a minibus! He moved towards the curtains, gripping one in each hand, making fists before ripping them open with a flourish. The dramatic gesture wasn't justified. The view was just of a large wall about ten feet away.

He slunk into the spotless bathroom, so polished it was almost unnerving, and stepped into the shower. As he massaged the shampoo into his hair, the lights went out. He half expected the water to cut out as well, but it didn't so he continued in the darkness. As he towelled himself dry, he thought about the day ahead: breakfast, find Michael, fly on to Dubai. He switched off the radio – those old stings were annoying him now, but at least he knew that old radio jingles didn't die, they just went to Beirut.

In the breakfast room, he ate a croissant and threw down some coffee before going to reception. There was something familiar about Kamal at the front desk. Perhaps that was what separated a good hotel from a bad one: they made you feel as if you knew them instantly. James made a mental note of this as he looked around: the adjacent bar was now closed, the television that people had been watching the night before switched off.

'Will you be staying tonight?' Kamal asked. James didn't answer straight away. The pace of the hotel was slow; none of the guests seemed to be going anywhere with any great speed. The walls were dark wood, and the bar a mock-up of an English pub. It was even raining outside.

'Will you be staying?' Kamal repeated.

A Scandinavian couple walked past James, nodding good morning to him as if they had already met. He smiled back, then remembered their faces from the minibus.

'Where are the people from the Dubai flight?' James asked Kamal.

'So you are not with the archaeologists,' Kamal replied, as if he had just been given the final clue to a puzzle.

'No.'

Kamal scanned down the check-ins. 'This flight, I think, went to the Bristol Hotel.'

Although James was now realising he had got on the wrong minibus, he was also marvelling how, at 7.30 a.m., Kamal not only knew about the flight, but also where its passengers were staying.

His mouth was dry, and the coffee hadn't helped. Kamal

was busy working the phones, tracking down Michael, so James decided to go and buy some water.

He stepped outside into the thundery February air, feeling a few spots of rain land on him. It was muggy and the warm, damp atmosphere made his clothes feel uncomfortable against his skin. A coffee roastery advertised its wares by sending wonderful smells down the street. There was a bullet hole in the wall opposite him. He looked up and saw square pockets of sky peeking through the tops of densely packed buildings.

And there was Beirut, looking back at him.

James brought his eyes down to street level and paused for a moment to take it all in. Multi-coloured mobile phones ringing and chiming, a car-stopping Wonderbra poster, a yellow Hizbollah flag, a mosque, a church, two battered Mercedes 200s narrowly missing each other. A female face surrounded by a headscarf above an ankle-length billowing coat walked past a café where the waiter was dressed in a tuxedo. People walked slowly on the pavement, no one was in a hurry. The street was sprinkled with shops selling lingerie and perfume and jewellery; there was one called Happiness, another called We Buy Gold. Signs in English, in French, in Arabic. Hollywood Boulevard-style stars engraved with the word 'Hamra' were dotted along the uneven pavement. On the corner stood a building peppered with bullet holes, a giant sponge about to collapse at the feet of the million-dollar apartment complex next door.

The scent of a woman's perfume as she walked past briefly overpowered the petrol fumes. She wore figure-hugging black trousers and had the shiny, glossy hair of a shampoo commercial. She glided down the pavement, past the flower shops, in between mini-markets that sold nuts and sweets, past the man selling lottery tickets, until she was out of sight. James took a step forward and lost his footing on the broken pavement. As he turned left down a smaller street, a Mercedes made a lunge at him, the driver gesturing for James to get in. When he did not appear interested, it carried on down the street, lunging and beeping at other people waiting on the pavement. James walked past freshly squeezed orange juice mixing in a glass container outside an open-fronted store; a French fry shop with any flavouring from interesting to disgusting; he passed Hardee's, Ben and Jerry's, and a policeman who was trying to stop drivers from triple and quadruple parking between the Pizza Hut and the university.

Uneven steps led to the ocean, beginning as abruptly as the country ended – exactly the path his aircraft had taken the night before on its approach. He walked alongside the sickly palm trees and the Mediterranean, noticing another thing that prevented the Corniche from pretending it was the French Riviera – the large picture of the Syrian president. From where James was standing, it appeared the president was wearing a Ferris-wheel halo, but somehow he still looked dignified with his crown of gaudy lights. Women with their children in pushchairs, roller bladers and kids on razor scooters all raced each other along the ocean front. Some of the racing pushchairs stopped to join a crowd of gaping pedestrians. Amidst all the intrigue was a large crane that had given up trying to lift an enormous boulder from the beach. Perhaps the crowd expected it to move again of its own accord, because James could see the crane operator sitting outside his vehicle, smoking a cigarette.

He pushed himself through the revolving door of the hotel, and when it spat him out on the inside realised he had forgotten his water. He had been too disoriented by the intense scribble of streets.

'I called,' Kamal announced. 'Your friend is at the Bristol Hotel.' He signalled for the driver, who doubled as the doorman, to get his car.

In ten minutes they were at the regal entrance to the Bristol Hotel. Flags from around the world were draped elegantly over the door, and the trees were peppered with white fairy lights. James walked up the steps into reception and asked for Michael. The receptionist called up to his room. No answer.

'I think they are having breakfast,' she said, pointing towards the restaurant.

'Hey, mate!' James looked round just in time to see Michael spatter the rest of his group with bits of scrambled egg. 'Where the fuck have you been?'

James entered the restaurant. 'I got on to the wrong minibus.'

'Should have shared a taxi,' Michael informed him. 'Our flight is at midday. They called this morning. We're upgraded.'

'I'll meet you back here at ten,' James said, turning and heading for the door.

'Stay! We don't have to pay for any of this. I think they have Jacuzzis.'

'I have to phone my girlfriend.'

James's taxi was no longer waiting outside, so he decided to walk back to his hotel. He was soon lost and stranded at an intersection, standing on the pavement for five minutes until an old woman took pity on him. She clutched his elbow with her bony fingers, saying, '*Yalla, yalla,*' and motioning for him to just cut through the traffic.

James was bewildered by what he saw – nothing had prepared him for this. Conference rooms were the same the world over, but outside, Beirut was a nasty little mess of low-slung electrical wires, overflowing rubbish bins and air thick with carbon monoxide. The buildings were stacked only a few feet apart, so close that people could almost hold hands with those in the apartment block opposite. The city taunted and threatened him. He didn't feel safe.

Back at his hotel, James took out his suitcase of mobile phones. He quickly rummaged through them, trying to find a handset that wasn't a display model. Only one actually had a SIM card inside, but the accompanying leaflet said that it worked across the world, so he switched it on with some excitement. Then he waited, watching the screen. After ten seconds it flashed a message at him.

'No *network*? What's the fucking point of having roaming if it's never—'. No one was listening so he didn't bother continuing. He checked the hotel call costs which were stuck above his bedside table, running his finger down to the prices for the UK. When he found them his eyes widened in amazement, and he quickly decided to find somewhere that didn't charge twenty dollars for a three-minute chat.

Downstairs, Kamal gave him directions to an international calling centre, and in ten minutes James had found it: four phones and a man in a booth. James wrote down Fran's number and passed it to the man, who punched the numbers then handed James the phone. It was still very early in England and the answering machine picked up. The new answering machine in a colour she didn't like. It spoke to him in its hollow computer voice, giving three different options. James pressed 5 on his keypad to leave a message. He waited. There was some beeping, then a pause.

Message one: 'Hi, James, this is Eddie. You've probably left by now. Just wanted to wish you a good trip and . . . uh . . . well, hope you enjoy Dubai.' *Clunk.* Either Fran was trying out a new outgoing message or James had hit the wrong button and the machine was playing his messages back to him. He pressed 5 again, trying to reset the machine. He had done this once before with their old machine, trying to send Fran a fax from a friend's house and accidentally rerecording his outgoing message as 'Shit, damn . . . fucking stupid thing. Shit. *Clunk.*'

Another message played while James jabbed at the keypad. The man in the booth looked at him strangely.

Message two: 'Fran, it's Becky. Do you have Caroline's e-mail in the States? Can you leave it on my machine as I'm going out? 'Bye.'

Message three: 'Hi. It's me. I thought about you all day. I miss you. I'll try and get off early tonight.'

End of messages.

It was just the kind of message James always left. The sort of thing he would do during his lunch break. When he was making videos he had often called to talk to the answering machine as a second best to speaking to Fran herself. It was similar to the pleasure he got from buying her a present when she wasn't around – while he chose the gift he felt that she was close to him, it was a moment of intimacy.

But the voice on the answering machine didn't belong to James.

It was male and it wasn't anyone James knew. He hung up, shaken. The man's voice had been warm and secretive, and he hadn't even said his name. No one reached that level of intimacy overnight.

James focused on the wall to try to keep himself breathing regularly. His heart thumped right up into his skull as he asked for the number again. The answering machine picked up and he pressed 5, skipping through the messages and repeating the last one. He definitely didn't know the voice.

End of messages.

James checked his watch, then slumped into a small plastic chair and waited for Fran to wake up. He picked up one of the old newspapers piled on the seat next to him. It was in English and he scanned the front page. It reported an Israeli politician announcing that if any of Hizbollah's rockets reached the Israeli town of Kiryat Shmona, then Lebanon would burn. James put the paper down and caught sight of a white sticker on the wall. It read: 'Burn our soil? Burn in hell first.'

He started to fidget nervously. He didn't want to be

caught in the middle of anything. He needed to get out of there. When he dialled again, a sleepy Fran picked up. When she heard his voice, she sounded bright and cheerful.

'Is it hot in Dubai?' she asked.

'I don't know. I'm in Beirut.'

'What?'

'I'm in Beirut.'

'Why're you there?' She paused. 'Beirut! Isn't that dangerous?'

James looked at the sticker, then the newspaper. 'I don't know. Look, the plane on the way here had a . . . something went wrong with it. I'm leaving for Dubai in a couple of hours. I miss—'

'You should get compensation,' Fran said, overlapping James, before adding, 'I miss you too.'

Fran's voice was so light that James took a deep, refreshing breath for the first time that day. He was completely at ease when he asked, 'Who was that on the answering machine?', already confident that Fran's explanation would be a simple and obvious one, and cursing himself for falling for the tricks his mind always played on him when he was tired and feeling displaced in a new country.

'What?'

'I just listened to our messages,' James said. 'There was a man saying he'd be over tonight.'

Fran didn't answer right away. James looked around him. The phone booth man was keeping an eye on the teletext exchange rates as he handed customers piles of Lebanese notes in exchange for US dollar bills.

'He's a friend.' Fran exhaled the line all in one word.

'Does he have a name? Why haven't you mentioned him?'

'Why don't we talk about this when you come back?'

The line went dead. James's first thought was that she had hung up on him. But it was the connection. The booth man dialled out again, then passed the phone to James. This time the line was scratchy and he could hardly hear what she was saying.

'Hello? Hello? It's me. *Me*,' he said. He listened to her speak, wondering whether there was guilt in her voice, but the line was so bad it was impossible to work out. 'So is something going on with this *friend*? What do you mean, how can I ask you like that? I can ask you because . . . What? I can't hear—'

When the crackle died down, there was a moment of silence before Fran said, 'I *have* met someone.'

'What does that mean? Be specific,' James said, looking at his watch; the hissing and clicking on the line told him he didn't have time to wait for the usual nausea that came with bad news. 'And brief.'

She was specific. And brief. James managed to shout, 'Get on the comput—' before the line went dead.

'The lines for other country not work today . . .' The man in the booth did a perfect representation of two fighter jets dropping bombs, using only his hands. James passed the phone back to him as a child passes food it doesn't like back to its mother. 'You want Internet?'

'Does it work?'

'Internet is local,' the booth man said, beckoning for James to follow him into a small room in the back which was packed with two rows of computers. 'Welcome,' he said, gesturing for James to sit down. James logged on to chat and waited. Fran logged on almost immediately.

> *Do not give out your phone number or credit card*
> *details to anyone during an on-line conversation.*
> Fran90: *can you call again?*
> JamesH: the international phone line is fucked. tell
> me you're joking about all this
> Fran90: *i'm sorry*
> JamesH: you're seeing someone?
> Fran90: *i'm so sorry, james*
> JamesH: stop saying that. who is it?
> Fran90: *doesn't matter*
> JamesH: yes it does. i love you
> Fran90: *i didn't want you to find out like this*
> JamesH: how did you want me to find out? by
> telegram?

James was worried that if he looked in the mirror he wouldn't recognise his reflection. He couldn't identify this as his life. He put his head in his hands and closed his eyes. When he opened them a few seconds later it was as if he had been in a car crash and was still trying to piece together the events that had led to impact. His racing mind came up with a photofit of the man from the sound of his voice. He thought about the back of Fran's neck, and how she liked it when he kissed her there. Now he imagined another man also knowing this, and he pictured her having private jokes with this person, having a favourite song. So this had been going on yesterday and would continue today and tomorrow. And no one had told him about it.

> Fran90: *what are you going to do?*
> JamesH: throw up
> Fran90: *just come back and we'll talk about this, okay?*
> JamesH: talk about what exactly?
> Fran90: *i wish it wasn't like this*
> JamesH: don't give me that bullshit. i fucking knew it as well, but i was too stupid to ask
> Fran90: *it hasn't been going on long*
> JamesH: why aren't you saying it was all a mistake and you won't do it again?
> Fran90: *because it's not a mistake*

James couldn't help it. He knew what he wanted to say. He wanted to say, 'How can you do this to me? I gave up my job for us. I'm doing everything I can for us to be together.' But he knew that a lot of people gave up things for the ones they loved, and they still never got a complimentary pancake roll when they ate Chinese; their lottery numbers didn't come up more often; people didn't stop cheating on them, lying to them, being human to them because of it.

> JamesH: i thought we were planning a future together?
> Fran90: *i didn't want this to happen*
> JamesH: stop saying that. you sound like a broken fucking record

WetNikki says: SPEAK TO HOT TEENS
RIGHT NOW!

James called over to the booth man, who looked sheepish
and logged off the other open chat programs.

James realised that this was probably not an awful
moment for Fran, this was what she *wanted*, a situation
that would give her the chance to be dumped. Had he not
heard the message, perhaps she would have allowed it to
continue, letting him dig a bigger and bigger hole until he
realised there was a problem. This was her opportunity to
bypass that plan.

Fran90: are you there?
JamesH: do you know what i gave up for you?
Fran90: what did you give up for me?
JamesH: i gave up the video thing. my whole career
Fran90: why did you do that?
JamesH: what – you've forgotten everything
already?
Fran90: tell me why you did it
JamesH: for us! so we had the two incomes that we
needed. i did that shitty job for that. do you think i
enjoyed it?
*Fran90: i fell in love with the guy that used to get
excited about his job, about his life*
JamesH: but i gave that up for you!
Fran90: i didn't ask you to!
JamesH: what?
*Fran90: why didn't you say you wanted to get back
to the videos – see if i'd go for it*

JamesH: all your friends have these important jobs,
they have money
Fran90: and?
JamesH: fran, i wanted us to be secure for our
future, that's all
Fran90: we have to be happy first
JamesH: let's just start again
Fran90: we can't. it's too late
JamesH: it's not too late
Fran90: it is

When James got back to his hotel, he collapsed on his bed
and shut his eyes. He kept them closed when he heard the
phone ringing. It rang four times. First he thought it was
Fran, but then he remembered that she didn't have the hotel
number. He thought it was Fran because he didn't want to
believe she had left him. When the phone rang for the fifth
time, he picked up. Kamal at the desk told James he had
a call from Michael, so James accepted it, then as soon as
he heard Michael's voice he hung up, before taking it off
the hook. After thirty seconds, the phone started to make
a noise that sounded like a distant ambulance siren. James
ignored it. The siren was then interrupted by knocking on
the door, which grew louder, and James could hear Michael
shouting his name. He was saying they would be late; they
would miss their plane; they had to leave *now*.

James was unable to move.

Eventually the banging on the door stopped. Michael
had given up. James shifted the pieces of the relationship
around in his head, spotting moments in restaurants, in the

bedroom, walking down the street, when Fran had given him clues. But they weren't really clues. James could twist even her choice of breakfast cereal into proof that he should have done things differently. What hurt more than the way he had found out, more than the idea of Fran with someone else, was that something solid in his life was now over.

He decided to examine the facts. He was en route to a job that he didn't like. His girlfriend was no longer his girlfriend. Beirut was not a nice place. He knew these three things for sure. He checked his watch while lying dead still, watching the minutes tick away until the absolute latest he could leave and still make the plane. He watched the seconds change until it got to the point where he would need to travel at the speed of light to catch it. And then finally it was too late. The flight had left. It was on its way to Dubai, and Seat 14B was empty; its listed occupant was in a Beirut hotel room. He wasn't leaving; he wasn't going anywhere. With the kind of bravery that only desperate men could pretend to have, James decided that he would never go back to Fran, no matter what she promised. Even if she begged. He would show her how little she meant to him; he would stay in Beirut and *demonstrate* it. He sat up on the bed, having a rush of energy, and a sick thrill of freedom. He would still have fallen into her arms if she had been there, but self-preservation had kicked in. He had to make something of the situation, or he would just sink into the folds of the bed, never to be seen again.

06

James was free-falling. His 'how to deal with foreign countries' bible seemed obsolete with no Fran waiting for him at home. But some kind of safety catch *did* click, and just as being stranded up a mountain can kick-start a survival instinct, James could feel the beginnings of a certain stay-alive mechanism of his own: buy shoes, get haircut, order cab, transfer to Marriott. He tried not to think too much about the cruelty of now finally being solvent but having no Fran to spend his money on, instead using it to pay for himself to stay *alone* in a hotel; and at the same time, he didn't dare work out how long being jobless was going to allow him to stay in the Marriott, or anywhere.

The shoes were the easy part. He walked in, tried them on, bought them. The shopkeeper impressed him by guessing his size just by looking at his feet. He wondered whether women had developed a similar ability to guess a man's size, but had chosen never to let on. He then bought some clothes from a large pine-floored open-plan store that was playing R&B chart hits while its discerning customers picked out the latest fashions. James paid for several items, then went back into the changing room and put them on. He left his old suit on the floor, and walked back out on to the street wearing his new purchases. Feeling slightly better, and a lot more comfortable, he strode along, stopping only occasionally to glance at the map Kamal had drawn for him. When he looked back up, a man was standing in front of him, blocking his path.

'Looking for Josef?' he asked. Maybe Josef had spotted James's hair and knew it was a safe bet that this man needed help. Perhaps all barbers could recognise a man trying to make sense of a finished relationship by having a haircut. Either way, James *was* looking for Josef, who smiled as he led his new customer into his barber's shop. Josef looked more Miami than Lebanon; he could have been a Florida loan shark with his pink shirt, big moustache and awesomely white teeth. Six chairs were all occupied by clients – from boys to old men. A small coffee machine whirred away in the corner. Josef handed James a small plastic cup of thick, strong coffee and talked about the weather in England, the price of a haircut in Paris, and how he didn't mind being a Christian in a Muslim area. James presumed this was just an extension of the Middle Eastern rule his out-of-date business travel book warned him about: never discuss business until you have asked after every member of a person's family and drunk enough coffee to fuel you for a triathlon.

'No one bothers me, I do good haircuts,' Josef explained. For good measure there was a poster on the wall: '*Please and with apologies refrain from discussing politics in this hair salon.*'

When a chair became available, Josef beckoned for James to take the space. He sat down in front of a barber who was making an effort to look as bored as possible. Josef translated James's request to him. This was a place for men, run by men. No sexy Lucy sticking her left breast in your eye as she cut that tricky bit, James thought. The barber readied himself by plugging in his mobile phone, rearranging his address book and checking his voicemail. After he was satisfied his phone was working at peak performance he looked at James as if to say 'What the hell do you want?' He took a piece of masking tape and wound it around James's neck so tightly that the skin coming out of either end looked as if it had been pleated. James threaded his arms through the shawl, and tried to measure his breathing. The barber was again briefly distracted by his phone – someone had had the audacity to unplug his charger in favour of a blow-dryer. He was too busy accusing anyone holding a hairdryer to hear James's pathetic pleas for him to loosen the deadly bib. James put his hands around the back of his neck, tried to locate the Velcro on the shawl, then grabbed hold of it and pulled the quick release. He then unravelled the masking tape.

He gasped for breath.

The barber noticed this, but chose to ignore it as he took his electrical clippers and, without shampoo, without wetting his hair, without 'How would you like it?' or 'Going anywhere nice this year?', just went to work. Every few seconds he would direct the blow-dryer directly into James's face, the hot air drying his eyes wide open. This was the barber's method of getting rid of unwanted hair from James's shoulders, lap and face.

In ten minutes, James was ready to join the army. The

barber had been silent the entire time. There was a brief halt to all activity when a man in an enormous Mercedes pulled up outside. The bass bins in his car shook the building. It took three barbers, including James's, to go out on the street shouting his name, 'Amer, Amer!', and help him locate a parking space. Amer wore a carefully crumpled Hugo Boss suit with an unbuttoned shirt. He seemed to walk in slow motion, and was greeted like the prodigal son. Josef had even stopped preening himself in the double mirror and started directing his barbers like a military commander.

'*Amoura habibi*,' Josef said, affectionately warping Amer's name, before turning to one of his barbers. 'Ramzi! Shampoo for Amer. *Yalla, yalla!*'

After every barber had kissed Amer three times, they reluctantly returned to their mortal customers. Amer looked like a daily visitor to Josef's, and had probably earned his welcome. James enviously eyed the shampoo treatment Amer was receiving, but then the crazed barber pulled his head back round so he could no longer watch.

Once the Amer commotion had completely calmed down, Josef returned to ask if everything was okay. The barber held James's stare in the mirror, daring him to say no. Just as James was wondering what would happen if he asked for something to be changed, he felt a razor blade on his neck. The barber was whipping off rogue hairs with the speed of a manic artist attacking a canvas. When he finished, he put his hands around James's neck and pretended to throttle him. He smiled, waiting for James to acknowledge his joke.

'*Na'eeman*,' Josef said, explaining it as a kind of an after-the-event *bon appetit* for haircuts, showers or general cleanliness. James checked his reflection and had to admit that, as far as ten-minute haircuts went, this was a very good one. He was now short haired and streamlined. He paid Josef, and then paused for a moment to watch his barber attack the next customer with the same aggression. This time he was on his mobile phone right from the start.

The taxi-driver sped along the coast, taking James to his new accommodation. He looked out of the back window as they passed a long, straight stretch of road by the beach where boy racers were gathering for their evening's entertainment. The taxi-driver slowed down so James could watch.

'*Wahad, itneen, taalete. Allahu Akbar!*' One, two, three, God is great! went the starter's orders. On 'God is great' they hit the accelerator. Until the police arrived and they scattered, screeching into local residents' garages to hide. James tried to imagine boy racers in Renault 5 turbos shouting 'Praise Jesus!' as they sped around Southend. A fly poster stapled to a lamp-post advertised a Palestinian revolutionary hip hop band. It wasn't clear whether the music was revolutionary, like DJ Shadow, or if the people were revolutionary, like Che Guevara. It had *Allahu Akbar* written at the bottom all the same.

James checked in at his beloved Marriott and went straight into the restaurant. A group of men were sitting at the bar drinking pints, but James took a table by himself. He was starting to feel safe again, and as he half listened to their conversation, he relaxed. Through the glass partitions separating the bar from reception, he watched a girl enter clutching a pile of papers. He knew he was staring, but he couldn't look away. He took in every part of her face, even though she went in and out of view, behind a pillar that obscured his line of vision. Her lips were glossed with a translucent pink lipstick, her dark eyes framed by curved eyebrows. She wore silver earrings that sparkled against her long dark hair.

'Don't get involved with the locals.'

James turned round with a jump. A short, slightly plump man with a red face was following James's eyeline to the girl. They both stared in awe for a moment.

'Come and join us at the bar,' the man said.

Jack had spent the previous day in the hills of Dbayeh, huffing and puffing his way up an incline, hoping a day outside would further improve his tan. The cool February weather was interrupted occasionally by a rogue summer day and Jack was sweating profusely as he started on the final stretch. He was bald, and wore very short shorts whenever he was abroad, no matter what the local weather was like.

Jack reached the finish just in time for the forfeits. He was made to drink a glass of beer in one go as he had been spotted taking a rest, sitting on a rock, smoking a cigarette. Everyone cheered as he downed his beer, then poured the dregs over his head. Another man drank beer from a child's potty as his penance for getting lost, while a Lebanese family stopped their car to watch what was going on. It didn't matter what Jack and his friends did at the weekends, how much beer they drank, how many times they fell over, they *still* missed home.

Jack bought James a drink and introduced him to everyone at the bar: accountant, insurance, construction, insurance. James was disappointed he had left his seat, and his view of the girl, for this. But he noticed, for the first time, that he didn't talk about his job and he didn't bring out some anecdote about selling phones. He felt awkward in this group, and it was strangely reassuring. He was silent, listening to them talk among themselves, not enjoying himself, and wondering whether he could catch another glimpse of the girl – the only break he'd had so far from thinking about Fran. Seeing her was like taking a little drug that kicked in for a few seconds to give him respite from his past. It was amazing how the libido could rush to the rescue of a broken heart, even if only for a short while.

'You came at a bad time,' said Jack. 'It'll be chaos soon. Aren't you worried?'

James had lost sight of the girl now, but his eyes were still searching. 'No, not really,' he said absent-mindedly.

'If the Israelis leave without a peace agreement . . .' one of Jack's friends said, tailing off.

'. . . the Syrians have all their troops here . . .' someone else pointed out.

'. . . Hizbollah will be able to reach Israel with their rockets . . .'

James had the feeling that the conversation was for his benefit, to somehow show their bravery. They seemed to him like very scared people.

'So why're you here?' Jack asked. 'Which company sent you?'

'I came out by myself,' James replied, catching Jack's surprised reaction.

'This country is a fucking shambles,' another voice added, finishing a fourth pint. 'Let's go to the Hard Rock.'

The Hard Rock had the usual giant guitar outside it. As soon as James entered, he wished he was back in his seat at the hotel, so he hid at the end of the bar and picked up the payphone attached to the wall. He dialled Fran's number, but hung up before she could answer, or the answering machine could imply that she was out having a good time.

'The thing about the Lebs, Malcolm,' Jack was telling his accountant friend, 'they don't know how to treat their women.'

Farther along the bar, a site manager for a large construction company had finished two more pints and had now solved the problems of the Middle East – a crisis that the greatest minds in the world couldn't untangle. Slowly, all these satellite conversations came to a close as the four of them arranged themselves in a circle and proudly compared suntans, each face more wind-burned than the last. James watched from a distance.

Later, Jack gravitated to the only Lebanese girl in the bar, who was standing close to the television which played silently in the corner. The closer Jack got, the more interested she became in the Sagesse basketball game on TV.

'How would you like to keep my bed warm tonight?' he asked her. James did a double take. Jack was the other side of the bar, but well within earshot. James finished his drink quickly, keeping an eye on the door ready for his escape. It was too late.

'Snooty bitch.' Jack returned rebuffed and sat himself squarely on the bar stool next to James. 'Do you have a girlfriend?'

'I did.'

'That's what's good about this place: the girls want to keep it *hush-hush* because they'll get into trouble. Hush-hush suits me fine.' Jack beamed. When he smiled his cheeks had the shine of the red leather on a brand-new cricket ball.

'No girlfriend, then?' James asked.

'I'm married, mate.'

'Is . . . your wife here?' James asked tentatively.

'Yeah. She doesn't like the place either. The kids love it, though, got loads of friends at school . . .'

'What does your wife do here?'

'Stays at home.'

James awoke in his hotel room the next morning feeling a little drowsy from the sleeping tablets. He hadn't needed them, he was exhausted, but he was determined not to disregard his plan entirely. On his list he had ticked off Marriott and sleeping tablets. He was feeling more normal. On his way to breakfast, he noticed that the girl he had seen the night before was in the reception area again. As James walked past, he had the awful thought, *Oh shit, I'm going to talk to her and there is nothing I can do to stop this from happening.*

'Hello,' he said.

'Hi,' the girl replied, looking a little surprised. James

nodded, as if she had given the right answer. He paused for a moment. Then he went and had breakfast.

A waiter broke his gaze this time. 'Would you like more toast?'

'Why not,' James said, not looking at him. This girl. The way she moved. Her long dark hair shone even in the artificial light. She had on a black top with a low-cut neck; her jeans were tight on her thighs, flaring slightly below the knee. They had a small embroidered flower pattern on the front. Her wide belt had an over-sized oval buckle, studded with sparkling stones. Her clothes exploited her curves enough to make James look, then feel guilty for doing so. Belt buckle apart, she wasn't dressed suggestively. It was in her eyes and her smile. It was in James's mind. He didn't notice the toast arriving. *What am I doing?* he thought. He couldn't look away. He got out of his seat, another foreigner stumbling blindly into something he didn't understand, and walked into reception again. He put his hand out.

'I'm James,' he said.

'Do I know you?' the girl asked.

'Yes. We spoke earlier.'

'About what?'

'I said hello, and you replied.'

'Is that speaking?'

'It's a start.'

'Are you here for . . .' She couldn't figure out whether she was being hit on or if this *ajnabi* might in some way be connected to her business and therefore required a degree of politeness.

'I make videos,' James said.

'That sounds ominous.'

'Music videos.'

'Oh yeah? Anyone I've seen?'

'Champagne.'

James was sure the girl stifled a laugh. He couldn't blame her. Champagne, an eighties band, had their short ironic comeback in the late nineties and James directed their video. It took off, and suddenly James could pay the rent. It meant he stopped working with the bands that had inspired him, the two-bit acts with passion and potential, but he was in demand elsewhere. Champagne had launched him into a world where the stakes were higher, where his opinion wasn't always respected – sometimes not even required – and where he had to deal with the likes of Bobby Del Pico.

'Champagne . . . they were funny.' The girl seemed to be calculating something in her head, trying to decide whether to continue the conversation or cut it off.

'I'm James,' he repeated.

She smiled at his persistence. 'You're going to keep telling me your name until I tell you mine, aren't you?'

James nodded.

'I'm Maya,' she said, visibly loosening up.

The woman from reception reappeared, handing Maya more papers. 'You have ten tomorrow,' she said.

'That's low. Have you been putting up our posters?' Maya spoke English with the smoothness of French and the efficiency of American. She pronounced double letters with more weight than single. When she told James the

Champagne video was funny, she had really paused on the n's. Fu*nnnn*y.

'What are you doing?' James asked.

'I manage a tour company. Unfortunately people don't seem to want to visit Roman ruins when bombs keep falling out of the sky.' She shrugged and made towards the exit. 'Why're you in Lebanon?' she asked, turning around in the open doorway. James knew the conversation was winding down. This needed to be good.

'Er . . . I'm making a music video here,' he said. It was less than a millimetre, perhaps only visible if you studied it closely, but James thought he saw her raise an eyebrow of interest. Then he watched her walk to her car and drive off.

The next morning James woke up and found himself getting ready for nothing. He stopped, standing in his room for a moment, then realised what his rush was. He was going to find Maya.

He wandered the streets, occasionally getting sidetracked at sandwich bars, or standing outside record shops, alone like a lost child, listening intently to the sounds coming from within. When, completely by chance, he spotted a road sign with an arrow pointing to the tourist office, he congratulated himself on his sense of direction and headed off towards it. He entered the building through a small doorway and, once inside, scanned the room for Maya. She wasn't there, and neither were the usual pictures of snow-capped peaks, beaches and valleys that all tourist offices displayed. Instead there were shelves, hundreds of them, packed with books sporting pictures of religious leaders on their covers. Similar pictures also hung on the walls. At the far end was an installation showing military equipment: artillery, ammunition, camouflage netting, all draped elegantly, like a modern art display you could walk through. Perhaps this was how the Lebanese did tourism. James didn't care – it had taken him so long to find he wasn't going to walk out with nothing to show for it. He asked the man behind the till for information about places to visit. The man stared blankly back at him, and James took that as a signal to end his touristic efforts in Lebanon. On his way out, as a memento, he bought a postcard of a bearded cleric. This brought an even more confused stare from the man behind the desk. James swiftly exited with his souvenir, and walked a couple of doors down, just as far as a small, easy-to-miss sign in the shape of a cedar tree that read 'Tourist Office'. There was a red arrow pointing inside. James rushed towards it, but before he entered he looked back at where he had just been, the phantom tourist office. The sign was in Arabic – perhaps it was better that he didn't know. Still, he thought to himself, it was just as well he didn't jump to conclusions.

Inside the real tourist office, two women were gossiping and smoking in French. Neither of them was Maya. They didn't feel James was a worthy reason for interrupting their conversation, and barely acknowledged him as he entered, clutching his postcard of the Iranian Supreme Leader. Grudgingly, the younger woman stood up and said hello to him. She handed him some brochures, eyeing the postcard in his hand.

'You want to go on a tour, isn't it?' she asked, pointing to the posters on the walls.

It was the poster which had given James the idea. As soon as he was back at the hotel, he raced around reception and the restaurant until he found one of Maya's posters, then indiscreetly ripped it down and stuffed it in his pocket. Despite his excitement, it was too late to leave by the time he had the poster safely in his possession, so he compensated by getting up pointlessly early the next morning. Clutching the poster and following the tiny map printed on the bottom, he navigated his way through the city. He wondered how Maya would react to him just turning up, but he put that to the back of his mind.

When he arrived, there were two large coaches parked outside the empty office. The early morning air was cold and one coach door was open so James climbed on board, settled into a seat near the back and dozed off. In his half-dream he heard a voice, but couldn't make out any words. The voice was female, singing by itself with no accompaniment. Sometimes it would stop for a moment, then resume. At times the voice became louder, and there was another noise, shuffling paper. James opened his eyes and saw Maya sitting cross-legged at the front of the coach stapling together brochures and putting them in a pile beside her. She was humming to herself. Then the hums became words.

James stood up, making Maya jump. 'What are you doing here?' she gasped.

'I'm coming on the trip.'

'Which trip?'

'Your trip?'

'You shouldn't be on the coach yet,' she said. 'You have to go and pay in the office and wait. There are chairs in there,' she added, as an incentive. James heard the order and walked down the steps. 'You could have caught the minibus – it picks up from the Marriott.'

'I don't like minibuses,' James replied. 'What were you singing?'

'You have to pay for the trip before you board.' She pointed to the office.

'What was the song you were singing? Is it famous? I think I've heard it before.'

She smiled at him, then turned back to stapling brochures. James walked towards the office. Just as he got to the door, she called out.

'Which trip are you going on?'

He turned round. 'Someone said Bcharreh was good.' He tried to add casually, 'Which one do you take?'

'I don't take them. I do their accounts and marketing and advertising and . . .' She exhaled. '. . . everything really.'

'You should go on strike,' James said.

'It's good for my résumé.'

'For what?' James walked back to the coach, closer to her.

'MBA.'

'Basketball?'

'MBA. Application to business school. I'm running this place.'

'Oh . . . so I should go to Bcharreh?'

'Yes, or perhaps go right up to the cedars, or down south to Sour, or if you like Crusader castles—'

'Someone told me Tyre is good.'

'Tyre *is* Sour.'

'It has two names?' James started it as a question and ended it as a statement.

'Most people prefer Bcharreh, it's the birthplace of Gibran Khalil Gibran.' Maya said the poet's three names as if they were one smooth word.

'So basically you know everywhere that's worth going to.'

'I do.'

'I'm trying to think where I'd send a tourist in England,' James said, needlessly extending the conversation.

'Stratford-upon-Avon?' she suggested.

For some reason this made James laugh. 'Well, yeah,' he agreed.

'I bet Gibran's town is a lot more fun than Shakespeare's,' she said. 'There's a joke about Bcharreh. A boy is having an argument with another boy in the village. The boy's mother shouts to him, "Roukoz, don't make problems! Now just shoot the boy and come up for dinner." So don't get into any arguments while you're there, okay?' she said.

James walked towards the tour office door. There were now two people behind desks, selling tickets. Again, James stopped and turned around.

'I didn't know Gibran was Lebanese,' he said.

Maya replied, 'You've not spoken to many Lebanese people yet, have you?'

'No. Why?'

'Because you haven't had the "everyone is Lebanese" and "everything was invented by the Lebanese" speeches. Don't worry, they'll come.'

'Everyone is Lebanese?'

'Neil Sedaka, Casey Kasem, Ralph Nader—'

'Casey Kasem? Scooby Doo is Lebanese?'

'No, Casey Kasem did Shaggy's voice. Shaggy is Lebanese. I don't know where Scooby is from. Not just that.' Maya put on a thick Lebanese accent. 'Paul Anka. Lebanese. Swatch watches. Lebanese. Kinko's photocopy shops. Lebanese. George Mitchell. Lebanese. Inventing the alphabet. Lebanese.'

'My guidebook just says that there are good banking laws and something about *hummus*.'

'Everyone is Lebanese until proven otherwise. Doesn't matter if their only connection to the Middle East is one great-grandfather from Jordan. They're still Lebanese if they are famous or successful.' Maya pushed a strand of hair away from her face and smiled. 'Look, if I keep talking I'll have to charge you.'

'Oh yeah? How much?' James enquired, making for his wallet.

'You'll have to buy every seat on the coach.'

James wished he had the credit card or the cash that would allow him to make the kind of bold gesture that appears in Hollywood movies.

The office was warm and people were gathered paying for their day trips. James found a Coke machine and got himself a drink. When he returned to the ticket desks, the queue had extended. He tried to recall the last time he had been on anything that could be described as a day trip as he handed over his fifty dollars.

'Which trip?' the woman behind the desk asked.

'Sour,' James said.

'Name?'

'Sour,' James repeated.

'*Your* name.'

James told her and spelt it.

'Sorry, no more places.'

'Really, are you sure?'

'It's full.'

'What about Bcharreh?'

She scanned up and down her list very carefully, before looking James up and down even more closely. 'Actually, you are already down for the cedars.'

'The cedars?'

'You have paid,' she said.

James looked around, waiting for the hidden camera to make itself known.

'You can get on board now,' she said. James tentatively made his way to the coach, looking around him as if someone might jump out of a bush at any minute. He found a seat and waited to be told he was in the wrong place. When Maya walked past him down the aisle, he grabbed her arm to stop her. She looked round suddenly. He was quickly aware that he was touching her. He didn't know whether to let go, or whether letting go would draw attention to what he was doing in the first place.

'Is the booking agency psychic?' James asked.

'Don't you like trees?'

'Me? I love them. Love everything about them. Leaves. Bark. Sap.'

She kept her eyes on him. The driver was calling her from the front of the coach, but she ignored him.

'I thought you didn't take the trips.'

'We have a new driver. I'm checking he knows the route.'

'How did my name get on the list?'

'I thought about it, and I decided you should see our national emblem. Besides, you need some Lebanese coaching if you're going to survive.'

The driver was still calling Maya so she finally gave in and went to speak to him. James looked around at the other passengers, catching conversations in German, Dutch and English. There was plenty of friendly eye contact between passengers, and every conversation started with 'What are you doing here?' James was the only one there because of a girl. Although he took comfort in knowing that, at any one time anywhere in the world, men were doing all kinds of things they usually wouldn't 'because of a girl'.

The coach took a long time to push its way through the city's tangle of cars, but once they were out of Beirut the tour guide got on the microphone and started pointing things out. She would do it once in English, then straight away in French. She succeeded in keeping the questions firmly on the Phoenicians, dodging the ones about Hizbollah. Maya sat up front with a man from the company, comparing important-looking papers. After a few miles the coach pulled into a dusty lay-by and everyone got off to buy coffee and expensive cakes – it looked like a nice little earner going on between shop owner and tour company. This break was Maya's down time – she seemed to have a permanent stack of work papers in front of her at all other times – so James left her alone to chat on her mobile phone and drink her coffee in peace. It didn't stop anyone else, though, and James wondered why he had bothered to hold back. Every other man on the coach just *had* to ask her some question. Just *had* to try to make her laugh. She looked like she had heard it all before.

The sight of the cedars ended all conversations as everyone gaped out of the window in respectful silence. James could see the thick cover of snow on the mountains sweating and glistening in the midday sun as the coach slowly hauled itself on to an embankment. Everyone disembarked and made their way, cameras in hand, towards the majestic trees. The large branches threw elegant silhouettes against the backdrop of snow, but Maya's dark hair looked even better, separating her from the white background, making her the centre of James's vision. Around her neck she wore a necklace made from many tiny slivers of silver thread. The boots she wore under her smart work trousers were knee length – but only she knew that. There was a thin smile of skin visible between her top and her belt. James wished Maya would fasten up her coat – so far all he had noticed about Lebanon's national symbol was a glimpse of Maya's tanned body. He decided to bring his focus back to the trees and wandered around dutifully, taking pictures, starting to feel as if he really *was* on holiday. He liked the feeling of being completely displaced – as if anything he did that day would have no bearing on his life and wouldn't stay in his memory. This was a bonus day outside of his normal life.

When he got back to the coach, Maya was sitting on a low wall, smoking a cigarette.

'The cedars are that way,' she said with a smirk.

'I like them.'

'So that's your treatise on the most famous trees in history? You know they cut down these *actual* trees to take to Jerusalem to build the temple. It's in the Bible.'

'The Bible, eh?'

'I have to ask you. Do you believe that Jesus looked like Peter O'Toole?'

'What?'

Maya flicked her cigarette away and stood up. 'Whenever I watch those old religious epics, Jesus always looks English or Irish. Didn't the producers know he was from the Middle East? I'm always waiting for him to offer his disciples tea and cucumber sandwiches.'

'No one has tea and cucumber sandwiches in England any more.'

'What do they have?'

'Tea and sun-dried tomato sandwiches.'

'Some tourists last week asked me if we had Christmas in Lebanon. I told them they were in the country where Jesus turned water into wine. They looked shocked. Anyway, we *invented* Christmas!'

James thought for a moment. 'Did Pete O'Toole ever play Jesus? Are you sure? I know he played Lawrence . . .'

'I'll have to look it up for you.'

'Are there more trees up there?' one of the eager day-trippers asked, as he approached them. He was a ruin fanatic: bearded, middle aged and single, the kind of enthusiast who travelled to places that most people in the West feared, seemingly oblivious to the regime or current political climate, just interested in ruins, digging and stones. Only seeing the world as it existed before. James didn't understand them, but he always liked people who were so interested in specific subjects that they missed the overall point entirely.

'You're not allowed into the field, but you can take pictures over the fence,' Maya told him. The man scuffled away happily.

'You were going to give me surviving Lebanon lessons,' he said, pulling her attention back to him.

'Okay. There are only three words you need to know,' Maya began. 'The first is *khalas*. It means "Enough already!", "That's final", "Stop bothering me", "I can't eat any more", "*forgetaboutit*", "Stop it!" and "It's been decided".'

'All that?'

'And about twenty other things. So you learn that word, and you've learned twenty words. Okay, the next is *habibi*. This means "my love" and it can also be "my friend" – like when you say "mate" or an American says "man".'

'How do you know how the person is using it?'

'If a girl is calling you *habibi* when she is lying naked next to you, it probably doesn't mean "mate". When the guy you buy your tomatoes from calls you it, he probably doesn't mean "my love".'

'Got it.'

'So now you know about thirty words.'

'What's the last one?'

'*Inshallah*. It means "God willing". But it can also mean "I hope so" or "possibly" or "no chance".'

'Will you meet me for a drink tonight?'

'*Inshallah, habibi.*'

No *chance, mate.*

As the rest of the day-trippers returned, Maya exchanged smiles and chit-chat with them. James couldn't work out whether their discussion about a blond-haired Jesus had been anything more than a diversion for her. On the way back to Beirut, they stopped for coffee again. James tried to revive the conversation, but received only clipped responses from her.

'This isn't the first time someone on a trip wanted to talk to you more than see the sights, is it?' he said.

'When do you start making your video?' she asked.

'Oh . . . er . . . soon.' James was starting to feel a little ashamed of his lie. But it wasn't that he was embarrassed by his salesman job, it was that he wanted to introduce to Maya a version of himself that he liked, even if he had to throw himself back to his past to do so.

'Can I call you some time?' he asked.

'When is some time?'

'In about five minutes? Later? Tomorrow? You could give me more Lebanese lessons.'

'Do you always go around asking nice Arab girls out?' Maya said, walking back to the coach.

'I don't know,' James answered, calling after her. 'Are you nice?'

07

Two weeks after Julien had burned a hole in Hassan's floor during the power station bombings, the dark holes the hot coals had made were still visible. Despite the destruction, his welcome at Hassan's house had never run out, but he was now happy on his own, in his new flat in Ashrafieh, east Beirut.

Julien stood across the road from McDonald's, watching the valet parking. He *had* to film that to show his friends back in Paris. He slipped a mini DV tape into his digital camera and pointed it at the subject. Clouds kept passing overhead, changing the lighting conditions. He swung around, focused his camera on the ocean for a moment, then went back to filming street life. Some kids were roller blading on a metal ramp, men on bicycles sold bread, others were fishing. There was a rumour that the men selling bread from their bikes were Syrian spies, so Julien scrutinised people standing around to see whether they stopped their conversations when the bread-sellers cycled past. He was so busy with his little experiment he didn't notice an angry Syrian soldier approaching him. The soldier grabbed his camera and carted him off. This wasn't Julien's first run-in with the authorities – even when he was filming a building for architectural interest, two seconds later a soldier would appear and demand the film. The emphasis on security was understandable, and a soldier guarding a patch of nothing was a familiar sight. A stack of breeze blocks – a soldier guarding them. A random piece of scrub land – a soldier guarding it. On Sunday mornings, as joggers ran along the Corniche, the ocean to one side of them, a long palm-tree-lined road to the other, they passed a series of armed soldiers guarding what appeared to be air.

James's three-week holiday – he felt that that was more than sufficient to let Fran know how little he cared about her – had nearly come to an end. How would she feel now, knowing he would rather spend *three weeks* in Beirut than see her? Was she missing the same things he was, was she remembering the same moments that filled his memory? His last recollection of them in bed together was New Year's Eve, spent at her parents' house. As the new millennium had swung into action in Trafalgar Square and Edinburgh Castle, James was fucking Fran silently in her old bedroom, trying not to make any sound that would carry through the thin partition walls to her parents next door. As the clock struck two and Fran slept, James pushed himself up on one elbow in bed, craning his neck so he could see his reflection in Fran's mirror. It was the mirror a teenage girl looked into to apply her make-up, a tiny Pooh Bear in the bottom right corner. James's eyes looked dead; yes, it was late, but there was something worrying in the very centre of them. There was a blankness that shocked him. He lay back down and touched Fran's arm, waiting for her pulse to inject life back into him.

As James walked up the Corniche, a refreshing breeze coming off the sea on one side, smog hanging over four lanes of traffic on the other, he fast-forwarded through different episodes of his relationship. He knew she wasn't thinking of any of the things that he was. Fran had moved on from him long ago; she had started moving on when they were still together. Whether James was in Beirut or London, it made no difference to her. He also realised that saying he would rather be in Beirut than see her implied that being in Beirut was undesirable. But he now had a café he visited every day; he was picking up bits of language; he was reading about where he was living. Michael would be back in England now, having made a great success of Dubai, probably promoted into James's vacant job. It was a given that if James dared to call his boss in London he would be fired long distance at a high per-minute cost. He decided to save his money.

James didn't understand what had changed. He had never liked *abroad*; the word itself conjured up the abrasive feel of old sunscreen peppered with sand, and the hidden threat of the non-English-speaker. He liked France, although he wasn't sure why after his holiday with Fran. It might have been because their truck drivers were anarchists. Now, as he walked along Beirut's streets, they were not the mad jumble he had first thought, but a perfect, damaged maze for him to get lost in.

Walking up the Corniche had become his daily morning

ritual, letting the fast pace of London life leave him completely. He flicked through his passport as he walked, as if to prove to himself he definitely *was* in Lebanon. He found the hard evidence near the back pages: a picture of two cedar trees and a large stamp that said he could stay for three months. As he approached the McDonald's on the corner, the pavement became busier and he started dodging the roller bladers and pushchairs. A couple of hundred feet ahead of him, close to the restaurant, a European man with a DV camera was being escorted away by a Syrian soldier. It was the camera which drew James in, then when he heard the man say 'I have a permit! I'm a director!' the intrigue was enough to cause him to start running to catch up with them. They disappeared inside an old bullet-riddled building that didn't look as if it had been inhabited for years. James's curiosity nudged him towards it. There was no door, just a gap into which the men had disappeared. On the outside wall was a picture of the Syrian president, Hafez al-Assad, and his two sons, the late Basil and the younger Bashar. Basil was depicted wearing Ray-Bans and had a well-groomed beard; Bashar had a thin moustache, and looked studious and serious. The picture didn't need words to express who was the rightful successor to the Syrian president, and therefore the main power broker in Lebanon. Power and leadership were genetically transmitted.

James peered inside the building and spotted the soldier and the cameraman standing over a table with the video camera opened up in front of them. A second soldier had joined them. James heard the cameraman try to

explain in French-accented English that he was shooting street scenes and didn't mean to film the soldiers.
He seemed shaken, and asked them what their problem was. The soldier understood the tone and didn't
look happy.

James felt a presence behind him. He turned around to
face another soldier. '*Shu baddak?*' he asked. *What do
you want?* He had a square face but little round glasses,
and stared at James, who was now motionless, standing
by the picture of the Syrian president. He tried to think
of something to say. Inside, the other soldiers and the
Frenchman had stopped what they were doing and were
now watching James in the doorway. Apart from the
words Maya had taught him, James knew three complete
sentences in Arabic. So he pointed to the picture of Hafez
al-Assad and said in pidgin Arabic, 'May God keep for
you the president.' The other two he had learned from his
ancient guidebook were 'I am not a spy' and 'Take me to
the petrochemical processing station'.

The soldier nearly choked with surprise, then burst
out laughing. He repeated what James had said to the
other two soldiers, who looked as if they had witnessed
some kind of miracle. James had said it with such deadly
seriousness. They asked him to repeat it.

James saw his chance. Repeating 'No problem, no problem', he motioned for the soldier holding the tape to put
it in the camera and watch it. Together the three soldiers,
James and the Frenchman watched the tape.

'Very nice,' James said, looking at the beautiful shots of
the coastline.

'Thank you,' the Frenchman replied, introducing himself as Julien.

'How do you find this digital tape?'

'It's good. Not as nice as thirty-five-millimetre, but I like it.'

One soldier had now taken the tape out of the machine and was examining it closely.

'Do you like it here?' James asked.

'Hospitality is amazing,' Julien said, while the soldier smacked his tape on the edge of the desk. 'The people are so friendly, it's fantastic.'

The tape was about to meet its end, so James made one last attempt. He asked the soldier to insert the tape back into the camera and, when he had done that, pointed the video camera at the wall and pressed record, letting it run for ten seconds before rewinding it. The soldiers watched as James demonstrated that the part of the tape on which their vehicle featured had now been erased by a shot of a blank wall. They conferred briefly, then ejected the tape and chucked it at Julien, who caught it.

'*Yalla,*' the tape-thrower said, motioning impatiently for them to leave.

Julien celebrated by buying James lunch in Ashrafieh, his part of town. The little streets had a more French feel, and James found it strange to be greeted with '*Bonjour, monsieur*' when he bought a bottle of water in a shop, while a ten-minute drive to the west shopkeepers spoke to him in English.

'I owe you,' Julien said, looking at the menu.

'So you're a director?'

'Oh, you heard?' Julien sighed. 'No, I'm not. I don't have a permit either.' He smiled.

'So you're a cameraman?'

'Yes.'

'What kind of stuff?'

'Documentaries, other TV things.'

James knew when someone was lying about their experience – he had done it himself enough times. But he liked Julien, so he didn't say anything. When they had finished eating, and Julien had made an extended speech about how he felt homesick in west Beirut but quite at home in the east, they exchanged phone numbers.

'You should move to Ashrafieh.'

'It's too French,' James replied.

'Of course, I forgot the English don't like good food.'

'I'm just scared I'll be made to listen to French music.'

The two of them started laughing, James's accent becoming steadily more *Laandahn*, Julien's more *Parisien*, as they joked with each other.

They shook hands. '*À plus*,' Julien said.

'See you later, mate,' James replied.

James watched his last few days of holiday slide away. He had booked himself a ticket to go home, and was now waiting out his last forty-eight hours.

With thirty-six hours to go, he opened his suitcase and started packing a few things that he would no longer need. He went out to his local café for a break, then came back and packed the rest of his stuff. With twenty-four hours to go, he reconfirmed his flight back to London and told the hotel receptionist what time he would be leaving. With twelve hours to go, he called Julien.

'I want to make a music video here. In Lebanon.'

James had already wasted precious days thinking about how his stay would affect Fran. Now he wanted to think about himself, and use the country to give him an edge.

'We find a Lebanese singer, someone up and coming, and we shoot it quickly and cheaply.'

James could hear his own words – he could almost hear his own thoughts, they were so clear. He would return to what he had become well known for: not Champagne and their quiffs, but interesting music, something that he could put on a reel, that would be his ticket back into the industry in London. He may have been shunned, but if anything would get him back, it was something fresh and new that they hadn't seen before.

There was a pause at the other end of the line. James spoke into the silence. 'What do you think?'

'I like it,' Julien said eventually. 'Do you know a singer?'

'No, but we can find one.'

'My friend Hassan knows everyone. I'll call him right now. We're having a party tonight. Why don't you come?'

The word party flashed the image of an evening with Fran's work colleagues and badly remixed flamenco music into James's mind. He hesitated. 'I don't know east Beirut at all. How will I find it?'

'Hassan lives in west Beirut. It's closer to you. Go to his house, then he will drive you to my flat. I'll let him know you're coming. Do you know Nabih Berri? He's the parliamentary speaker. Hassan lives in one of those big apartment blocks close to him. It's called al-Sultan building.'

'Just give me the address and I can tell the taxi-driver.'

'People don't use addresses here. Say you want to go to Nabih Berri's house.'

That night James found himself stuck in Friday night traffic, trying to remember Julien's directions. He had checked his map of Beirut before he had left, and memorised the names of the closest streets. He still couldn't accept that this was a waste of time – that no one went by street names, or if they did, they used local slang names. If he knew the Arabic for 'It's next to Faisal's bakery' or 'Near the second tree on the right after the pistachio shop' then he would find it. But with only a street name, he didn't stand a chance. He tried to describe where he wanted to go to the driver, who replied '*Sprechen zie Deutsche?*' On the dashboard there was a sticker that read: *Die Autoreparaturwerkstatt Abu Ali*. It wasn't hard to work out which country the driver, and his mechanic, had lived in during the war.

James remembered what Julien had said about Hassan's house being near Nabih Berri's, so he looked up the Arabic word for 'house' in his old guidebook. Just below 'Is this the drilling site?' was the word he wanted.

'*Beit* Nabih Berri,' James said, wondering what would happen if he got into a taxi in Washington, DC, and said, 'Take me to Newt Gingrich's place.' The driver repeated the address and nodded. From now on, James decided, he would just find someone famous who lived near wherever he wanted to go. The driver threaded his prayer beads through his fingers as they flew along, then hawked up some phlegm and spat it out of the window. The taxi stopped; some people got in, others got out. This was a *servis* taxi, part of a system of merry-go-round Mercedes that constantly circled the city. People got on and off at different points along the way, but as far as James could work out there were no fixed routes. He watched as the driver slowed down for people standing by the side of the road. When they shouted out their destination, the driver would sometimes tut at them. At first James presumed he didn't approve of where they were going. Perhaps they had given him the name of an area in the opposite direction and he was chastising them for being stupid. James also noticed that he would give a little head tilt, different to the tut, a sort of non-verbal *back there, mate*, to customers he wanted to get into the taxi.

James offered his bottle of water to a young boy who was sitting in the back seat with him. The boy took it and, holding it a couple of inches above his lips, he poured. Germ free. He didn't spill a drop. James decided he had to somehow get the boy to refuse so he could check his tutting theory. He offered it repeatedly, but the boy continued to take it. Finally, when James volunteered the last drop, the boy tutted. Success. Tutting meant *no*.

James looked through his stack of Lebanese notes and tried to work out what to give the driver. The boy took one single blue note from James and passed it forward for him. James did a quick calculation: it cost fifty pence. The driver

took the note but didn't look back; he was arguing passion-
ately with his great friend, or perhaps brother or cousin, in
the passenger seat. James didn't need to understand Arabic
to know that this was what they were doing. They seemed
incredibly agitated. Noticing the concerned expression
on James's face, the young boy wondered whether the
foreigner understood that the driver and his passenger,
a complete stranger, were happily discussing the recent
storms, and whether they were worse than the previous
year's. He knew that Westerners always interpreted even
the mildest discussion as 'passionate arguments'. The boy
got out just as a man leaned in the window on the other
side and said, 'Raoucheh.'

'*Wayn bil* Raoucheh?' the driver asked.

'TGI Fridays,' the man replied. The driver thought for a
second. Yes, he was going that way. He motioned for the
man to get in.

'Two minutes, two minutes,' the driver said, somehow
communicating with his hands and face that they were going
to drop the man off in Raoucheh first. The car sped along the
jagged coastline. The five or ten small fishing boats, each with
a little light that made them look like tiny floating candles out
on the water, had given up on their day's fishing. The weather
had deteriorated; the wind whipped up waves that jumped
out of the sea, cleared the pavement easily, and landed on
the cars in the middle of the road. Parked vehicles stood in
salty puddles of dizzy single-cell sea life. As the ocean grew
angrier and angrier, the usual stream of aircraft still passed
low over Hamra on the way to the airport.

*   *   *

It was so dark in Beirut. Half the lights were out; half the stars were out. Mahmoud strained his neck to watch the aircraft as it went out of sight. He always loved watching the planes, although he really preferred the military helicopters that sometimes circled the city. They flew so low he could see the pilots' faces. Mahmoud was already late for his second round of that evening's deliveries. His bicycle – the frame bent from excessive wheelies – was in retirement. Not that he minded, he was now a moped man. Thirteen years old and owner of a 50cc engine. Hassan had broken his promise to take Mahmoud and his friends out for his birthday, but at least Mahmoud's special day had brought him something with an engine. The girls would love it. Attached to the back of his moped was a square metal box with a Welcome Pizza sticker on it. Haj Ahmad was big on free advertising and Mahmoud wore his Welcome Pizza baseball cap backwards, and his T-shirt untucked. He had spent the afternoon engaged in a wheelie competition with a rival pizza delivery restaurant. They were seeing who could wheelie the farthest up Bliss Street. Mahmoud had got as far as Bliss House sandwich shop, but his rival had reached SubStation, before hitting the kerb and falling off. It didn't matter, Mahmoud had lost. But only the battle, not the war. He would be back.

Mahmoud had developed a knee-jerk show-off reaction whenever he sped past girls on the pavement. He just *had* to do a wheelie in front of them, risking the stack of hot pizzas falling out and the telling-off of a lifetime which always started with Haj Ahmad shouting, '*Ibnil*

Kalb!' Son of a dog! Mahmoud still wasn't sure why his father insulted himself when he scolded his son. Part of his brain knew he should be careful as he rode around the city, but his hormones insisted he show off wherever a female was in sight. It was as if someone else was in control of that part of his decision-making. He zoomed off down the street, stopping outside an Internet café to peer in the window. There were nice girls everywhere. It was torture. Mahmoud tried to read a girl's e-mail through the window. His father had said he could have his own e-mail account when he was older. Mahmoud already *was* old – how much older could he get than thirteen? At that moment, all the lights went out in the Internet café. The only illumination was the eerie blue light from computer screens that were seemingly immune to the power cuts. In the café, no one moved or looked at anyone else. They just kept typing. They were used to it. The sound of the generator starting up inhibited Mahmoud's ability to listen to the conversations going on inside. The pizzas would get even colder if he stayed around any longer, and then he would definitely be in trouble. He spotted a girl walking along the pavement and shot off after her like a moth to a light bulb. She was in her twenties and took absolutely no notice of him as he did a long wheelie past her, the engine of his moped screaming like a tortured lawnmower. It was when he tried to repeat the trick while waving that the trouble started.

The taxi pulled a U-turn after its drop-off at TGI Fridays and shot off along a small back road. James had been promoted to the front passenger seat now no one else was in the cab. He checked the time on his watch.

There was a dull thud.

The driver slammed on the brakes and the car skidded to a halt. James flew forward, hitting the dashboard hard. The prayer beads fell out of the driver's hand on to the floor as the car came to a rest. James and the driver exchanged looks. Sprawled on the road in front of the car was a young boy, his moped on its side, its handlebars bent like metal antlers. There were splinters of wood scattered on the asphalt, along with blobs of cheese and tomato and a baseball cap. The driver got out and approached the boy, helped him up, and put him in the back of the car. James and the driver managed to haul the moped half into the boot and tie it down while the boy sat very still in the back seat. The driver said he would take the boy home.

'*Shu ismak?*' the driver asked the boy. The boy didn't reply. '*Shu ismak?*' the driver repeated, louder this time.

'Mahmoud,' the boy answered, his voice timid. The girl that he had done a wheelie for had been standing on the pavement when the crash happened. She walked over to see if everyone was okay, leaning into the back of the taxi and ruffling Mahmoud's hair maternally, asking him if he was hurt. Mahmoud gestured that he was fine, a smile breaking on his face. The girl said something to the driver that made him laugh, but Mahmoud didn't hear. She then left and Mahmoud would never see her again. But now he knew that, although love hurt, it was always worth it.

The driver left with Mahmoud in the back, the remains of his moped sticking out of the boot. James waited by the side of the road for a few seconds before hopping into the next passing *servis*, which dropped him off near a glitzy shopping mall, not far from a blocked-off road and an expensive-looking, fenced-off house. 'Nabih Berri's place,' James whispered to himself. As he approached on foot, a soldier appeared, a sub-machine gun slung around him.

'*Beit* Nabih Berri?' James asked, wondering whether it was a good idea for him to be asking for the home of one of Lebanon's highest-ranking politicians, and leader of the *Shi'a* organisation Amal, at 10 p.m. on a Friday night. The soldier nodded in response.

'I'm looking for al-Sultan building.'

The soldier pointed down the road. At the bottom, James found two more soldiers.

'I'm looking for al-Sultan building,' he said. This time there was less certainty in his voice, and the soldiers either didn't understand or didn't know where it was, so one of them called over to a young girl, no older than ten, who was playing in a car park. One soldier spoke to her in Arabic, then called up to her mother, who was shaking rugs over the balcony on the third floor of an apartment block. A four-way discussion started: two soldiers, a girl with a skipping rope, and her mother leaning out over the balcony. They all seemed to be agreeing that if al-Sultan really *was* near Nabih Berri's place, then James couldn't be far away. The young girl was given instructions as to where to lead him, then she skipped off with James tagging along behind.

The men with guns waved.

'*Shukran*,' James plucked out of his guidebook. *Thank you.*

'*Tikram.*' *You're welcome* echoed back in military stereo. The girl got as far as the next main road, then their communication broke down and confusion set in. James thanked her and she disappeared round the corner and returned to her skipping rope. James heard a car beeping behind him but didn't bother to turn around – he was getting used to taxis hooting, constantly soliciting business. The noise didn't let up, so finally he relented. A man was leaning out of a large BMW, mobile phone pressed to his ear, waving for James to get in. James approached the window.

'I'm Hassan,' the man said. 'Yeah, yeah, I found him,' he said into his mobile phone, then flipped it shut. James gave him the once-over: expensively tousled hair, piercing eyes, well doused in aftershave. 'Julien thought you might be lost,' Hassan continued. '*Yalla*, get in.'

They could hear the Faudel song blasting through Julien's apartment from down in the parking lot. When they got to his door it was deafening. Julien let them in, and Hassan, James and the rest of the people who had been in the car entered his apartment. Julien's living room was already heaving: Americans, Arabs, Europeans, all talking and drinking and eating. The French kissed the Lebanese kissed the French. And the paler Europeans looked a little brittle.

Outside, a storm was racing towards the city. The weather came in from the sea then immediately hit the mountains and was trapped. It built up until it exploded over Beirut, setting off car alarms, making Westerners run for their embassies, and turning the streets into five-minute rivers. Thunder didn't rumble, it crashed. The lightning lit up the sky with a violent blue light. The roads were instantly full of water and the taxis floated down the narrow streets.

Julien, Hassan and James left the party after a couple of hours and headed for rue Monot. The rest were staying dry at Julien's house and would follow later.

'Where are we going?' James asked, as they jogged down the drenched street.

'I have a surprise. Hassan used his *wasta*,' Julien said breathlessly, trying to light a cigarette while running.

'His what?'

'Connections,' Hassan cut in.

'He knows a singer,' Julien shouted, giving up on the cigarette, water splashing up from the pavement on to his trousers. The three of them jogged on, their jackets pulled over their heads, until Hassan stopped outside a doorway.

'This is it,' he said, checking the long queue trying to shelter from the rain. Hassan's doorman immunity seemed to extend to James and Julien, and he led them smoothly down twisting stone steps and into the club.

'The women,' Julien said evenly, looking around. He left it at that. The riff from Pink Floyd's 'The Wall' was coming from the speakers, fused with Arabic beats. The walls were decorated with Algerian-style mosaics. James and Julien made their way to the bar, somewhere between walking and dancing, as if they were crossing hot coals. The whole room was moving, swaying.

'*Trois bières,*' Julien said to the barman.

'Twenty-one dollars,' came the reply.

'Just like in Algeria,' Hassan deadpanned, appearing behind them. James took a four-dollar sip. He was tired – his journey to Hassan's had taken most of the evening, and now it was past midnight and he wanted to sleep. Cushions and low seats were set up in corners, just waiting for him to sink into. They beckoned him. The beer, costing a few pence in the local shop, didn't taste better with the five hundred per cent mark-up. As in any capital city, people paid good money to come to a place that ripped them off.

'You think of this the wrong way round,' Julien explained, when James complained about the prices. 'It's important for the man to say he spent two hundred dollars.' Julien was starting to understand how it worked – he spent every evening on this street, and had visited almost every club and bar. His favourite, although he wasn't sure why, was a nightclub that always had at least ten identical-model BMWs parked outside. The only thing distinguishing one from another was the colour. He liked to watch and listen to the smartly dressed clubbers chatting on their mobile phones in the long queue, waiting to be let in. He could pick out words: 'Cellular' (pronounced *celluleur*, as if it were a French word), '*meesed* call' (French again), 'BM' (a car so popular it didn't need its final initial), and finally 'Armani'. There was a giant curtain behind the main entrance, so when you entered, you really *entered*. There was something 1980s New York about the place, and Julien imagined that at any moment Kiefer Sutherland was going to show up in an expensive suit and order a Scotch.

But tonight they were visiting Julien's second-favourite place, its Algerian décor, low lighting and *rai* music already combining to make him forget that a few minutes ago he had been caught in a winter storm.

Hassan watched James as he looked around him. 'What?' he asked.

'I don't know,' James said, looking at the people dancing. 'There are no constraints, it's just . . . I don't know what I imagined, but it wasn't this.'

Hassan shrugged. 'This place isn't normal life.'

James nodded, but didn't understand. 'So do you really live next to a politician?'

'Pretty close. It's my uncle's house.'

'You live with him?'

'Kind of,' Hassan replied. 'Unless you're married, people don't really leave home. Occasionally it happens, maybe brothers living together, or a brother and a sister. But most people don't move out until they get married.'

James was suddenly thankful for the breakdown of the Western family if it meant being able to leave home.

'Do you live with your brother or sister?' James asked.

'My situation is a little different.'

James didn't press him. Hassan seemed a little ill at ease. 'I have a brother,' James offered, taking the conversation in a different direction. 'He married a girl he went to primary school with and now works for a bank in Hong Kong.'

'Do you talk to him?' Hassan suddenly seemed more interested in the conversation.

'I send him e-mails. They're expecting their first child soon.'

'You should make sure you speak to him when you can.'

'Uh, yeah,' James replied, suddenly feeling guilty.

'Really,' Hassan said. 'It's important.'

'So, what's this singer like?' James said, changing the subject.

'She's good. Not your typical Lebanese pop star,' Hassan replied as the crowd surged towards the stage. A tabla player had come on, and was now sitting down, beating out a rhythm. Then two more band members ambled onstage. The sound from the speakers was so clear James thought he could hear the ridges of the tabla player's fingers as they hit the skins. The keyboardist and drummer soon slid into the rhythm, as the beat became deeper and fuller and irresistible. A jazz flautist and a trumpeter then arrived onstage, filling out the band, the sound building until it challenged anyone not to dance.

The singer walked casually onstage. Everyone's eyes, that is everyone's apart from James's, went straight to her and didn't leave. James was watching people's reactions to her: she hadn't started singing, but the crowd were on her side already. She was wearing a flowing skirt and a blue tube top with a thin metal belly chain.

'That's Joelle,' Hassan said, in admiration, as if already in love.

Over a slow breakbeat, she sang in Arabic as she swayed just one inch to the left, then to the right.

'This isn't the stuff that gets in the charts,' Hassan whispered.

When the first song ended, she took a sip of water and looked at the crowd. She smiled, then launched into the next song. Her voice was pure, no effects were being used on it. When she messed up a lyric, she giggled and carried on.

'You didn't say . . .' James started.

'Say what?'

'She was so . . .'

'Good?'

'You said she was good, but you didn't say she was *this* good.'

'Now you see what I'm talking about?' Hassan said.

James waded through the crowd and found Julien. He tapped him on the shoulder.

Julien turned around, a broad smile on his face. 'Perfect for a video, eh?' he said.

'I can do something great with this music,' James said. 'And look at her, everyone is entranced.' James could feel a rush of adrenalin surging through his body; he wanted to watch her sing more, but he also wanted to find some paper and start drawing storyboards; he wanted to get in a car and find locations; he wanted to do everything at once. He wanted to find Maya and tell her that he really was making a video, that *this* was what he did, and this was who he was.

'We're making this video.'

'I know we are,' Julien replied.

'No, but I mean we're really going to do this.' James's eyes sparkled.

When the band had finished their set, James saw Joelle

walk to the bar and had to stop himself from actually running up to her. He settled for a fast walk. Just as he reached her, he felt suddenly tentative. 'You were great,' he said. 'The whole band.'

'Thanks,' Joelle replied. She was petite, somehow smaller than she had appeared onstage.

'Did Hassan mention . . . I'd like to talk to you about making a music video.'

The two of them found a table, James now with renewed energy, happily discussing business in the middle of the night. Joelle had a quiet confidence that James had read as shyness, then quickly realised was not. She was intrigued by his video proposal, but coolly left James with only a maybe.

'Well?' Julien asked.

'She's thinking about it,' James said. 'She wants to see a showreel, so I'm getting one sent over.'

'If we do this, we need some *wasta*,' Julien said. 'We can't just shoot it the way you would in England or France.'

'Okay, we'll get some *wasta*.'

'No, we need Hassan. He knows the right people.'

'Are you in, Hassan?' James asked.

'I might be,' he hedged.

'I'm appointing Hassan . . . assistant director,' James announced.

'I prefer chief assistant director.'

'Well, there isn't actually a position called chief assis—
Fine. The *chief* assistant director will be Hassan.'

The evening's business completed, James lay back on a deep cushion that enveloped him. People stood on chairs, on tables, all dancing. It was not stopping. The music and movement drifted into the background of James's consciousness, dissolving into the sound of the faulty aircraft that had brought him there in the first place. As he closed his eyes, as Maya finished her paperwork just five hours before she had to get up again, as Mahmoud slept fitfully, plasters over the scratches on his arm and a bandage around his leg, the city settled down to sleep. Outside the club, the rain had stopped. There were clear skies over Beirut.

08

James walked proudly down Hamra Street holding a bag containing at least twenty CDs (including *Now That's What I Call Arabia 2000*) in one hand, and a *felafel* sandwich in the other, its white sauce trailing down his arm. He tripped over an uneven paving slab and nearly catapulted himself into a 'Stop' sign by the post office from where he had just sent his brother a postcard.

He still had no real recollection of his first night in Beirut, when the power had come back on and fed eight hours of Arabic pop into his subconscious, planting it there for ever. His head was now full of string sections, dance beats and women singing '*habibi*'.

He looked happy holding the heavy bag of CDs, mostly because coming to own them (and the *felafel* sandwich, which was a self-awarded prize) had been so arduous. His first blind pilgrimage to Abed's Records had been a disaster, full of the 'Have you got this one? It sort of goes like this . . .' questions all record shop owners dread, the whole thing taking on a new level of insanity given that the songs were in a different language. His second trip hadn't been much better, and had involved James humming and singing the songs he wanted (not a pleasant experience for him or Abed), with little success. He hadn't given up. This was research – he needed to understand this new world. So for his third trip he decided to first record songs from the TV with his Dictaphone and then play them back to Abed. The experiment worked perfectly for the first two songs, then came to an abrupt end when the Dictaphone chewed up the tape.

Seeing James's disappointment, Abed took things into his own hands as he gently guided James through the mounds of CDs that were arranged ten deep on the shelves. He started with the great Egyptian diva Umm Kulthoum, the mother of Arabic music, he told James, then past the Lebanese singer Fairuz, whose beautiful, haunting vocals seemed to hang in the air long after the music had stopped. (James asked, if Umm Kulthoum was the mother, then who was Fairuz? 'Also the mother,' Abed replied, as he pointed out CDs on the shelves, taking out their booklets, translating lyrics, selecting his favourite moments.) The tour continued with Abdel Halim Hafez, a 1940s singer and film star, whose songs of lost love ade him sound as if he was about to break down and cry any minute. Then Abed fast-forwarded through the decades, touching on so many names that James lost count, before reaching the present day and the sound of Algerian *rai*, its lyrics the blues, its music a fusion of Western pop, reggae and Arabic rhythms which brought back to James memories of his first nightclub experience. Abed finished his tour by throwing some modern Egyptian and Lebanese pop into the bag, just for good measure, and James grabbed a copy of Joelle's CD so he could get right to work on a pitch that she couldn't refuse. Satisfied with his purchases, he had headed straight to the *felafel* place to celebrate.

He didn't blame Maya for not giving him her phone number. But now there was a chance he might be staying he wanted to see her again. He would have wanted to see her even if he was leaving, but he had tried to keep his feelings where they belonged, in denial. He couldn't just turn up on another coach trip, but he had another plan. After they had returned to the depot from the trip to the cedars, Maya introduced him to her friend, Nadia, who was keen to practise her English with a native speaker like James, and said she was studying it at the Lebanese International Language Centre. James figured this was as good a place as any to track Maya down.

The LILC was situated next to the Arabian Sands Trading Establishment. The rickety signs on the narrow doorways could barely cope with the length of the names they had been given. The LILC had been started several years earlier by Raja, a chain-smoking entrepreneur in his mid-thirties. One year into its existence, a disgruntled employee left and set up the rival LILCE: Lebanese International Language Centre *for English*. This itself then splintered two years later, creating the LILCEL. The final l was for language. Then in 1999 the two factions dissolved, rejoined LILC and resumed working for Raja.

James stopped on his way to the LILC and grabbed a can of Mirinda orange drink from Arabian Sands, briefly trying to decipher what had been written on the fridge door. He got as far as something about a *sexy overdose*, then gave up and waited at the till. The shopkeeper seemed to be looking at him, expecting him to do something. Then James realised that the man was actually asleep with his eyes half open. A helper appeared from behind the singed spice rack and, bypassing James, greeted the customer behind him.

'Hi, *key-fak?*'

'*Ça va?*'

Three languages in five words, all overlapping. The customer was looking for cigarettes and pointed at the brand he wanted.

'One diet Marlboro,' the helper said, handing him a pack of Lights. James was wrestling with the top of his can as the multi-lingual transaction between customer and shop helper climaxed with the fusion of two languages.

'*Yallabye.*'

The helper disappeared, so James threw a coin in front of the owner, who twitched slightly but didn't pick it up. James then walked back out on to the street, where he caught snippets of conversations he hadn't been able to pick up before, finally able to tune into a frequency that had previously been out of reach. He caught scraps of dialogue taken from the past and the present; Turkish and French words, English and Arabic, New York expressions and *Friends*isms were all welded together into an old-new language. A girl on her mobile phone talked excitedly, gesticulating wildly, her accent straight from the San Fernando Valley.

'And I was like, "We're *so* over." But Karim totally didn't get it, so I was like, "Helloo? *Khalas!* It's o-ver. What's your problem anyways?"'

James was pretty sure that if evolution sped up a bit, in fifty years Beirutis would be born with mobile phones attached to their ears. It was the spiritual home of mobile communications. The little phone shops James walked past were stacked with brightly coloured gadgets, twinkling in the lights like new toys. There was even a twenty-four-hour phone shop. At least Beirutis had the excuse of an unreliable regular phone service, he thought. It was the same with the generators that everyone owned: the state had let people down with electricity and communications, so they bypassed the system.

As James entered the building, the final round of qualifiers for Miss LILC had just finished. The judging table was being packed away and he could see an array of happy and sad female faces, their owners pondering whether their fate was to be a beauty queen or to serve burgers in a Dairy Queen. On the wall, as if to tempt future candidates, were details of the many different beauty competitions held by all the schools and universities throughout the year. James tried to shake the confused look off his face, but it wouldn't go away.

'What are you doing here?'

He spun around quickly. Maya was standing behind him. He couldn't think of anything to say.

'Thinking of entering a beauty contest?'

'Is this some kind of ironic thing that I'm not understanding?'

'No, it's serious business.'

'Maya, I wanted to ask you out some time. Just for a drink. I didn't get your phone number.'

'You're leaving, and I work the whole time,' Maya said,

as if this was just the start of the list of reasons for them not to see each other again.

'I'm not leaving. Not yet. I'm making a video here.'

'Are you? Really? I thought that was just a line.'

James hesitated. 'Well . . . it was just a line. But now I'm actually going to do it.'

'I don't get very much free time,' she said. Her tone didn't make it sound like a brush-off. 'And I have to drop Nadia off here every day.'

'Well, that works out perfectly,' James said.

'How is that?'

James thought quickly. 'I'm working here now.'

'You teach English?'

'Yup,' James said, trying to suppress a gulp. 'To keep me going while we prep the video.' He was getting into the habit of lying, but realised that his lies were the basis of good ideas. His hotel allowance was fast running out, his bank balance was draining quickly now that nothing was going into it every month, and the extra he had brought along to buy Fran a new necklace from Dubai's gold souk was also disappearing fast.

Maya was suspicious. 'Which class are you taking?'

'Not sure yet, we haven't worked out all the details,' James blustered. 'I start next week.'

'Well, Nadia's teacher has an Israeli helicopter gunship hovering over her house so she won't be here today. Why don't you substitute?' Maya challenged him.

James couldn't find a way out that would keep Maya in the same room as him. 'Why is it hovering?' was his best attempt.

'She just lives near some Hizbollah offices or something. Why? Is it important?'

'I'm just not used to things hovering, that's all.'

'It's nothing.'

'Where does she live?' James asked.

'Near Tyre, I think.'

'Isn't that breaking some kind of airspace law?'

'Well, we're still in a technical state of war with Israel. Haven't you heard the F-16s fly over Beirut in the day?'

'Those booms?'

'Yeah.'

'I thought that was your insane thunder.'

'When the sky goes dark and it rains, thunder. On a clear day, if you see a trail of vapour and hear a boom, then it's an F-16.'

The war had ended, but it wasn't quite over. James thought back to his lunch with Julien in Ashrafieh the day they had first met. After the meal, he had decided to walk home past the Place des Martyrs – the old centre of the city. He had subconsciously looked for the three lanes of traffic encircling the large, palm-tree-lined square, the different-coloured canopies on the shops, the Rivoli cinema with its perfect painted renditions of Hollywood stars – the Beirut that was framed and hung on the walls of Lebanese restaurants. Like Maya's casual words about fighter jets, what he saw shocked him out of his comfortable belief in this artificial picture, this fake portrait of a slightly battered, but almost European, Mediterranean country. It no longer existed, if it ever had, and the proof was in front of him: there, in the old centre of the city, there was nothing, not even rubble any more. It was complete disintegration, the buildings now levelled and cleared by bulldozers. Now not even the greatest romantic could have imagined David Niven dashing across the road towards a waiting taxi-driver, who would call out to him in the Queen's English: 'Sir, wood you layk a tex-yeah?' That was how Lebanese taxi-drivers always spoke in old films, those films in which the bad guy was always called Agent Z.

Feeling a little disoriented and shocked, James had approached the newly rebuilt downtown that bordered the Place des Martyrs. Cafés and tourist trinket shops were slowly appearing, although many buildings remained empty. The friendly sound of tinkling cutlery and waiters serving food at an outdoor café was suddenly interrupted by one loud explosion, then another. The sound was so loud the glass windows rattled in their frames. It was as if all of Hamra had gone up in flames and they were just getting the aftershock downtown. James couldn't stop his mind tracking back to the destruction he had just walked past, and wondered whether something else was being levelled at that very moment. He decided to gauge the reaction of the other patrons. They were eating their salads as if nothing had happened. He noticed only one man looking up at the sky, cursing through a mouthful of *kafta*. James glanced upwards to locate the target of this torrent of swear words. Miles above in the cloudless sky there was a jet, dirtying the perfect blue with its white trail.

Now, back in the language school James realised that it must have been an Israeli F-16, breaking the sound barrier. He was about to relate this story to Maya, but she was now talking to Nadia and a group of male students. James convinced himself that his first reaction to this, which felt an awful lot like jealousy, was just his stomach getting used to a new diet.

He attracted Maya's attention and extracted her from the group. 'How do you know so much about F-16s and helicopter gunships?' he asked.

'When I was a child I could name military hardware like I could name colours in the rainbow. When the fighting stopped from time to time, we'd go into the street, collect old mortar shells and bullet casings, and swap them with other kids.'

The male students had migrated over to the coffee machine, so Nadia joined James and Maya. 'I think you met Nadia at the depot?' Maya asked, looking at James and then at Nadia before saying something to Nadia in Arabic that James didn't understand. Nadia and Maya always spoke to each other in Arabic, but Nadia was French educated and knew the days when French was the desirable second language were gone. American English had arrived, and she needed to learn it.

Maya and Nadia had known each other since child-hood, and they still saw each other every day, having roughly the same conversation as Maya drove Nadia to her English class:

'Should I stop my classes?' Nadia would ask.

'No,' reasoned Maya, knowing that the key to Nadia getting her own car lay in her first getting a promotion, and the route to *that* was through the magic TOEFL, Test of English as a Foreign Language, certificate. 'I can't drive you around for the rest of your life, and don't you want to leave home?' Maya envied Nadia for having a father who would consider letting her move into an apartment with a female friend.

'Should I put more henna in my hair?'

'No,' reasoned Maya again, persuading her friend to keep it in its current golden brown incarnation.

Nadia amused Maya, and driving her to class was the best part of her day, especially if she had enough time – which she rarely did – to hang around the LILC. Nadia flirted with men, but she never went much farther than that. She was a 'good girl' and did everything in life – whether eating breakfast, driving or talking – as if it was the best thing in the world, as if she was doing it for the first time, eyes wide, face expectant. Maya wondered what would happen when Nadia finally found out that sex made the world go around. She had only recently started seeing Hakim – for Nadia 'seeing' involved letting a man take her out for Dunkin' Donuts and that was it – but Maya didn't see a big future there.

'Nice to see you,' Nadia said to James, shaking his hand, while in the background a small army of English teachers tried to manoeuvre the remainder of their students away from the coffee machine and into the classrooms. Nadia's accent was thick, as if it had travelled once around France and a couple of times around Lebanon. When she spotted Hakim smoking a cigarette and sitting on the couch outside one of the classrooms, a broad grin broke over her face and she blushed, excusing herself and walking quickly over to him, then turning and beckoning for James and Maya to follow. 'New boyfriend,' Maya whispered to James by way of explanation.

Nadia performed the introductions. Hakim didn't get up; he probably couldn't as he was sitting so low on the couch – his neck was where most people's arse would be. The only part of his body that seemed to move was his mouth.

'Whassup?' he mumbled to James and Maya. When one of his friends called to him from the other side of the room, he got up and excused himself with 'I'll see y'all later, aa'iight?'

When he was out of sight, Nadia turned to Maya and beamed a smile that said *he's great, isn't he?*

'Why does he speak like that?' Maya asked.

'He's black,' Nadia explained.

'He's not black. He's from Saudi Arabia.'

James couldn't stop himself from laughing at Maya's short, sharp dismissal. Nadia noticed James's reaction, and read it perfectly: Maya *was* sharp, but then he would have laughed at anything she said. Nadia turned to Maya and said in Arabic, 'He likes you. Does he know about Walid?'

Maya tutted her answer, *No*, then turned to James, 'So we'll be seeing each other from time to time, then.' She left a pause long enough for James to fall into, then added slyly, 'Now that you're teaching here.'

James nodded robotically.

'Nadia will explain to the students who you are,' Maya continued.

All James could manage in reply was 'Uh . . .'

He looked at Maya, then at Nadia. He realised Maya wasn't going to go, so he had to at least pretend to enter the classroom and hope that she would leave once the class started. Then he could make a run for it.

She didn't leave.

James faced sixteen staring pairs of eyes as he sat down.

Nadia stood up. 'I tell them you teach today. Okay?'

James made an expression of pained agreement, as if being dragged into a high-stakes poker game that he knew he couldn't win. Nadia addressed the class in Arabic: 'This is James. He is here because he fancies my friend Maya.' The class laughed. James convinced himself it was an encouraging laugh, especially when each member of the class welcomed him individually.

'Welcome in Lebanon.'

'Welcome to you.'

'Welcome.'

James absorbed all the welcomes and thanked Nadia for her introduction. The door was still open and James could see Maya sitting outside on a low chair reading a letter and smirking to herself. She caught James's eye and gave him an 'everything okay?' look, then went back to her letter.

Maya had printed out all her e-mails that morning to read later. Unfortunately a university acceptance was not among them, and even though Maya knew not to expect any kind of answer so soon after she had sent her application in, she couldn't help but nervously, obsessively check her mail at least once an hour. She turned to her next page of e-mails.

To: MayaHayek@qserv.net
From: Maroun2@mfaasolutions.com

Dear Mayoush,

How're you? I hope to God you are fine. Im'
fine and my works is very successful (Thanks
God). Next week I'm going for business in Dubai.
I can't wait to go out from Kuwait, there is
nothing to do here. I am so boring in this place!!
Anyway, Mayoush I just want to say you are
so soft and sweet girl, and very beauty as well.
Also polite. From the first time what I saw you
I felt a prisoner of your eyelashes. Please don't
think that I am just making compliments for you
but I really have to say what I think although
we only seen each others one time. If its okay
I will telephone to you because I love to hear
your voice.

Personal Best Regards,
Maroun F. Abu Abdullah

NB. Tell to your mother and father that I say
hello very much.

Maya folded up the print-outs and put them in her pocket.
When she looked back over at James, he hid a grimace and
smiled back.

James introduced himself to the class. No response at all.
He spoke slowly, but there was still no reaction from them.
Perhaps they were shy. The group conferred together, then
the appointed spokeswoman took the floor.

'We cannot understand you. You speak English with a strange accent,' she informed him.

'It's an English accent,' James offered feebly.

More conferring took place before the spokeswoman said, 'It sounds funny.'

Maya was *still* sitting outside, blocking his chance of an exit, so James decided to take a roll-call. That was something he could get through without too much trouble, and it would make him look busy. He read through the list of students' names as they winced at his pronunciation, and spotted two boxes without ticks.

'Where is Amal?'

'Sir, she have an exam for anozer class,' Nadia answered.

'Where is Michel?' James asked.

Nadia answered again. 'Sir, he is in . . . *shu ismo?*' Someone provided the word she wanted. '. . . jail.'

James wasn't sure what to say about that, so he kept quiet.

'*Sorry*, Mr James, we can do good . . . speaking practice today? I want to speak very nice in English.'

The rest of the class was getting restless as Nadia hogged the floor.

'Yes, Nadia. You speak London very best,' a boy said sarcastically.

When the door opened, James spun round to see whether he had been busted. It was Michel. He started conversing excitedly with the students in Arabic before explaining to James, in good English, what the problem was.

'They put me in jail because I say the Syrians must go!' Michel shouted.

'You can sit down,' James said nervously, hoping Michel would lower his voice if he lowered his body.

Michel was clearly an activist. The rest of the class laughed at his interest in politics.

'I tell to you. The problem in Lebanon is not *Isra-eel*. It is *Sooriya*. The workers come from *Sooriya* and take jobs, make money and go spend in *Sooriya*. We have many of their troops here. You see them, yes? *Isra-eel* occupies maybe ten per cent, but *Sooriya* has *miyeh bel miyeh*! One hundred per cent!'

With James's persuasion, Michel finally sat down, before outlining the reasons for his lateness at class. It made the 'I missed the bus' English school excuse look like the work of an amateur. All along the highway were Syrians selling vegetables without work permits, Michel explained to James, his voice getting louder and louder as he spoke. James suspected his English wasn't as good as it had at first seemed, and that this was a speech he kept well rehearsed. Michel had set up a vegetable stall on the highway, an old cart with three wheels, and waited for the police to come and arrest him for not having a permit. When the police duly took him away, leaving the Syrian stall owners well alone, he shouted, 'Why don't you arrest them? They are Syrian – at least I am Lebanese!' This was a regular performance and had cost him several days in jail.

The bell rang for a ten-minute break. There were questions during the intermission – ninety per cent of which were focused on what James thought of Lebanese girls. He had avoided the questions before, but was now running out of ways to dodge them. Michel then started a meandering speech about why he was Phoenician and not Arab, which luckily took up the second half of the lesson and was only curtailed by the bell finally ringing and Amal – whose lateness excuse was a shrug – cutting him off in Arabic.

'She say of course he is Arab, and stop be stupid,' Nadia translated for James.

When James left the classroom, he felt as if he had been there for a week.

'So what do you think of Lebanese girls?' he heard behind him. Michel had shared so much about his time as a jailbird, James felt obliged to answer this time.

'They're okay if you like that kind of thing.' He paused, thinking about Maya. 'And by that kind of thing I mean style and elegance, beautiful eyes, very tight-fitting clothes and tanned skin.'

As he finished his sentence, he realised Maya was well within earshot. He held his breath, then asked her, 'Do you think they learned anything?', looking at the students milling around.

'I think we all learned something.' She smiled. There was a long pause.

'Well, I'll see you around,' James said, his voice now expressionless. She wasn't going to give in. Resigned, he made for the exit. On the street a man was rewiring the neon sign on the front of Arabian Sands; five other men were watching and pointing. James stopped to look, becoming the sixth man.

'Listen, James,' Maya said, walking up to him, taking his attention away from the neon sign. Every time a Lebanese person used 'Listen' before his name, James assumed they were annoyed with him for not paying attention, or wanted to get a serious point across, like the English when they used it: *Listen, Dave, I've told you, keep your dog off my garden!* But Lebanese people used 'Listen' – followed by the name of the person they were addressing – the same way they used olive oil: with everything. *Listen, Karim, which club are you going to tonight? Listen, can we get a ride with you? Listen, Karim, when are you leaving?*

'Listen, thanks for doing that class. You amused them,' Maya said.

'No problem,' he replied.

'You need help with anything?'

'No, I don't think so.'

'Where are you staying?'

'In the hotel,' James said. 'Where I met you.'

'Okay, we have to sort that out. I'll give you a lift.'

As they walked towards her car, Maya watched James peer into Arabian Sands. 'Have you been in there?' she asked.

'This morning.'

'They're always stoned.' She laughed. 'But if you call Abu Khalil at any time of the day he'll send one of his boys around with a delivery.'

James was impressed: a corner shop that delivered to your home.

Back at the Marriott, James had already packed his bags and was waiting in the restaurant while Maya talked business with the assistant manager in reception. Jack and Malcolm were sitting at the bar, playing cards.

'Back to England, then?' Jack said triumphantly, as if he had won something by James giving up.

'I'm moving to a flat,' James replied, taking a seat next to them.

'You're *staying*?' Jack asked, looking first at Malcolm for a reaction but getting nothing, then glancing at James only to find he had turned around in his chair and was waving to a Lebanese girl, trying to get her attention as she entered the restaurant. 'Who's that?' Jack asked grumpily, putting his cards down.

'She's a friend. She's helping me move.'

Jack processed the information slowly, again looking at Malcolm, but getting no reply, only an expression that said, *Leave me out of this*.

'Do you . . . *like* it here?' Jack was determined to get to the bottom of this; he couldn't work out what was going on. James didn't answer – he was too busy watching Maya approach – and Jack quickly gave up on his line of questioning so he too could turn his gaze and watch her walk towards them.

'This is Jack and . . .' James started his introductions but then tailed off when he realised he remembered only one name.

'Malcolm,' Malcolm muttered to the table.

'Hello,' Maya said, without giving her name. She looked at James. 'Shall we go?'

'I have to settle my bill. Do you want a drink?'

Maya didn't look enthusiastic. 'Not really.'

'Wine, beer, whisky?' Jack butted in. Maya didn't even register him. 'Bacardi, Martini—'

'No thanks,' she stopped him. Jack listed the alcoholic contents of the bar and took Maya's refusals as if her not accepting a drink were a crime.

'What *do* you drink, then?' Jack asked her.

'How long will it take you to pay?' Maya asked James, ignoring Jack.

'Two minutes,' James promised.

Jack rammed himself into the conversation. 'What's your name again?'

'Maya.' She sighed, then turned to James. 'I'll have a Coke, then, but I want to get going soon.'

While James was at the bar, Jack tried to make small talk. Malcolm, meanwhile, sat there wishing he could speak to her himself – he didn't like Jack's tone of voice with Lebanese women, it incriminated everyone who sat with him. But Malcolm could do nothing and say nothing; he didn't look directly at Maya, or at any Lebanese woman, even though he had been living in Beirut for four months. He didn't know what he feared, but he let his eyes rest on his beer while Maya sat at the table. And at work, when the awesome cleavage of his assistant was proudly displayed as she walked around the office, bursting out of a tight, low-cut top, always leaning over the desk to hand Malcolm some papers and simultaneously giving him vertigo, he forced himself to move his stare away from her and subsequently spent hours gazing at filing cabinets, at staplers, at *anything*, as if only he could truly understand the fascination of office equipment. It wasn't the same as working in the bank back in Uxbridge, Malcolm thought

– here everything took twice as long as it needed to and everyone who was employed was related vaguely to someone else working there. And his assistant seemed to flirt with him, but perhaps that was his imagination. He found himself stuttering and stammering; he started dropping things and his mind spun with questions that he was sure, somehow, perhaps through an extra sense, she could hear. He didn't know that everything she did in the office, every little tease, she was just doing for sport, because watching her boss stutter made her day pass more quickly.

The sound of glass on wood brought Malcolm back to what was going on at the table. He watched James put a Coke in front of Maya.

'I'll pay the bill, then we'll go,' James said.

Malcolm watched Maya nod approval, then once James had left the bar and was safely in reception Jack ended the silence.

'Haven't seen you in here before.'

'That's right,' Maya replied, evenly. Her response would have crushed Malcolm, who was still only observing. The reply was not offensive, but so direct and honest that it would floor anyone with a thinner skin than Jack. Malcolm played with his beer glass, twisting it around on the damp coaster, wondering why Maya hadn't wanted an alcoholic drink. Perhaps it meant she was Muslim . . . but then, he thought, her hair wasn't covered, so did that mean she was Christian? Or did some Muslims not cover up, or was that dependent on which branch of Islam they followed, or was it because of something else? How would he know if she was Druze? Or if she was Armenian or Syrian or

Palestinian, or if she had a father with a gun to protect her honour? He didn't dare speak because he knew he would say the wrong thing. None of the European employees at work ever said the word 'Israel'. But it struck Malcolm that the euphemism they all used, 'the neighbours', was so weak, and used so often, that anyone, *anyone*, could work it out. And why couldn't he use that word? He had heard plenty of Lebanese say it.

'Are you okay?'

The softness of the voice comforted Malcolm for a moment. His fourth pint was really taking effect now. Then he realised that he had to answer, he had to answer this girl who was speaking to him.

He turned to Maya. 'I'm fine, thanks,' he replied.

Maya smiled at the silent Englishman, then excused herself and went to the bathroom to wash her hands. She didn't notice the other man get up and follow her. When she came out, he was standing in front of her.

When he didn't move out of the way, she said, 'Can I help you?'

'I'm sure you can,' he said. 'Has anyone ever told you that you look Italian?'

'Is that the best you can do?'

Jack was not put off. 'So how about getting together soon?'

'Go fuck yourself,' Maya said, trying to get past, but Jack blocked her way.

'We can both keep a secret.'

Maya could see the excitement in his beady eyes. She pushed him out of the way hard.

'Let's go,' Maya shouted to James, flying through reception. James caught up with her in the car park.

'What's the matter?'

'Just another prick who thinks he's in Bangkok.' Maya lit a cigarette as she started up the car.

As they drove, it became clear that she didn't want to say anything more, so James changed the subject. 'Tell me about the apartment.'

'It's on Bliss.'

'What?'

'Bliss Street. It's only two streets away from Arabian Sands and the LILC,' Maya said as she pulled up outside the apartment building. 'How long did you stay in that hotel?'

'I don't know. A month?'

'Well, this won't be as nice, but it'll be a lot better. You know what I mean?'

As they entered the building, James realised he was breaking his hotel-only rule. It felt as if he were slowly shedding a skin.

'Is this place nice, though?'

'It's de luxe.' Maya smiled.

'Everything here is de luxe or super de luxe.'

'Ah, so you've noticed,' she said.

The concierge wore a thick gold necklace, and his car, which was parked outside, had stripes down the side and 'Schumacher' written on the back window. 'What a *waz-waz*,' Maya whispered, as she watched the concierge turn up a Marc Anthony song on the radio. When he had finished writing down James's passport details, he handed him a key.

James tried to contain a laugh. 'What's a *waz-waz*?'

'I'm sure you can work it out from the evidence,' Maya said, looking at the concierge's car. *Don't follow me, I'm crazy* was written in white along the top of the windscreen.

James entered the studio flat with Maya right behind him. This was *his*. From the disgusting lime green walls to the 1970s carpet and the single stove. *All his*. Maya had negotiated a price on his behalf, and he didn't tell her he had only enough cash to see him through one month, before he would have to start earning or leave.

Out of the window he could check the time on the university clock tower. He could see into the campus of AUB – the American University of Beirut. It was like being able to look into California while standing in the Middle East, an oasis of trees and grass that could have been any West Coast campus. James had been told of the many prominent people who had studied there, but at the moment all he could see was the Lebanese students exchanging hip hop handshakes and 'S'up?' greetings on the grass oval. James could also see the ocean, even the snow-capped Sannine mountains in the distance. Ethiopian and Sri Lankan maids hung out the laundry on balconies, below the hundreds of satellite dishes that sprouted out of every roof.

'Thanks for doing this, Maya,' James said. He liked the sound of her name – he felt an intimacy simply saying it.

'You're welcome.'

'So shall we go out somewhere?'

'We can have a drink here. Toast your new apartment.'

James called Arabian Sands and asked for six mini Almaza beers and some crisps. Eight beers and a bag of tortilla chips duly arrived and James paid the kid who delivered them. His change was 1,250 Lebanese pounds – about fifty pence. The boy didn't have the change, so he handed James a five-hundred-pound coin and a pack of chewing gum. Gum was currency. James had already learned that the one-hundred-poundandfifty-poundcoinsincirculationwere not used. He had tried to buy a can of Coke with a pile of them at Arabian Sands, but they hadn't been accepted.

'What are they for, then?' James had asked.

'Just for fun,' Abu Khalil had deadpanned.

James was beginning to realise that now he had allowed himself to experience more than just a hotel room and an air-conditioned taxi he found himself in a country where he had no idea of the rules. Since he had been in Beirut he had not once heard the words 'boyfriend' or 'girlfriend' or 'partner'. It was always fiancé or fiancée. When he met Fran, the only question had been whether they liked each other or not. With Maya – even starting to think these thoughts about her seemed crazy – he was lost. Here, he didn't know how anything worked. They clinked their bottles of beer together and James settled for just enjoying the good feeling of being in the same room as her. He didn't care how long the rebound factor was supposed to last – it already seemed irrelevant, and he wondered whether in fact he would have left Fran, or anyone, at any stage of *any* relationship, for this person sitting opposite him. His life, everyone's life, was a series of rebounds, he decided, of departures and arrivals, endings and beginnings, and we carry our experiences with us into every moment, every second. James was on a roll now – the beer was strong. We're all pinballs, he thought, constantly rebounding from things that happened last week, last year, in our childhood.

'Why are so many people engaged here?' he asked, wondering whether Maya would drop a hint about herself. 'Half the class today was engaged.'

'To stop the neighbours talking,' Maya said with disgust in her voice. 'It makes it less of a scandal if a couple are at least "intending to marry".'

'Isn't wearing skimpy outfits a scandal, then?'

'No, that's okay. In the right place at the right time. Being engaged isn't probably like it is in England. It doesn't necessarily mean you'll get married. Engagements get broken off quite often.'

As she spoke, and James found himself unable to take his eyes away from her lips, he understood that the last thing she was thinking about was kissing the person she was sharing a beer with. She would probably be shocked if he tried to do anything. It was strange how, although a kiss was just a kiss, it was absolutely *everything*, no matter where you were.

'Is there anyone at home who is missing you?' she asked.

'I did have someone, but she doesn't miss me any more.'

Maya nodded. 'Well, I better go,' she said, standing up. She knew Mrs Jihad would be lurking behind a large plant on the balcony, noting her arrival time in her logbook. As James walked her to the door, she said, 'You know, you should talk to Raja, he's the boss of the LILC. You could go from pretending to teach and earning nothing to *actually* teaching and earning some dollars.'

James was lying on the bed, the scent of Maya's perfume still in the room, when there was a knock at the door. The creepy concierge peered past James and had a good look around. This concierge said little, but stared a lot. His bright blue eyes glinted with serial-killer-mugshot intensity. James preferred the *waz-waz* concierge who had checked him in.

'Yeah?' James said.

'Your *friend* Miss Maya has left?' he said. When he said 'your friend' the term was so loaded it hit the ground and made a dent.

'What do you want?' James asked.

'You have a phone call.' James had a phone in his room, and they were able to put calls through, but he didn't bother to question why the concierge needed to personally deliver this message. He was now standing on his toes, straining to see over James's shoulder and into the apartment. James thanked him, and shut the door on his nose.

The call was put through. 'It's Hassan . . . where are you? I called the hotel and they told me to call here.'

'I moved house. Maya found me a place on Bliss Street,' James said.

'Who's Maya? Listen, James. Be careful, okay?'

'Be careful of what?'

'You know this expression? "Don't trust any woman, except your mother. And if your father divorces her, then don't trust her either."'

James laughed.

'I'm serious. The women here are just after the next man with the bigger bank account or better car.'

'Maya isn't like that.' James could sense Hassan wanted to say more, but was censoring himself.

'How is the video going?' Hassan asked.

'I've got my reel. It arrived from England yesterday. I sent it to Joelle.'

'Want me to call her, help it along?'

'That'd be great. You know where we can get a crew?'

'We'll think of something,' Hassan replied. 'Look, I'm going out for a drink with Julien. Want to come?'

It seemed that friendships here developed at the speed of light, and James liked the fact that Hassan had called to invite him out, even though they hardly knew each other. English cities could be lonely places, but James wondered how much lonelier they would feel if you were used only to life in Lebanon. After chatting to Hassan for a few minutes, James made an excuse and arranged to see him another time. His mind was on other things – he was thinking about Maya, about how he wished she was still sitting there, casually chatting to him while his mind did somersaults. He flicked over from an episode of *Ellen* dubbed into German and watched an old Egyptian comedy. There were three people in the shot: one sat in bed and two standing. They argued, cried and laughed, then moved on to the next scene for more of the same. At one point a man took his sandal off and started beating another man over the shoulder with it. Towards the end, a guy with a curly moustache was scolding his wife while he lay in bed. When she made him some tea and then started belly-dancing in front of him, he started clapping in time to her moves, a huge smile on his face. He seemed to have forgiven her.

09

The zigzag stone staircases didn't always lead somewhere. The building this one had been attached to had now disappeared, collapsed, leaving the staircase behind, looking like a point of ascension to the sky. Perhaps if you kept walking up it you would just float into the atmosphere. The building, someone's home, had a simple history: first its walls had been irreparably blistered with bullet holes, then its foundations rocked with small explosions, and finally its weak construction disintegrated by heavy shelling.

A young child sat on the bottom rung of the steps, playing with a yo-yo. Across the street, from a VW camper van with a makeshift corrugated-iron canopy, a man sold old car parts. Next to him, in a building with no front at all, sat two old men on plastic chairs. The owner was making *man'ousheh*, sprinkling the bread circles with thyme, olive oil and sesame seeds before putting them into a large, open oven. With its gas-fuelled flames it looked like a miniature torture chamber from an Indiana Jones movie.

Aisha had flawless skin and a perfectly round face, framed by a pastel-coloured *hejab* concealing her hair. She picked up some *man'ousheh* for her family and greeted the two men sitting at the entrance. She was exhausted from another four hours comforting her mother; she no longer knew what to say to her, so she left the house for five minutes, with the excuse of finding them something to eat.

Fatima had been separated from her sister for fifty years, for longer than Aisha had been alive. As Aisha entered the house holding the food, she could see her mother, still sitting at the kitchen table where she had left her, her wrinkled face catching the tears, providing empty river beds for them to flow down. Fatima repeated her question, the same question that she always asked, which her daughter never knew how to answer: 'Will I be able to see my sister at the border if the Israeli army leaves Lebanon?'

'*Inshallah*,' Aisha answered, as she had been doing all afternoon. *God willing*. She didn't want to get into it. She didn't talk politics – it was too tiring and too depressing, and it didn't change the fact that her aunt, Fatima's sister, was in a place they still called Palestine while Fatima was with Aisha, in the kitchen of a small house in a crowded refugee camp in Lebanon. As far as Aisha could see, that was where they were all going to stay.

Fatima was alone, having lost her husband, Aisha's father, in the massacre eighteen years earlier, which, Aisha suspected, had fuelled her obsession with seeing her sister. Fatima's husband had been so sure something terrible was going to happen when Yasser Arafat and his guerrillas left Beirut for Tunisia that he had sent the family out of the camp. He was right. Something did happen. The guarantees regarding their safety did not hold.

'If I see Dalia,' Fatima said, as Aisha spread the food

out on the table, 'my hand on the *Qu'ran*, I will be happy. I will sleep peacefully.'

Aisha passed her mother a *man'ousheh*, and they both started eating.

'I will never see my husband again, but why can't I at least see my sister once more?' Fatima asked, taking a bite of her *man'ousheh*. Her hands were shaking slightly, not always responding to the messages that her brain was sending them. She looked out of the kitchen window at a roughly painted picture of Yasser Arafat on a wall. Fatima trusted no one to secure her return home. She knew she was alone. When she had finished eating, she took out a small wooden box from her drawer and then walked back into the kitchen and rested it on her lap. Inside, she still kept an old folded map of Palestine, along with some jewellery and her faded British mandate papers. Aisha sighed as she saw the elderly lady take out a rusted key and place it on the crumpled map. She knew Fatima was going to start her familiar lament.

'When we fled our homes in 1948, during the *nakba*, I dropped this key in the mud. I lost it, but I got on my knees and dug until I found it.' Fatima was no longer speaking to Aisha. She was speaking to herself.

That night, when it was dark outside and everyone in the house was asleep, Aisha walked around her little home. Her husband, Marwan, a mechanic, was sleeping peacefully, and she could hear Fatima's laboured breathing in her room. Aisha went into the cramped hallway and opened her front door. The streets of Sabra-Shatila that were once blood-soaked were now sewage-soaked, and she watched as spots of rain deepened the puddles. The rain sounded like solid matter as it smacked on their corrugated roof, held on by a few breeze blocks. It was the first time Aisha had enjoyed any peace all day. Her young son had returned home that afternoon wearing a T-shirt with 'Terrorist' written on the back. Her daughter had told her she wanted to be a doctor when she was older. Aisha wasn't sure which upset her more.

She closed the front door and went into her children's room, just big enough for two tiny beds. She stood in the doorway and watched them sleep. She'd had to hold back the tears when she heard her little girl say she wanted to heal people. Safaa was never going to be a doctor – as a refugee, she wasn't eligible for most jobs. Aisha didn't mind housekeeping herself, but her parental instinct of wanting something better for her children was strong, and it crushed her that her little girl's future had been decided before she had even had a chance to shape it. She had no status. They were not welcome guests in Lebanon. Sometimes it felt as if they didn't exist.

Aisha was unable to look at her daughter's face any longer. She found it hard to admit to herself that things could have been worse, but she knew it was true. Thank God, Safaa hadn't been alive when the name of their camp had been flashed around the world. Thank God Safaa never saw her grandfather cut down with a machete, and would never smell the stench of rotting bodies, never know the sound of flares being let off to illuminate the sky so the killing could continue into the night. The Israeli army were occupying the Sabra-Shatila sector of Beirut at the time, and did nothing to stop their Lebanese Phalangist allies from committing the massacre. Aisha remembered as a young girl watching the television pictures of four hundred thousand Israelis demonstrating against the massacre, calling for the defence minister Ariel Sharon to resign after their own inquiry into his role in the tragedy. Every year since, as she grew into adulthood and then had children of her own, she had watched the annual commemoration that took place in the camp, but there were never any answers. Hundreds of bodies were found after the massacre, but hundreds remained missing – including Fatima's husband – a bulldozer having been used to dig mass graves to hide the corpses.

Aisha arrived at work at 7 a.m. having slept fitfully for only a few hours. As usual, she started on the first floor of the building, and worked her way up. She had been a housekeeper at this Bliss Street apartment block for three years – it was the best job she could hope for. She had the skills to work in an office, typing, answering the phone, filing, and she would have preferred to have been doing that. But she put this out of her mind as she took the bucket, the mop and some bleach and started work.

James looked around his room suspiciously. Someone had been in there. He instinctively rushed around, checking that his passport was still there, along with his wallet and the pile of dollars – his rent money – that he had stuffed in a drawer. He had only been out to buy himself breakfast.

There was no sign that anything had been taken – nothing was overturned, no drawers had been rifled through. In fact the place looked tidier than when he had left. His clothes were now in a neat pile, his bed had been made, and the bathroom floor had been washed. This was some strange burglar.

There was a knock at the door. When he opened it the woman standing there said something in Arabic, then made an action that looked as if she was rubbing two items of clothing together.

'Er . . . washing?' James asked. The woman nodded. She picked up a pile of James's dirty clothes and put them in a huge washing bag as he stood and observed, unable to do anything to help. His 350-dollar-a-month apartment came with a housekeeper. He may have shared her with several other rooms, but it made him feel like a king and a slave-driver in equal measures.

'*Ismi* James,' he said, using something he had picked up.

'*Ismi* Aisha,' she replied. '*Tcherafna*,' she added, putting her hand to her heart, then apologising quietly in English for not shaking hands with a man.

Aisha stuffed the washing bag under one arm and disappeared – that night James's T-shirts and trousers would hang drying from a line in Sabra-Shatila, before being brought back and exchanged for a few dollars the next day. Aisha used more and more English each time they saw each other. It turned out that she knew quite a lot, but she had just been too shy to say anything the first time they had met. 'My daughter learns English,' she explained.

So the next day James stole a suitable book from the LILC and brought it back for her.

Each time Aisha came to clean his room he felt a teenage guilt, in case she should stumble on any more remnants of Maya's single visit. She had already found a hair clip of Maya's from the night they had shared a beer together. Yet James half hoped she *would* find something else to remind him of her. Aisha didn't seem to take any notice of the evidence of a female presence, and every morning her visits were extended by twenty minutes: ten for her to teach James Arabic, ten for him to teach her English. He also used his new-found Arabic to take Maya's advice and call Raja to offer his services as a full-time teacher. His Arabic took him only as far as basic greetings, but slipping into English he discovered that Raja had already heard about his impromptu performance and was amused rather than angry – having an English face teaching English would help enrolment, so he set James up with a series of classes, adopting him as a teacher, rather than employing him, with no contract, and no fixed hours. But the money was good.

James had agreed to meet Joelle in his regular café. He didn't like the waiter there, and each time promised himself he was going to find somewhere else. But he never did, perhaps because it had become familiar. He looked at his watch as he listened to the waiter's predictable chatter. It was still only 10.30 a.m. – surely no one could talk about sex at this time of day. The waiter's descriptions of what he had done or *wanted* to do were so lurid that the thought of him engaging in such acrobatics had ruined breakfast for James more than once.

'So, have you sampled the fruits of the Orient yet?' the waiter asked, putting James's coffee down in front of him.

'Yes, I like pomegranates.'

'No, I was talking about the women.'

'I'll have the waffles when you're ready.' James didn't really like waffles, but they took so long to make he hoped it would keep the waiter out of the way until Joelle showed up and could protect him.

The waffles arrived before Joelle did. 'So, guess what?' the waiter said.

'Can I have another coffee, please,' James replied, not looking at him.

'I met this girl.' The waiter was determined to get his story out.

'And you kissed her.'

'More.'

'You got her into bed.' James yawned, trying to show as much boredom as possible.

'*More.*'

'You got her into a canoe.'

'Hi, sorry I'm late,' Joelle said, sitting down. James resisted the urge to hug her for getting the waiter out of his face. 'I got the reel.'

'What did you think?'

'I thought the stuff at the beginning was great, and the stuff at the end was . . . *different.*'

'The stuff at the end was all the commercial artists. Don't worry about that.'

Joelle's body language suggested she had cooked up a master plan. 'Our kind of music doesn't sell here. But maybe we could do two versions: one minimal and like the stuff you used to do. That would be for Europe. Then we'll do another version, like all the videos you see on TV here. That'll be our Lebanese market covered.'

'So you want two videos?' James asked.

'I want two videos.'

'Look, I think getting one video for free is pretty good.' James tried to wrestle back control of the meeting.

'Oh, and you're getting *nothing* out of this, are you?' She smiled. 'You're just doing this to help me out?'

'Well . . .'

'Exactly. Look, if we do the Lebanese version we'll get paid when it gets on TV. That'll at least cover our expenses and give us a chance to do something good as well.'

James thought for a moment, then found himself nodding in agreement with her.

It took several public holidays to get there – at least one for each of the nineteen recognised religious groups, a couple because of an important pan-Arab meeting, and one more because a regular holiday fell on top of a new holiday, causing a kind of holiday avalanche, leaving James helplessly watching the days tick by on his three-month visa – but finally the shoot day arrived. James hadn't slept all night. He was excited, nervous and hyper with adrenalin, and when he caught sight of himself in the mirror, he looked slightly manic.

Julien showed up, beeping his horn outside James's

apartment, anxious to get going. The camera equipment, which seemed to have grown in size since James last saw it, was piled in the back.

'Where did all this come from?' James asked, getting in.

'Local TV station.'

'And what about our crew?'

'Our crew is you, me and Hassan,' Julien said, dodging a parked car that was pulling out without the driver looking.

'What? We need people to haul equipment around. Didn't Hassan sort something out?' James said, fastening his seat belt.

'Have you noticed how you go out with four Lebanese friends for the evening and by the end of the night there are a hundred – brothers, cousins, old friends – who all dropped by without calling?'

'Well, yeah . . .'

'We'll have enough crew.' Julien smiled, glancing at a road sign, then taking a corner so late James shut his eyes.

'So, where's Joelle?' James asked, opening his eyes again.

'She's coming with her fiancé.'

The route took them out of west Beirut and through the city's southern suburbs, where the central reservation dividing the road was no longer a row of concrete blocks but a long track cluttered with large green overflowing rubbish bins. The air smelt of oil. Every second shop was either a mechanic's or was selling spare parts for cars. One shop had hundreds of hub caps lining the walls.

They regularly popped off cars as they hit potholes – if you waited by the side of the road for ten minutes something to fit your own vehicle would surely roll along. In between the oil and the tyres and the hub caps was the occasional shop selling furniture: beautiful hand-made chairs that sat patiently by the dusty road, waiting to be purchased.

When they were free of south Beirut, Julien took the road along the coast, past tired banana trees and checkpoints. At a brightly painted Hizbollah arch a collection was taking place, people moving from car to car with buckets and pots, taking donations.

Julien stopped to buy a drink at a shop selling plastic Father Christmases. A large sign next to the road read 'All our problems caused by USA' against a bastardised flag. The stars had been replaced with bombs and skulls. Just past this sign was a giant Marlboro man, complete with horse, big Stetson and cigarette. 'Welcome to Marlboro country,' the caption read.

'Look at this! The Lebanese can't drive!' Julien yelled, overtaking a truck. He drove at a hundred miles an hour where possible, and a little faster given the chance. He had that 'the maddest patient in the asylum is the one who thinks he's a doctor' syndrome: the more he criticised Lebanese driving, the more insane manoeuvres he would pull himself. He attacked roads as if he was playing a PlayStation game and had infinite lives left. James was glad for the endless military checkpoints along the way that forced them to slow down.

In Tyre it was sometimes hard to distinguish where

ancient ruins ended and modern ruins began. Mortar-shelled buildings hung precariously over Roman ruins. When James and Julien arrived at the meeting point – a restaurant, of course – Joelle was already there, along with her fiancé, Tony, as well as Hassan and various other hangers-on. After several *felafels*, they piled back into their cars and headed for their final destination.

The beach was impressive. It was miles long, reaching from Tyre right down to the Rashedieh refugee camp. At the other end was a half-built hotel, now abandoned. A hundred feet away, some UNIFIL men on their day off had spread out their towels. Boys played football in the car park. Occasionally a man would run past, jogging in the shallows, his stomach bouncing, fighting gravity as best it could. This was not the beach for the beautiful people, and it suited James just fine.

'We've got to make this really stand out,' he said as they unloaded the gear, while in another car Joelle's friend applied her make-up in true Lebanese pop singer fashion: a silver shade on her eyelids, large bright lips, flawless skin. Joelle had the complexion and Lebanon had the natural sunlight to pull this off for the camera. Julien started doing lighting tests, directing helpers to hold large silver discs to bounce sunlight wherever he asked.

'What do you want to start with?' he asked James.

'Something simple to begin with. Warm things up. Let's do a wide shot through the whole song. Then we know we're safe and we'll move on to close-ups.'

'Okay,' Julien said.

Hassan walked up. 'Is it lunch-time yet?'

'We just had lunch,' James said.

'I thought that was breakfast.'

'Hassan,' James said, spotting a person about to become very bored, 'show someone how to work the playback, then go and tell that guy on the horse to get out of our shot.'

'When am I going to meet your girl?' Hassan asked.

'Tonight probably,' James said. 'Now go and deal with the horse.'

Brothers and cousins were scattered everywhere – the crew expanded by the hour. Everyone knew somebody who knew something about film-making. All of them had shown up. Someone's mother was setting out lunch on an enormous picnic rug. James had to conceal a smile when he remembered the catering in London: a man in a van. He walked around the set, surveying his domain. He was *back*. Joelle was sitting in the shade, listening to the radio, looking relaxed as he approached. He experienced a sudden flashback to Kitty and stopped. He cleared his mind, then spoke.

'Joelle, we're going to start wide and just let the song play out for the first take to get us into the swing. What I want you to do is just sing along to your song, and kind of—'

'I know,' she said, immediately putting James at ease. 'It's no problem.'

Hassan returned with bad news. 'The guy on the horse won't move. He wants to be in the shot.'

'Tell him to get out of the bloody way,' James said, walking up to the man on the horse, who was in the shallows, a cowboy hat on his head.

'*Marhaba,*' James said, looking up at the man, shielding his eyes against the bright sunlight.

'*Ahlan,*' the man said, looking down.

'Can you move?'

'For who you make a video?'

'Just a singer. You don't know her.'

Hassan watched the conversation from a distance and saw that James was making no progress with the 'You'll be on MTV if you just move over there' line. He walked up and whispered in his ear.

'You know, Arabs love horses. Why don't you get this guy in it? It'll be good. Stick it in the Gulf version.'

'Action!' James shouted ten minutes later. Ibrahim on the horse galloped along the shallows, spray flying up behind him, melting against the burning sunlight.

Joelle was giggling when James shouted, '*Cut!*'

'You really understand Lebanese pop – that's a classic,' she said.

'I've done a lot of research: girl being pursued by man, or girl being rescued by man, and him using a lot of powerboats in the process.'

Joelle smiled. 'And remember: you can *never* go too far over the top.'

'Joelle, we'll finish this horse stuff, then I want to show you some storyboards for the other version. *Our* version. Do you remember "Nothing Compares 2 U"?'

'Sinéad O'Connor. I love that video.'

'Right, because I was thinking of something like that.'

Ibrahim, the cowboy, was not an attractive man, so when he went to collect his pay James quickly reshot the close-up with Tony, who at least had all his own teeth. This was also a neat political move as it seemed to put Tony at ease with the idea of having all these strange men hanging around his soon-to-be bride. Ibrahim stayed for the rest of the day, smoking his payment: a few boxes of Marlboro Lights. His horse was bored by the whole thing and faced away from the action, but James tried not to let this get to him. He didn't want to be the overly sensitive director. Horses aside, he knew that in London people had been going crazy for anything from Mexico and South America: the dancing, the beats, the new artists. The Arab world could offer all that *and* far better food. James was going to knock Del Pico's baseball cap off his head with this; he was going to show him a video that was so sharp he would have to re-sign him simply from fear of someone else taking him.

James asked Julien to mount a smaller camera on to a mini-steadicam so he could operate with just one hand, the camera smoothly reflecting his every move. Julien looked like a magician, gracefully moving his arm, the technology following the human arcs his body made. His free hand was out behind him to give him balance, like a fencer's.

'Okay, d'Artagnan?' James asked, but Julien was concentrating too hard to hear him, so James went back to showing Joelle his storyboards for their non-horse version.

'We're losing light!' Hassan cried from far down the beach.

'What do you know about light?' someone shouted back.

'Let's shoot one,' James said, checking that everyone was in position.

'Playback!' Hassan yelled and Joelle's song started blasting from the portable stereo. She began singing along, and James motioned for Julien to get in closer. He got out of the way, and sat on the sand, looking at the images that Julien was capturing as he swung the steadicam into a close-up on Joelle's face, bathed in gold light. Joelle would sing into the air, then look back at the camera – one minute the camera was a friend she was whispering a secret to, the next it was the lover who had walked out on her, a split second later it was the empty space left by the end of a relationship. James had to stop himself from shouting out his appreciation. This was *their* version. Just a face, perfectly shot. As Joelle reached the end of the song, she looked up at the camera, her eyes sparkling through her long eyelashes. It was the look that James and Julien had named 'The Samira Saeed' after the absolute queen of great glances at the camera. Joelle could capture it. She barely moved because she didn't need to, the sign of a powerful actor.

'Cut!' James said. He had it. Finally. *Sensuous.*

'What next?' Joelle asked.

'We have it. I want to centre the whole thing around this shot,' James said, excitedly. 'I want to do some different variations on it.'

Julien said, 'What about the dancing? For the other version.'

James thought about it for a second. 'Okay, we'll do a few more on the steadicam, then we'll break and start again when the dancers show up.'

A few takes and a brief picnic later, the dancers did show up.

'Who's this?' Hassan laughed, as a packed minibus pulled up on the beach.

'I don't have *wasta*. But I have dancers,' James replied.

'Are they professional?'

'Oh yeah,' James said, as his students tumbled out of the bus. He was pleased that he was fulfilling Raja's requirement that he take them on at least one field trip, and as Hassan started funnelling them into position he set up the next shot with Julien. Only Michel was absent from the group – a day of protest outside a university had ended with him behind bars.

The Mediterranean sparkled as the sun lit the dancers' faces. Joelle's tape was at full volume, so loud that the entire crew was dancing. James smiled as he watched Nadia and the others unselfconsciously swaying on the beach, following Joelle's lead. He would multiply the Joelles in post-production, putting her all over the beach, shimmering in infinite numbers. When the sun went for the day, Julien looked at James, trying to contain his enthusiasm.

'Well?' he said.

'That's a wrap,' James shouted.

James and Julien reviewed the tapes, spinning through the images, checking what they had captured.

'Is the camerawork what you want?' Julien asked tentatively.

'It's exactly what we want,' James replied, already cutting the pictures together in his head.

'We need an engineer for next time, though. The camera needs some work done on it,' Julien said, as the two of them walked to the car. 'By the way, I have to confess something.'

'What's that?'

'This is my first proper job operating. Usually I'm a camera assistant.'

James smiled. 'Don't worry, this is my first time filming galloping horses.'

'I thought the French and the British were supposed to hate each other,' Hassan said, walking past, leading the horse off the set. '*Does anyone know where Ibrahim is?*' he shouted. When no one answered, he mumbled, 'Looks like we own a horse now.'

James tried to explain that wrap parties happened only when the *whole* shoot was finished, but no one was interested in details. Hassan and the crew, and Joelle and the students, were in the mood to celebrate. James was too, but he felt nervous as he called Maya from the car. His plan to see her every day hadn't worked out: she was rarely at the LILC, just dropping Nadia off, and having time only for a quick hello before disappearing again. Over two weeks they had exchanged about as many words. Maya seemed to be endlessly late for important appointments, although James wasn't sure what those appointments were, so he was surprised when she answered, and tripped over his words with excitement when she agreed to come to the party.

She walked into the bar wearing a black asymmetrical

top that was hooked over one shoulder, showing the smooth lines of the other. James jumped out of his seat as soon as he spotted her.

'I like your top,' he said, apprehensively. Suddenly, with Maya sitting next to him, he felt as if each word he said counted that much more. He introduced her to Hassan, who nodded his greeting. After a couple of drinks, James and Maya retreated to a corner, where James tried to control his attempts to impress her but had difficulty stopping his enthusiasm for the video. He heard himself tell her for some reason how they had only located Ibrahim just before leaving Tyre, and how by then an argument had already broken out among the crew as to who should rightfully take ownership of the horse. When she laughed at this, James continued, 'All the crew wanted to know about this amazing girl who was coming to the wrap party with me.'

'You should be careful what you say and who you say it to,' Maya replied.

'What?'

'Everyone knows everyone in Beirut. There is one degree of separation.'

'You're losing me.'

'*Ma'lesh*,' Maya said, gesturing with her hand that it was time for a new subject. 'Have you seen any belly-dancing since you've been here?'

'Isn't that a bit of a Middle East cliché?'

'You can decide if it's a cliché,' she said. 'Do you want to dance?'

James stood up and followed Maya on to the dance

floor. He had learned to dance in the early nineties, so his moves were the product of dancing to people called DJ Tanith playing 150 bpm techno. Then, when he started making videos, he developed a slow head-nod-to-the-beat-type move while filming unknown hip hop bands every day. Neither of these had set him up very well for Arabic music, so he copied what most of the other men were doing, which was very little, while the women did all the work. Maya didn't so much dance as unleash some kind of slow-burning electric current which took hold of her body. James felt like a cartoon character with his eyes out on stalks. In the 1960s, the Twist had been banned in Lebanon, while in the United States it had been illegal to film Elvis below his waist because – whether it was the Twist or the King – everyone knew what happened to young people once they were exposed to wiggling hips. James was a perfect example. The only thing that was more of an aphrodisiac than wiggling hips was the *thought* of them. It was still impossible to ban the imagination.

Maya kept her shoulders quite still, her hands making elegant patterns in the air, while her hips swished to the beat of the music. James could hear her shout to the DJ, asking him to play a song she liked. The DJ obliged and Maya danced, her arms in the air, her upper body moving slowly and gracefully, but some other force entirely was in control of her hips, which swished and rocked. As she moved close to James, he could see her mouth open slightly, her lips pursed. He couldn't stand it any more, and grabbed her arm.

'What?' she said, smiling.

'Let's get out of here.'

'You don't like belly-dancing?' she teased.

'Oh, I *like* it.'

Julien didn't even notice them leave, he was too busy dancing; Joelle was arguing with Tony about what top she should wear for the next part of the shoot, and Nadia was leading the students in a game of poker in a corner.

They arrived at James's apartment. 'So do you like your new place?' Maya asked, sitting down. It was hot in the room and she was still perspiring; her honey-coloured skin glistened in the low light. James leaned over and kissed her on the mouth. The ease between them disappeared and he felt her tense up. He did the same. It wasn't what he expected, but he continued kissing her. She put her hand on the back of his head, her fingers threading through his hair. He kissed her neck, then stood up, bringing her to her feet. For a moment it was like in the club, the mood lightened. They were both smiling at each other stupidly, knowing what was about to happen. Maya caught James trying not to look at her thong, which had ridden a fraction above her jeans.

'If you wanted to see my underwear you could have just asked me.'

'Well, can I see it?'

She tugged at the string of her top and took it off. His eyes followed her fingers as they worked their way down the buttons on her jeans. She lay back on the bed, easing them slowly over her hips. James impatiently took them by the ankles and pulled. She slipped out of her knickers, then propped herself up on one elbow to watch him undress. His performance was far less elegant.

Maya arched her back as his lips touched her neck, feeling the weight of him pressing her into the soft mattress. There was a short pause while he located a condom before turning his attention back to her. Maya's nails dug into his sides as he pushed inside her.

Afterwards, as they lay in bed, the atmosphere became tense again. James didn't know where it had come from or how to dispel it. Maya got out of bed and made a whispered phone call, but James couldn't make out anything she said apart from the word 'mother'. Then she got back into bed and curled herself around him, and they slept.

When James woke early in the morning, Maya was putting on her clothes.

'Are you going?' he asked.

'I have to. I have so much to do.'

'Can I call you later?' James said. 'I still don't have your number.'

She wrote it down on a piece of paper and handed it to him. 'Actually, I'll call you,' she said. 'It's easier.'

James jumped out of bed to catch her before she left. He didn't want her to leave this way, and he knew he *had* to kiss her again. He put his arms around her as he moved his lips to hers. The tension of their conversation disappeared. The kiss lasted and lasted.

10

The kiss seemed to go on for hours. Maya didn't know when it would stop. She felt his tongue play with hers; she could see how turned on he was. Walid always kissed her this way and he didn't stop, even though the mobile phone in his hand was ringing, its numbers glowing ultraviolet blue. The two of them were standing in the middle of his bedroom, silently looking at each other, but when Maya didn't start undressing, as Walid clearly expected her to do, he shrugged and put his arm around her. As they walked into the living room arm in arm – the dull thump of him closing the bedroom door behind them making Maya jump slightly – she felt herself break into the kind of cold sweat that came from food poisoning. She covered up by reaching up to kiss him again. She could taste toothpaste in his kiss, combined with menthol-flavoured tobacco. She tried to pull away casually, but he kept kissing her.

'I missed you, *habibte*,' Walid said. Maya looked around the living room in the hope of finding something that could spark a different conversation. His phone was still ringing. Walid poured himself a brandy and very calmly said, 'I want to know where the fuck you were last night.'

Before Maya had fallen asleep at James's apartment she

had called Nadia. When she left his apartment that morning she had called her again.

'It's me. Did my mother check up?'

'I said you were staying at my house, but had gone out to buy pizza,' Nadia replied.

Friends covered for friends in an intricate web of lies every Saturday night.

'Is your mother being crazy?' Nadia asked. 'You sound edgy.'

'Just the usual. But it's not that.'

'The English guy?'

'I don't know what to do. I have to go and see Walid now.'

'He called last night. The pizza excuse didn't work so well.'

'I'm going straight to his house now,' Maya said, unlocking her car.

'You want me to call you later with an "emergency"?' Nadia asked.

'In a couple of hours.'

'No problem.'

'Okay, Nadia. *Yallabye.*'

Maya put the phone in her pocket, relocked her car and hailed a taxi. She felt that if she were behind the wheel, if *she* were in control, then she would never be able to bring herself to go through with it. Someone else would have to take her to Walid's, then at least she would feel as if she was somehow not complicit in what she was doing. The taxi-driver sped past Armani and Tiffany's on rue Verdun, the only street in the world where the women walking around were better dressed than the ones in the fashion magazines they read; the beauty salons and gyms and shops did good business plucking and oiling, glossing and curving, waxing and sculpting. In a nearby mall with an open front, teenage Prada-clad princesses darted around in small groups, mobile phones in hand.

Maya signalled the driver to stop. When she got to the front door, she rang the bell. Walid opened it wearing his usual Sunday attire: suede Birkenstocks, black jeans and a Gucci open-neck shirt. He was smoking a cigarette. He wasn't particularly tall but he was well built and Maya shrank in front of him. He kissed her as she entered his apartment and then motioned for her to follow him into the bedroom. His mobile phone started ringing.

Every year, the world's gem-makers produce over $6 billion worth of diamonds. The global diamond retail trade is thought to be worth around $56 billion, and about four per cent of that comes from war zones in Africa. The illegal sale of these blood diamonds helps to bankroll the militias and revolutionaries that continue these wars so their profits don't dry up. They mine them in areas they are operating in, then sell them or trade them in exchange for arms. The diamonds leave the mines by any means necessary: bribery, murder, carrier pigeon. In one South African mine the order was given to shoot any unregistered pigeons as the birds were being used to smuggle the uncut diamonds out of the mine, a couple of million dollars having flown out in one year. Diamonds are a smuggler's delight: a concealable and easily convertible form of wealth. It was once believed that the gods blessed only India with diamonds. But Walid knew the Devil had given them to Africa as well.

András had been smuggling for five years and used several different names. He was originally from eastern Europe, but he had a Belgian passport and took different routes each time, sometimes through France, sometimes through Switzerland, then on to Turkey, finishing in Freetown in Sierra Leone. At a hotel he would meet his contact, inspect the diamonds, and then pack them into children's toys or bags and suitcases with secret compartments. He favoured expensive leather bags as the material was thick and he could slit it and sew in a pocket before closing it up. He then returned via Liberia, where he could bribe his way out if he was stopped. When the diamonds were safely in Antwerp, the back-flow of money and arms to Sierra Leone started. The diamonds were the breaking waves, and the arms were the undertow, the deadly rip tide. The diamonds were cut in Antwerp, then sold to a dealer who would mix them with legitimate diamonds. The blood diamonds would disappear. András did three or four smuggling runs every year, but he didn't cut the deals. He was just the mule.

During the war, Walid had acted as an intermediary, a facilitator for András, organising the cash and arms flow back to Africa, and it had made him very rich. Many Lebanese were legitimate diamond dealers in Africa, but Walid was not one of them. He knew who to bribe, he understood how Africa and Europe worked; he knew his way around customs and he knew diamonds.

Walid was now banned from ever entering the continent

of Africa. It specified this on his passport. He was one of the lucky ones; over the years some of his contacts involved in diamond smuggling had been killed in Sierra Leone. Walid had bought his way out of the situation that had ended his diamond-smuggling career. András had been searched in Liberia on his way to meet Walid in Europe, and they had found several hundred thousand dollars' worth of diamonds in his belongings. The documentation that András was carrying was false as always, and although he had been able to bribe his way to freedom, the bad luck had followed him to Belgium, where Walid was waiting. Someone in Liberia had tipped off the authorities in Antwerp, who were keen to make a bust after reports of their sloppy customs inspections had become public. Walid made a hasty exit back to Lebanon.

Now the war was over and Walid was just a 'successful businessman'. No more diamonds – apart from the odd little personal deal, but he didn't feel that really counted. His arrogance and past ability to keep his record clean meant that he still travelled freely around the world, Africa being the only exception, in the naive belief that he held some kind of divine immunity, not realising that all over the globe the files on him had not been closed. Maya had known straight away that there was something strange about him, something hidden, although she wasn't sure exactly what. For a start, he was *very* rich. He had all the trappings: several houses, several Mercedes, several gold watches. But he wasn't a rich Lebanese who had earned his money working in the USA or the Gulf, or had very successful children or other family members who worked abroad and sent money back. Walid was part of the Lebanese economic miracle that puzzled economists all over the world: how could so many people in the society be so wealthy considering the GDP was tiny and the national debt was huge. And the explanation wasn't simply that most people lived in houses they had inherited, or were rich because of land that had been passed down through family. Walid didn't have any of these things. But what the economists had failed to grasp was that if you took Lebanon apart, you wouldn't have enough pieces to put a country back together again. No one knew how it worked financially, because money came from so many untaxable and untraceable sources. Smuggling raw diamonds from Africa was just one of the ways in which people like Walid had earned money during the war. Now he was making a stab at legitimacy. He had offices, he had secretaries, and although Maya knew his import business was above board – he purchased Persian rugs from Iran then shipped them to Europe – she guessed he was running a little sideline of money laundering. It was like giving up smoking: she was sure Walid had quit, but who was to say whether or not he occasionally had one at a party? Walid never told her about the diamonds, and those who did know his past valued his friendship above the gossip kudos they would gain from telling all. No one would have dared to cross him.

Walid swilled his brandy around in the glass. He repeated, 'I *said*, I want to know where you were last night. I called you but you didn't answer. Then I called Nadia.'

'My phone's battery ran out.'

Walid took a sip of his drink, an action he performed so calmly that Maya felt immediately threatened by it. 'Why didn't you call me from Nadia's?'

'We were watching a movie! Calm down.'

'She said you went out to get a pizza.'

'We were hungry,' Maya said, exasperated.

'I called you but your phone was off,' he said, sitting down next to her and draining his glass.

'I told you, the battery ran out.'

'What movie?'

'What?'

'What movie did you watch?'

Maya couldn't decide whether this was another trick to see if she would stumble, or if he was trying to change the subject and have a normal conversation.

'Something with Pacino,' she said. 'Anyway, how are you?' she asked, softening her voice. She patted his thigh and gently kissed his cheek. She could feel him relax.

'What's that in your bag?' Walid pointed to some papers sticking out.

'Applications.'

'For what?'

'Nothing. It's for Nadia.'

'Tell me what you need. I can get it for you.'

You can't get me an MBA, Maya said to herself. She wanted to spit in his face. She hated the way he smoked his cigarette; she hated the ring tone on his phone; and she hated the fact that he was the key, he was absolutely her *only* route out of the country and an arranged marriage.

'Why do you make things hard for yourself?' Walid

asked, taking a handful of *bizzer* and expertly cracking the pumpkin seeds in his teeth to extricate the nut inside. The line seemed to echo from her mother to Walid and back to her.

When Maya had first met Walid, when she had thought for a split second that maybe she could spend some time with him, she had told him about her wish to study abroad. He had given her a look that said, *You'll grow out of these ideas soon.* Whenever Maya used to tell her parents her plans, they acted as if she was a child who had told them she was going to the moon at the weekend. It was just *silliness.* Now she never mentioned anything: work, hopes, ideas for the future. She was disgusted with herself for staying with Walid; she was disgusted that she had no other choice. Maya didn't want Walid to know her plan; she didn't want him to know anything about her. He was right about one thing. She did make things hard on herself. There was no way she was going to get out if she didn't.

Maya gritted her teeth as Walid fucked her. If only she could think about something else, if only she could focus her mind on *anything.* Her whole jaw was tensed up so she was unable to kiss him back. She held the back of Walid's head and gently applied pressure, pushing his face into her shoulder. It turned him on even more – he thought she wanted him to kiss her neck. He didn't know it was so she didn't have to look at his face.

Everyone disappeared. James hadn't seen Maya for a week, and Aisha hadn't been at the apartment block for two days.

He had been busy earning a living, teaching, putting dollars in his pocket, paying Mr Toufic, the landlord. It would keep him afloat while they made the video.

But James was worried about Aisha – she was always very prompt, arriving before ten every morning. But there had been no sign of her. He had no number to call, and Mr Toufic just said she was taking some time off to be with her family. Without contact from Aisha or Maya, James became involved in the lives of his students: Michel and his politics, Omar and his *nargileh*, which they smoked after class, the apple-scented smoke drifting from the bubbling pipe down the corridor, Nadia and her harmless flirting. He often wanted to ask her about Maya, but he had to respect the unwritten rule that they would not talk about her best friend. He could feel Nadia become uncomfortable if she thought he was even approaching the subject, so they kept their relationship strictly that of teacher and student.

James dialled Maya's number but she didn't answer. She hadn't answered for a week. The cold, hollow sound of her voicemail message seemed to mirror the mocking tone of his own answering machine when it had played back Fran's messages to him. James could always hear that stranger's voice with its comfortable intimacy, arranging to meet Fran on the first night James was away. But now he found that Maya's silence was having a worse effect on him. It was over with Fran, but the *possibility* of Maya was enough for him, for the moment; the thrill of talking to her, the way she laughed, watching her dance, kept him going. But if he had no contact with her, then that possibility faded.

*   *   *

Fatima looked tired, lying in the hospital bed. It had started with shivering fits at home, leading Aisha to believe it was a fever, but then she developed pains in her chest and the coughing got worse. It was dry to begin with, then she started to cough up bloodstained phlegm. Aisha had brought her in straight away and had stayed at her bedside for two days. Now she watched the sheet that covered her mother as it moved quickly up and down, in time with her fast, shallow breathing. Sometimes Fatima gasped for breath. It upset Aisha to see her mother in pain, and in this increasingly confused state. She had always been such a strong woman, but the pneumonia had taken a grip on her and was winning. Pneumonia was a killer for the elderly and Aisha knew it as she gently held her mother's frail hand, closing her eyes from time to time to escape the situation. She experienced a range of feelings: guilt, sadness, anger. They all coursed through her veins when she remembered how many times Fatima had brought up the subject of trying to reach the border over the last few years; even falling ill hadn't stopped her from talking about it. But there was no way a Lebanese checkpoint – let alone an Israeli-controlled one – would let a Palestinian close to the border. The Palestinian cross-border attacks that had helped ignite one front of the war had now been replaced by the actions of Hizbollah, but no one was taking any chances. The closest Fatima could get to the border was a few miles. It may as well have been a thousand. As she looked at her mother's face, Aisha promised herself that if God helped Fatima survive this, if the Israeli army left Lebanon, then she would do everything she could to allow her mother to visit the border. If she had to wheel her there herself, then she would do it.

Aisha struck up a conversation with a friendly doctor who brought more antibiotics, and told him of her mother's wish. He nodded when she informed him he had to get Fatima through it; he *had to* give her something to stop the pneumonia worsening. Aisha decided right then that if her mother died at the border, then so be it. She would accept that and never ask for anything more. She knew that until her mother had touched her own flesh and blood through the metal fence, no one in their home would be at peace. She didn't believe Fatima would ever live in her land again, although she never said so. She didn't know why the old lady kept her useless door key. To Aisha it was like willingly bringing back a nightmare; to Fatima it was her only connection to the wood and stone and soil of her past. Aisha usually left the room when the family watched the news, but now she was starting reluctantly to pay more attention. She found herself wanting to hear the latest on the border situation.

When Aisha returned home from the hospital, Marwan was having an argument with their son, Tareq. As soon as Marwan lost one job he had to search for another one. Nothing was secure – he had already worked as a mechanic and a plumber in the last year. In between jobs, his pride wouldn't allow him to stay at home during the day so he would help out at a local shop. That was his entire world. Their lives were as shaky and fragile as the walls of their house. Strict laws prohibiting certain building materials in the camps were designed to stop anything too permanent being constructed, and their cars were regularly searched as they entered. Each year the house managed to hold together despite the conditions, and Aisha's family did much the same.

Aisha could do nothing about their living conditions, and she could do nothing about ending the occupation that her mother had become obsessed with. Perhaps Fatima had also given up on the hope of ever living in her old home again, so she would accept just *seeing* some of the land. Aisha couldn't imagine her mother giving up anything, but she had looked so weak in the hospital bed. All Aisha could do was offer as much love to her children as she herself had received, and leave the rest in God's hands. As she watched the aggression and frustration her son was starting to display, she worried what Tareq and his generation would become: young men growing up knowing nothing but being strangers in a country that would never be theirs. He couldn't help but be changed by his surroundings. In the home Aisha felt she had some influence, but outside, at school, or when he was playing in the dirt tracks of the camp, who was his role model there? If someone offered a route out, would he be attracted to it? Aisha didn't want to think of him as a boy with no future, but he was a boy who every day saw his parents struggle to put food on the table, who had no right to medical care and relied on UNRWA hospitals, no right to work, or education. No human rights. Most refugees fled and asked for asylum so they would not be returned home. Palestinian refugees thought *only* of returning home. It was the one thing that bound the community together in the squalid living conditions.

'Tareq, go and wash for dinner,' Aisha said, breaking up the argument. Marwan looked tired, but Tareq had an intense expression in his eyes, a look that said soon he would be old enough to take on a nation's anger. Aisha knew that Tareq's only identity, his only notion of being Palestinian, was through the idea of the return home. Where else would it come from? His football team was the only one without a homeland; he was registered at school under the Palestine address where his grandfather had lived, not his address in the camp. The little houses and narrow cluttered streets of the camp may have suggested that this was something temporary, but it had been temporary for fifty years, and the leadership – far away in Ramallah – hadn't offered them anything yet. Aisha continually heard rumours that a deal might be struck to send some refugees to Switzerland or Canada, or that their rights would be signed away by an ageing leader. But then the rumours disappeared, as weak as the foundations of the camp.

A pale face appeared at the kitchen window as Aisha was putting dinner together. It made her jump, then she realised who it was.

'Kathy!' Aisha's eyes lit up. 'Come in, come in.'

Kathy walked into the kitchen and spoke to Aisha in Arabic. 'Tell me about your mother, what's the news?'

'She is living,' Aisha replied solemnly, as if that was enough to be thankful for.

'But she will recover,' Kathy said.

'As God wills it.'

Kathy nodded, and tried to smile reassuringly. 'I actually wanted to speak to you about Tareq.' As she spoke she could see Aisha hide a faint smile: Kathy had moved from Canada to Syria several years earlier and had learned Arabic there. Her Syrian accent amused Aisha, but Kathy didn't mind, she was just glad to be a light-hearted distraction for her friend.

'What has he done?' Aisha asked, her voice full of dread. 'Marwan is too tired to spend much time with him. He needs a good influence.'

'I think I've found something,' Kathy said. 'We have a few computers now and Safaa sends thousands of e-mails every day to Dseisheh camp in Bethlehem, but Tareq never seemed interested. Then this afternoon two of the computers went down, and he wouldn't leave the engineer's side as he repaired them.'

Aisha turned around from chopping up parsley. 'Really?'

Kathy continued. 'If the back is off a computer, Tareq's nose is there, watching closely. Anyway, is he here?'

'Yes – Tareq, come in here, Miss Kathy wants to talk to you.'

The boy ambled into the room, then his eyes sparkled when he saw Kathy.

'I have a job for you, Tareq,' Kathy said.

'What is it?'

'You're going to be in charge of starting up the system every morning and logging on the other children.'

'Really?'

'What do you say to Miss Kathy?' Aisha cut in.

'Thank you.'

Kathy had more work to do and had then organised to meet up with some other camp workers later, so she tried to excuse herself, but should have known by now that she wasn't getting out of the house until she had been fed. Aisha had adopted her, and became very maternal whenever she was around. She did Kathy's washing and made sure she didn't say anything when she found out that Kathy lived with several men, none of whom she was married to. Kathy lived not far from the camp, and some local boys – posing as electricity repair men – had managed to get inside her flat and have a good look around. The den of decadence wasn't much to look at: a Norwegian man studying Islamic finance law, a German man who imported Mercedes, and Kathy, an Ontario-born camp worker. There didn't seem to be any evidence of seedy sexual practices, just laptops, stacks of paper and separate rooms. It confused the boys. They didn't bother to waste their time going back again. It was no fun.

The next day, Aisha kissed her mother's hand as she slept in the hospital. When she arrived home, Marwan was already back from the garage and looking after the children. Safaa was doing her homework and Tareq was watching a Stallone film on SuperMovies. Aisha took the remote control and scanned for news on the border situation.

'I'm watching a movie,' Tareq protested as Aisha switched channels.

'What would Miss Kathy think of you speaking to me like that?' she replied, and the boy became quiet.

'You hate the news,' Marwan said.

In a crowded camp in a tiny Middle Eastern country, Aisha flicked from CNN to BBC World to al-Jazeera to the Hizbollah channel al-Manar and back again. Her hand was getting tired. Non-stop information was being beamed at people around the world from satellites, but as far as Aisha could see very little wisdom went along for the ride.

She didn't find what she wanted. There wasn't a single news anchor to tell her 'Aisha, the pull-out will happen before your mother becomes too weak', and she felt no comfort that night. Like everyone in the camp, she waited for other forces to move and change her life. She had little control over anything, apart from what time her children went to bed.

11

Maya still wasn't answering her phone. James sat on his bed, editing the pictures from the shoot on Julien's Powerbook. When the phone rang he leapt for it, only to be disappointed by Raja's voice breaking through the din of the LILC in the background.

'Can you come down for extra hours today?' Raja asked. The Powerbook was flashing James an error message – the same message it had been giving him frequently during a morning of crashes and lost information – so he left it whirring away by itself and ran out of the door. He reached the bottom of the stairs and bumped into Mr Toufic, who had a landlordy glint in his eye. After a high-speed Q&A about respective families, Mr Toufic enquired as to when he could expect the next rent cheque.

'In two days,' James offered, hoping Raja would pay quickly.

'What are we doing today?' Omar asked. The students were still buzzing from their unorthodox music video field trip. James was starting to remember names, although people whose names began with the 'kh' or 'gh' sound still winced when James tried to pronounce them. He played this to his advantage as the students themselves became embarrassed when pronouncing the English 'th' sound – saying 'wezzer' instead of 'weather'. One morning James had written a sentence on the board with a lot of these sounds. Then Nadia – ahead of everyone else's mad dash to beat her to it – had sidled up to the board and written a sentence in transliterated Arabic which James read aloud for everyone's amusement. When they had finished laughing they were relaxed enough to read the 'th' sentences, and bit by bit their pronunciation improved.

'Today we are doing listening comprehension,' James said.

'What are we listening to?'

James popped a Beatles tape into a portable stereo. He handed out sheets with fill-in-the-gap slots for the song 'I'm Only Sleeping'. After an initial reluctance, and a lot of puzzled looks, the students started listening to the tape, and were soon agreeing that Mr Lennon was not, in fact, literally floating upstream, it was just in his mind. James was feeling pleased with himself at having won them over, until the ten-minute break, when Omar told him that they had found the exercise very useful, but next time could they bring in some good music.

An apple had started appearing on James's desk each day. Nadia was determined to pass the semester if she had to take down an orchard. James wasn't sure whether she was playing the 'apple for the teacher' joke or if it was for real, but each day she brought two, and ate hers noisily during the class, ignoring the large sign on the door that said 'No food or drink allowed in the classrooms'. When James heard the crunching sound he gave Nadia his best disapproving look. She smiled, held out the half-eaten apple in her hand.

'You want ay-pple?' she purred.

'No thanks, Eve.'

'*Shu?*'

James sighed. 'Nothing.'

Bringing James things to eat had become a pastime for the students. In the break, Noura – a quiet girl in the corner wearing a black *hejab* – often offered James a piece of Turkish delight sandwiched between two biscuits. She exchanged sweets for information on David Beckham, who she regularly reminded everyone she was in love with. She apparently didn't share this information with her fiancé. James happily worked his way through the Turkish delight during the breaks that never *were* breaks because none of the students bothered to leave. They were too busy having classroom picnics (someone eventually took down the 'No food or drink allowed' sign), and talking about Mexican soap operas and the latest happenings on *Zee Bold* – their stylish abbreviation for *The Bold and the Beautiful*.

'Do you want another class?' Raja asked later, between puffs of his ever-present cigarette. James thought about his landlord's face that morning.

'Yes,' he replied. 'Any chance of an advance?'

James stood at the side of the road, his advance safe in his pocket, repeating his destination to every *servis* driver that passed. The only things that were cheap in Beirut were cigarettes and *servis* taxis. If James could ride around in circles all day while smoking, he felt he could really save some cash. Finally one stopped and James told him his destination, about two miles south-east of Hamra, according to Raja. The driver asked James a question in Arabic which he didn't understand, so he just motioned for James to get in. James was becoming wilfully entangled with the city. It was a good feeling. He had classes. He had somewhere to live. He liked it that the guy at the sandwich shop by Arabian Sands remembered his order after only one visit; that people from shops he had gone into said hello as he walked down the street. It was nice to be somewhere where everyone knew everyone. Maya was right – you were only one person away from anyone in Beirut.

The twenty-minute stop-start journey took James through areas that were towns within towns, worlds within worlds. On one street, women in black *chadors* walked past pictures of religious leaders stuck on every wall, then in another there were expensive boutiques and restaurants, and a large painting of Leonardo DiCaprio adorning one wall. The subjects of all the pictures and paintings seemed to be looking skyward. At a large roundabout the driver stopped for a man to get in. He wore a black shirt, unbuttoned about as far down as the 1970s, exposing a mat of tangled chest hair.

He looked at James. 'From where?'

'*Ingiliterra*,' James said.

'Welcome,' the man said. 'From Iraq.' He put his hand out and James shook it. Then the man brought his right hand to his chest, just as Aisha had done. 'What's your name?' he asked.

'James. What's yours?'

The man answered by pointing to the thick gold necklace around his neck, framed by his half-open shirt. 'Nasser.'

James looked at the Arabic writing hanging from his necklace on a cushion of chest hair. 'This says "Nasser"?' James asked, trying to work out which letter corresponded to which sound.

'No,' the man said, pointing to the word below, 'this say Nasser. *This*' – he moved his finger over the word James was examining – 'say *Allah.*'

The taxi bumped along the road as Nasser chatted, sitting sideways on the back seat, occasionally stealing a glance at the overwhelmingly perfumed girl sitting in the front. 'My sister is in Canada,' he said sadly. 'I leave Iraq, but for me no Canada. But *Lubnen* is good. Iraq is big problem.'

Nasser then spent a long time trying to mime a word that he could not translate. The driver picked up a medical student outside the hospital who pitched in with the translation. Eventually the three of them got there: the word Nasser wanted was obstetrician. Just before he left, he told them, he had been watching Iraqi television when the daily execution list came up and he noticed the name of the man who had delivered him as a baby.

James couldn't believe how long a two-mile journey was taking. The traffic moved so slowly it felt as if he must have at least crossed into another country by now. The driver took them through the area that had held the PLO headquarters during the war. It was from here that Arafat and his guerrillas said they defended the city. A city that was not theirs. They passed a Phoenicia petrol station and huge cemeteries full of the dead from the First World War.

'What do you do?' James asked Nasser.

'Computer engineer.'

'Know anything about digital cameras?'

'*Yaani*,' Nasser hedged.

The driver stopped by a large mosque in a busy main street. There was a row of shops on the other side of the road, one of which had a rickety sign that read LILC2. Raja was obviously trying to branch out across the city. The driver motioned for James to get out, which he did, watching the *servis* quickly disappear and blend into the Mercedes ocean.

Nasser was standing next to him. James and the latest addition to his flock of students entered the shop, then were shown a special door through which they went upstairs and into the language centre.

It was obvious immediately that the new group didn't want to be there. No Nadia with her apple; no Noura and her production line of Turkish delight sandwiches; no Michel and his occasional incarceration. One man in the class was dressed in full camouflage combat gear; two adolescents stared at James, looking very unimpressed. One girl was interested only in making jokes in Arabic and disrupting the class. At least Nasser was enthusiastic, James thought.

'That is not correct!' the entire class erupted after James wrote a sentence on the board.

'"Colour" does not have "u".'

'And "favourite" is also with no "u".'

James changed the sentence to stay in line with the students' American textbooks, and silently mourned the death of British English. What would happen to sarcasm? The students were a grudging lot, staying as far away from him as possible, muttering monosyllabic answers at best.

At the end of his first week with the new class, the students had to deliver speeches to earn their pass grade. As James listened to Nasser read out his piece in English (his fourth language, if you didn't include a good grounding in Russian), about how he hoped a more unified Europe might change the West's Middle East policies, a girl at the back was conversing loudly with her boyfriend on her phone. James tried to engage her by asking a question.

'What did you do at the weekend?'

'I visited the sister.'

No one offered the correction.

'I visited *my* sister,' James said.

'No, *the* sister,' she corrected him back.

Hussein, the soldier still wearing his army fatigues, asked her something in Arabic which she answered. 'She went to Syria for the weekend,' Hussein said. 'We call it the sister.'

'There is a joke,' another student said. 'You do not choose your family.'

Routine was bringing James comfort. As soon as he started thinking about Fran, he added something else to his schedule. But every time he thought about Maya, he called her only to get no answer. Just as he felt Fran fade in his memory the tiniest amount, he found he couldn't relax for thinking about Maya and the empty ringing sound her phone made when it went unanswered. He spent his evenings at his apartment, and having bought dinner for himself and Nasser, he would edit while Nasser worked on the camera or the computer. They would sit in contented near-silence, speaking only to comment on rendering times for different special effects. In the classroom things also picked up: it took four plays of a Britney Spears listening exercise to get there, but James did finally win some ground with his students. The soldier, Hussein, became James's chief of discipline and helped keep order. Nasser was quiet, and just made copious notes throughout the class. When the students finished an exercise now, they no longer sat in their seats passively, waiting for him to ask them to read it or hand it in. They gathered around him and rewrote their papers as he made comments. One boy used James's back as a desk, the phone girl – who had broken up with her boyfriend so now concentrated less on her mobile and more on English – pulled up a chair and sat next to him. Another student sat on the floor, resting his paper on James's knee. Hussein's holstered gun knocked against James's chair leg. He got used to his personal space being invaded.

The textbook warned him to stay away from politics, and James had initially attempted to do that by talking about films and music. It made no difference – the discussions always ended up on more interesting subjects as the students jumped from conspiracy to conspiracy, solving the giant, intricate plots that had apparently changed the world. And their pronunciation improved.

James wondered whether the endless plots that his students concocted were getting to him. They had conspiracy theories for everything that happened in the Middle East. James had unconsciously started to create a few theories of his own. He had been introduced to the other teachers at the LILC – there were two or three middle-aged Lebanese women who had been working there for a long time, and the occasional university student coming in to teach as a way to help with tuition fees. But it turned out that James was not the only foreigner. He had met three young American men, all extremely polite and pleasant. Unlike James, they were qualified English teachers and were more than capable of earning even better money teaching elsewhere. So the question of what they were doing in Lebanon planted itself in James's mind. He decided that there was something almost too eager about them, and that they were always far too enthusiastic about everything. One of them, Jerry, had eyes that were impossibly pale and watery, but appeared to be in a constant state of pleasure. Filled with joy.

James decided they were Christian missionaries. Secret ones, at that.

As James left the building after Nadia's class, he was wondering whether Jerry owned a guitar. That would be a sure sign of a Christian missionary. As he walked down the stairs, Raja caught his eye.

'Everything okay?' Raja asked.

'Pretty good,' James said. 'I wanted to ask you something.'

'What's that?'

'That guy Jerry. The teacher.'

'Yes.'

'Is he . . . I mean . . . I wondered if he . . . Oh, hi, Jerry,' James said as Jerry appeared behind him. 'How're the classes?'

'Awesome,' Jerry said. 'You?'

'What did you want to know?' Raja asked James.

'Nothing.' James grimaced, before turning back to Jerry. 'Yeah. Listen, Jerry. What are you doing later?'

Jerry held up a large black case. 'Guitar practice,' he said. James was certain his eyes looked even more watery than usual.

'Okay-see-you-later,' James machine-gunned, and fled to Arabian Sands to buy a drink. He had only large bills, so Abu Khalil gave him the drink for free saying he could pay '*Bukra, bukra*'. A Lebanese *bukra* was at least a day later than a Spanish *mañana*.

When James exited the shop, there was a familiar car parked outside. Maya was inside, engine running, window rolled down.

'Where've you been?' James asked, crouching down to speak to her. She shrugged. 'I get a shrug? That's my answer?'

'What answer do you want? Get in the car.'

'You never pick up when I call.'

'The last week has been difficult,' Maya said with forced calmness. James walked round to the passenger side, and opened the door. '*Yalla*, close the door. We'll get seen,' she said.

'Seen?' James said as he got in. When she didn't answer, he said, 'I missed you.'

Maya was edgy and nervous. The bar they ended up in may have pulsed to the soothing sounds of Café del Mar, but Maya tensed when anyone walked in. 'This actually *tastes* of peach ice cream,' she said, passing her drink to James as if he were one half of an old married couple. It was the first thing she had done all day that seemed like the old Maya. It gave him a little kick: even the thought of the two of them being middle aged and doing their taxes together somehow made him happy. As he took his second sip she reached her hand out, accidentally brushing the side of his face with her fingers, and took the glass back from him.

Young men in sleeveless T-shirts eyed each other up, college girls laughed in dark corners with their friends. Tables were crowded with cocktails, beer, pastel-coloured shots, baskets of popcorn. James sipped his drink, and tried not to give in to the impulse to bury his head in Maya's neck, as if all the answers might be in her soft, perfumed skin, set off perfectly by a silver earring. She had her hair up, showing off her elegant neck. He tried to resist, but it was drawing him in.

'How does it work here, Maya?'

'How does what work?'

'I can sit here with you, right? In public. That's not a problem. There are college boys and girls in the corner all mixed, that's okay.'

'What's your point?'

'So people have relationships. I thought it might be kind of secretive.'

'Kind of? Okay, the girls' and boys' dorms are separated on campus with very strict visiting hours. None of those girls' parents know they're here, though, unless perhaps they're engaged to someone and it's all approved.'

'But it's not like an arranged marriage when you meet your husband on the wedding day, is it?'

'It depends on the family. Sometimes it feels like it's a deal,' Maya said.

James looked around the bar. 'What about the men?'

'Boys will be boys,' she said.

'So they can . . .'

'Do what they like.'

The room was filled with music so cool it probably didn't have a title. James leaned over and kissed Maya. She put her hand gently to his face and kissed him back. Then she grabbed his hand and, almost throwing their table over, dragged him towards the toilets. James tried not to laugh at her impulsiveness. When they got to the bathroom door, James looked at her, waiting.

'What's going on?'

'Just someone I don't want to see,' she said.

James looked around. 'Ex-boyfriend?'

'Yeah,' she said, hesitantly. James peered round the corner, but couldn't see anyone who looked like an ex-boyfriend – ex-boyfriends seemed to share a look, especially in the eyes of next-boyfriends. Maya lurked behind James, her hand on his arm.

James laughed. 'Where is he?'

'I can't see him. Maybe he's gone.'

Maya seemed so serious, James tried to make light of the situation. 'I remember when I bumped into this girl I went out with when I was sixteen. She looked really different without two litres of cider inside me . . . so in focus.'

Maya didn't react.

'You sure you haven't murdered someone?'

Maya hushed him. When she was sure it was safe, the two of them sneaked out. James threw some money at the barman as Maya dragged him outside.

At his apartment, Maya was still tense. Her mobile phone rang, but she silenced it. It rang again.

'What's going on, Maya?'

'James.'

'Yeah?'

'It's complicated.'

'Complicated as in you've got a lot on your mind, or complicated as in you're secretly married to a goose?'

'*Habibi*,' she said softly. 'Stop asking so many questions.'

'Maya, I just wanted to see you. That's why I kept calling.'

She sighed and switched her phone off completely. 'And I came to tell you we couldn't see each other again.'

12

It was a familiar routine for Maya, standing at Walid's front door with her heart pounding. Each time she prayed he hadn't seen her or heard something from one of his friends. She was easily spotted: she was so striking, men noticed her. Many people wanted to ingratiate themselves with Walid and, as long as they put it subtly, they could gain favour by feeding him information on her whereabouts.

'Where were you last night?' he asked, opening the door.

'At Nadia's.' Maya sighed, thoroughly bored by the routine and walking casually past him.

He grabbed her arm and pulled her to him. 'I don't believe that.'

'Well, it's true.' She dismissed his comment with a wave of her hand.

'Antoine saw you in a bar last night.'

Maya froze.

'With some guy,' Walid said.

'Antoine is full of shit,' she responded.

'He told me you were wearing your black boots and you had your hair up.'

Maya was silent for a moment. 'So Antoine told you some bullshit and you immediately believe him.'

'I called you. Why didn't you pick up?'

'Walid, what's your problem?'

His hand smacked against the side of her face, immediately bringing tears to her eyes. She blinked several times, taking in the shock of being struck. She instinctively moved away from him into the corner of the room.

'*Sharmouta*, you're fucking around on me,' he shouted. He paced around the room, rubbing a hand over his day's growth of stubble, considering the situation. He was solidly built: stocky and thick necked, as if he had been cut from a block, not formed in a womb. He looked as though he was pondering a deal that he had been offered. Just as he would be about to say something else, he would shake his head, his lips pursed, his eyes glaring at her. She could smell the mixture of his sweat and cologne. He was exhaling deeply through his nose.

Maya held her hand to her face. She was crying now. She slumped down into a chair and Walid sat next to her. He put his arm around her, but his grip was too strong to be comforting.

'If I hear you're out with another man, *ever*, your parents will know what a little slut their daughter is.'

Maya knew what this meant, that they would take Walid's word over hers. They turned a semi-blind eye to him – it was okay if he took Maya out to dinner. Mrs Jihad always shut up when Walid pulled up in his Mercedes. But they could never find out that Walid had slept with her – that her virginity was fictional. A tarnished reputation would have to be saved by an almost immediate marriage. To Walid probably, or another suitable suitor.

He knew this. Once her reputation was damaged, she was through.

Why do you make life hard for yourself?

Maya had scrunched tissues into a hard nut in her fist. She didn't answer. Walid went into his bedroom to take a business call, leaving her in front of his wide-screen television. Even though she had told James they couldn't see each other any more, she found herself calling him from her mobile. She started crying again as soon as he picked up, but she loved it that his initial coldness towards her, which she had expected, melted when he realised something was very wrong and she needed cheering up, even though he had no idea what was upsetting her. He told her how one of his students had made him a birthday card with 'Happy to you' written on it. But Maya closed up. She didn't want to tell him what had happened – it would be like admitting it to herself. As long as it had taken place between these private walls, it didn't exist. As she spoke, she could hear Walid in the other room, making deals.

'You sound really upset,' James said.

'I'm okay.'

'I know you said yesterday that we couldn't see each other again, but *before* we never see each other again, I think we should have dinner tonight.'

Maya almost managed a laugh. 'Happy birthday, by the way,' she said, wiping her eyes. 'I better go.'

'Are you going to tell me what's going on?'

'I have to go,' she replied.

'Will you come over?'

James could hear Maya sigh on the other end of the line, before whispering, 'I'll try,' and hanging up.

Walid was smiling as he entered the room. He could see that Maya was still upset, but he was looking pleased with himself. He handed her a rectangular box covered in green velvet. She knew the ritual by now. He would get upset, then angry, then she would cry, then:

'It's beautiful,' Maya said, opening the box. A studded diamond necklace reflected little stones of light on her face.

'Put it on,' Walid said softly. She held her hair up as he put it around her neck. The touch of his fingers made her shiver. She knew what this felt like; it was ownership. She wanted to scream and run for the door, but she remained still as he fastened the clasp. The necklace suddenly became something of pure ugliness to her; something grotesque, a diamond noose.

'It's beautiful,' she repeated.

'That's not all,' Walid said. 'We're going to Paris tonight.'

Maya struggled to stop any sound coming out of her mouth. She decided she had misheard. 'Why're you going to Paris?'

'No, *we* are.'

'I can't, Walid.'

'Why not? You can tell your parents you are at a friend's house for the night. No problem.'

'Why do you want to go to Paris anyway?'

'A new hotel wants thirty Persian rugs. I have about two hours' business to do. Then we can do what we like.'

'I can't go.'

'I can call your parents. I can assure them it is separate hotel rooms. They will understand.'

Maya shook her head and gave up. She was going. 'I have to go and get some clothes from home first,' she said.

'We can buy clothes there. Anything you want.'

'Walid, I have to get some things from home,' she persisted. 'What time are we leaving?'

He looked at his watch. 'Around eight,' he said.

Maya left Walid's and jumped into a taxi, getting out at a jewellery shop on Hamra Street.

'Hello, Miss Maya,' the owner said. 'How you are doing?' He always practised his English with her, even though she answered him in Arabic.

When Maya presented the diamond necklace, even the shop owner looked a little taken aback by its beauty. In the glass cabinets all around the little shop were the sparkling apologies of Walid's possessiveness. Some had been sold on, others were still there. Maya noticed some earrings which were supposed to erase a black eye; a ring that compensated for a day of being yelled at. Maya couldn't keep looking around the shop, it depressed her too much. Her history was written on those walls. The shopkeeper was out the back, discussing the piece with his brother. When he returned, he put the necklace on the counter, gently positioning it on a piece of cloth.

'Three thousand dollars,' he said.

It was worth more than that; Maya knew it just from looking at the mark-up on the earrings she had pawned three weeks earlier. It didn't matter; she knew how this went. She nodded agreement and the shopkeeper's brother appeared from the back to start counting out her cash in hundred-dollar bills. As he did, an elderly woman entered the shop. She had a red dye in her permed hair, enormous glasses and thick gold earrings like heavy tears. She saw the necklace and exclaimed something to herself.

'He must really love you,' she said, turning to Maya. Maya didn't reply, imagining the woman probably thought she was just having it valued for insurance. When the brother finished counting out the cash, he slipped it into an envelope and the transaction was complete. From Walid to Maya to pawn shop, then transferred to a bank account in the US for college funds. Maya was almost there – she just had to hold on a little longer.

She left the shop, making sure the cash was stuffed safely in her bag. She was concerned only that it might fall out. She felt secure carrying cash in Beirut – it was a city where a woman could walk alone at 2 a.m. and *know* she was perfectly safe. That didn't stop the comments, though, especially to foreign women with no potential angry husbands or brothers. There was a strange unspoken law on the streets which Maya felt evened things out slightly: although some men would make comments from their cars or as they walked past – the kind of comments most teenagers would think showed sexual immaturity – there were other men who, when they overheard this, would have a go at the perpetrators: 'Shame on you. What if she was your sister?'

Maya walked quickly down to Bliss Street and was soon outside James's apartment block. She flew in through the door, saying hello to the *waz-waz* concierge, before jumping into the lift. When James opened his door, he looked angry, his voice displaying the same cold tone that she had heard when he had answered her phone call from Walid's house.

'I thought we weren't seeing each other again.'

'I know . . .' Maya said, sliding her arms around him. James didn't know what to do with his hands, but then gave in and wrapped them around her.

'Why did you change your mind?' he asked softly. Hearing this was like a sharp knife cutting into her skin. Maya knew nothing had changed, and she wondered whether she was using him to make herself feel better, to put an invisible barrier between her and Walid that neither of them knew about. Maya was a terrible liar, had told only a handful of lies in her life so far. She couldn't tell James about Walid, though. She was so close to finding her route out of the country, she couldn't stop now. She had to see it through, even if it made her feel terrible.

James wanted to stay angry, but as he kissed Maya he relented and gave in to the feeling of not wanting to be without her even for a second. It was scary, but it was a relief. To know for sure how he felt about something, *someone*, eased his mind, even if it ultimately caused more problems. He kissed her neck, completely losing himself in her breathing rhythms. As he looked down at her, lying naked, she slowly trailed a hand down her body, keeping her eyes on him the whole time. Her nails were painted baby pink and they crossed her stomach and reached down between her legs. Then she took her glistening finger and traced it along his lips. She pulled him close, whispering in his ear, her lips brushing the skin on his neck. Their bodies were slick with sweat, her nails leaving small red trails on his body.

Later, she lay on her side with James behind her, her back arched against his chest, his hand in her hair, his lips kissing the back of her neck. They didn't notice it grow dark outside, they were completely lost in each other – laughing, teasing, a never-ending stream of power switches, clicking on and off, submission and power. Little unrehearsed games that said, *I won't ever be able to leave you.*

'I have to go,' Maya said quietly.

'We're having dinner in an hour.'

'I can't go tonight.'

'I booked it.'

'I'm sorry. Something came up. I have to go away for the weekend.'

'Why? Where are you going?'

'Paris,' Maya said, her insides twisting when she heard herself say, 'It's a stupid family thing,' without hesitation.

'Great, so I get to spend a romantic evening editing with Nasser,' James said sarcastically, dialling his friend's number.

Maya didn't reply. She was out of the door in two minutes. Once outside, standing on the street, she wondered what James was thinking. She knew she had probably left his room before he had even registered that she really was leaving. She had made her escape without telling him that she felt comfortable with him, that she enjoyed his company, that she could be herself with him. Any admission like that would just make things worse. She waited for a taxi, wondering why she didn't deserve something normal in her life, one thing that made her happy. Why should she feel guilty for her time with James? But she did feel guilty. She felt an ingrained guilt towards her parents that ran deep. And when she thought about Walid, she felt full of fear.

Maya arrived back at Walid's house late, but he was on the phone and didn't register the time.

'Why aren't you wearing your necklace?' he asked as he hung up.

'It's too precious.'

'It's for you to wear,' he stated, pouring himself a drink. He offered one to Maya but she refused.

'I want to keep it safe.'

'Go home and get it,' he said.

'It's late, Walid.'

'Okay,' he relented eventually. 'Anyway, we're going tomorrow night now.'

'What?'

Walid caught her reaction. 'Why, did you have other plans?'

Maya hesitated, then said, 'Just going over to Nadia's,' before realising what he was doing. It was such a simple game: he'd had no intention of leaving that evening, it had just been a ploy to keep her there for the whole weekend.

*   *   *

Mahmoud watched Hassan get into his new BMW Z8 convertible. He knew Hassan had been sent to Beirut when Majed was kidnapped, in case the same thing happened to him. He knew all that now, his father had explained. But he didn't understand why Haj Ahmad had spoilt Hassan so much. Why was he so special? Mahmoud was his *son*. Hassan was just a nephew. More importantly, Hassan had a great car and never gave Mahmoud a ride anywhere; he had his own apartment within the house and he hardly ever let Mahmoud watch TV in there.

Hassan had been a very quiet and studious boy on his arrival in Beirut. As he had got older, his confidence had grown and he had become lazy, in the way someone who is truly intelligent can afford to be. Now he enrolled and dropped out of postgrad courses at will. Meanwhile Mahmoud was stuck in puberty hell with no older brother figure around to ask questions of or get lifts from.

Even in the darkness, the silver finish on Hassan's new car sparkled; the red-and-white interior put every car on the street to shame. The other vehicles seemed embarrassed to be parked next to it.

'Is that a Z8?' Mahmoud asked as Hassan started it up.

'Unitary aluminium spaceframe, high-performance V8 engine,' Hassan said.

Mahmoud liked it when Hassan wasn't shouting at him or telling him to do something. It made a change. He ran his hand across the wing and down to the head-light.

'Don't touch it,' Hassan scolded. Mahmoud jumped back. 'The design curve is a homage to the BMW 507.'

'How fast to sixty?' Mahmoud enquired. It was the longest conversation he could remember ever having with his cousin.

'Four point seven seconds,' Hassan answered.

The conversation was going well, so Mahmoud thought he would try his luck. 'I want to meet my friends at PC Mania. Can I have a ride? I can walk home.' It would kill his friends to see him show up in that car, driven by his cool older cousin.

'Ride your moped.'

'It's being repaired. The handlebars are broken.'

'That's because you were doing wheelies and showing off,' Hassan said, revving the Beemer's engine as two girls walked past and smiled at him.

'No, someone ran into me. A stupid taxi,' Mahmoud pleaded. 'I only need a ride there. You don't have to pick me up.'

'Ask your father,' Hassan said.

'*Baba* is busy with the restaurant tonight. Please, Hassan.'

'*Inshallah*,' Hassan dismissed him, then sped off.

Hassan entered James's apartment, immediately noticing the clothes, cups and ashtrays that were strewn every-where. It looked as if James and Maya had been living there for years, not hours.

'*Habibi*,' Hassan said, shaking James's hand. 'What the hell happened here?'

'Housekeeper is away. She's disappeared.'

'For how long, a month?' Hassan said, glancing around. 'Who's this?' he asked, looking at the small figure in the corner of the room, hunched over a laptop.

'That's Nasser. Maya is away tonight so we're doing some work.'

'You want to go and have a drink?' Hassan asked.

James turned to Nasser. 'You want a drink, Nasser?'

'No thank you.' Nasser looked up and nodded towards Hassan, then went back to work. Their editing area had grown slowly, but it now boasted a large table borrowed from the landlord, two plastic seats and two ashtrays. Half-empty cans of Crush lurked dangerously close to the keyboard. Numerous external hard drives, jazz drives and things James didn't recognise but had hired and paid for with his earnings from Raja turned the computer into a Medusa, giant cords sprouting from its head.

'What's he doing?' Hassan asked.

'Do you really want to know?'

'Uh, yeah?'

'We're relinking consolidated media clips.'

Hassan sighed. 'I need a cigarette.'

'Do you want to see it so far?'

Hassan perked up. They were silent while Nasser, with the slow confidence of a Russian chess player, hit two buttons and played back the rough cut. It still gave James a little shock, to see the images on a screen, even at low quality, cut together for the first time, an almost childlike feeling of not understanding how all that weather could get into such a small box. There was Joelle on the beach, but no smells of the ocean, no sounds of gulls or people shouting orders around the set. Just music.

When it was over, Hassan turned to James and smiled. 'You're good at this,' he said, then realised he sounded surprised and covered up with a joke. 'Where's the guy on the horse?'

'Other version. Haven't started on that one yet.'

Hassan stood up and walked over to the fridge, selecting a beer for himself. 'So, are we going out?'

'We can do. I wouldn't mind something to eat. I was supposed to be having dinner with Maya tonight,' James said.

'Where is she?'

'She had something else on.'

Hassan said, 'James, you're too trusting. Right, Nasser?' But Nasser was too busy to answer.

'It's not about trust,' James replied. 'I just wanted to have dinner with her, that's all.'

'You can never believe what a Lebanese woman says. I've told you.'

James felt a chill go through his body. He didn't believe his friend, but just hearing Maya spoken of in those terms had a physical effect on him. This led to the thought of Maya with another man, whether in the past or present. These images crowded James, stopping him from thinking clearly. Why don't all men just admit it, he thought angrily, trying to dismiss the images from his mind: we're all possessive, it's in our nature.

'You would say that about any woman,' he said.

'I had this girlfriend once. I fell in love with her, she

told me she loved me.' Hassan recounted his story in a matter-of-fact tone. 'We were together for a year, then I found out that from the *first week* she'd been sleeping with other men.'

'So really this is your problem, not mine.'

'So you've got no reason not to trust her, then?'

James could hear the voice of the man on Fran's answering machine. It echoed around his head. 'Not *no* reason.' He caved in a little. 'You just don't have any evidence for what you're saying.'

'Don't need evidence. Just ask her. "Same sex as Eve."'

'Proverbs are McWisdom, Hassan. Anyway, don't you want to see the shot of the guy riding the horse?' James asked, trying to get Hassan off the subject. His words had got through to him, though, and now James wanted more than anything to know *exactly* where Maya was and what she was doing.

When Hassan arrived home, Mahmoud was sitting slumped in a chair, looking pissed off. He had spent the evening trying to cut his own hair and he now had a small bald patch above his right ear. All his friends were at PC Mania, playing Counterstrike to the sounds of Rachid Taha booming from the speakers at ear-splitting volume. Tonight was supposed to be the big night when Mahmoud exacted revenge on his rival, KISSMYASSOK, who, bespectacled and a good few inches shorter than Mahmoud, had a hell of a cheek giving himself such a cocky user name. But that wasn't the main problem. The main problem was that KISSMYASSOK had a nasty habit of sniping. Mahmoud and his friends had been shot in the back so many times by the little bastard it had been decided that tonight was going to be payback time. Mahmoud had even spent the day conjuring up a new user name for himself, a new assassin alias, but alas, AREYOUFUCKENTALKENTOME? couldn't get a lift, so stayed at home and gave himself a haircut.

Mahmoud brightened up as soon as Hassan entered.

'Can we go to PC Mania now?'

'Maybe tomorrow,' Hassan said, going into his room.

Mahmoud sat there by himself for a moment, then took out the hair clippers again.

13

The next morning, Maya slipped out of Walid's apartment while he was still sleeping. They weren't leaving for Paris until that evening, but his little trick of keeping her there the whole weekend had almost worked. She stepped out on to the street, into 425 Day. One day every March, the streets were full of posters and flags – the annual reminder of UN Resolution 425, calling for Israel to end its twenty-year occupation of the south.

There were traffic jams as far as Maya could see. Her *servis* got tangled up on Bliss Street where students stood in the middle of the road, tables set up and large flags displaying the number 425 in blue. Bliss Street felt like *Beirut 90210* most of the time, a street packed with Americana, but today yellow Hizbollah and green Amal flags fluttered in the breeze. Pictures of political and spiritual leaders hung from every tree. Students leaned into passing cars, handing out plastic packages of literature about the south. Taxis were parked on the pavement, hitched up like old women trying to hoist themselves up stairs, their drivers sitting by the kerb, listening to the radio.

The city was an illogical jigsaw of parked cars, some next to an already parked car, others half up on the pavement, bisecting it, taking up the maximum amount of space. Sometimes an empty parked car would suddenly twitch into life as it was gently shunted by someone trying to park in front of it. It was easier for a pedestrian to walk down the middle of the road.

It was early when Maya arrived at reception at James's apartment; the night concierge was just ending his shift. There were four concierges in total, each with two or three hangers-on, so there were at least twelve faces to get to know. There was *waz-waz*, and also the creepy blue-eyed one who stared at Maya while she waited for the lift, tried to peer into James's flat, and listened in on her and James's phone calls. Then there was the one who sang Umm Kulthoum songs to himself and said 'Welcome to you, Mr James' no matter what James asked for. He also listened in to their phone calls. The night concierge just slept in his chair, waking only to give a resident his or her key, or to accidentally forget to hang up the downstairs phone when he put Maya's calls through. Perhaps it was the content of their calls, the fact that Maya had sometimes started their conversations with a graphic description of her underwear, which had caused this interest and led to them staying on the line. But in return they had to put up with James calling Arabian Sands fourteen times in one evening to try to get two cans of Sprite delivered.

As she got into the lift the night concierge handed Maya a piece of paper to give to James.

Each of James's relationships, if he looked back over the last six or seven years, had been getting progressively longer, or at least it felt that way. Perhaps they were just getting slower. He had never felt the rush of madness, the *I miss her even when she's with me* feeling. He had almost taken it for granted that the strong attachment he had formed with Fran was love. He used to tell her he loved her, as if to force the feeling out of him, but now he was sure those feelings had just been ghosts masquerading as love. With Maya, he realised he had fallen in love with the way she had spoken to him right from the start. He had been caught by the intimacy with which she had addressed him. When he had touched her arm on the coach trip on their first day, it had felt like a moment of real closeness. He had almost flinched when he had noticed what he was doing, before realising his only crime had been to try to stop her from walking past. But somehow everything that was said between them, and the way she moved, the way he reacted to her, felt so loaded. He loved her laugh, loved her hair, loved her skin, loved the way she walked. There had always been a question mark attached to his past relationships, even with Fran, although he would never have admitted it to himself at the time, because everyone wants to believe they have it all. There were many tricks James had played on himself to convince himself he was happy, and it had taken Maya to puncture those illusions. He knew he now risked being unhappy, but it was worth it for this new feeling, this dangerous feeling: knowing what he wanted.

James was relieved when Aisha turned up for work again with Safaa in tow – she had brought her to work because the school was closed down for 425 Day. The weather was getting hotter – it hadn't rained for a while and didn't look like it ever would again. Six weeks of Beirut and James still wasn't used to the choking exhaust fumes, so he welcomed any company that didn't involve him leaving his flat, particularly Aisha.

Safaa had eyelashes that were so long it looked as if she might tip over under the weight of them. She was busy writing a letter to her penpal in Bethlehem, and sat quietly on the couch while Aisha explained to James what had happened with Fatima. While James listened, he also kept glancing at Safaa, marvelling at the beautiful Arabic that flowed from her pen. That what she was writing was mostly about boys she fancied didn't matter – to James it looked like poetry. Arabic didn't sound as he had imagined, especially when spoken by the Lebanese. It was graceful and poetic, but also economic and direct. 'Me here' would stop a taxi, yet it took 'Peace be with you' followed by 'God be with you' before you could leave someone's house. There was a satisfying protocol about the replies that certain greetings required. *Marhaba* – hello – was answered with *Marhabtein:* two hellos.

James stood by while Maya exchanged elaborate greetings with Aisha as she entered the apartment, before handing him a piece of paper from the concierge. It was a rent invoice, so James filed it in his pocket. Maya then casually poured herself a glass of water, complaining about the creepy concierge who always stared at her when she waited for the lift. Aisha passed on some gossip about him, and told Maya what to say the next time he did it. The four of them sat and drank coffee for a while, James containing his irritation at Maya. He didn't even know what she was doing here; she was supposed to be in Paris. She had run out on him the night before without a real explanation, then turned up now as if nothing had happened.

When Aisha and Safaa had to move on to the next room, and the two of them were alone, James turned to her, and spoke coldly: 'I thought you were in Paris.'

'I didn't go,' Maya replied defensively.

'Why?'

'Going tonight instead,' she said, lighting a cigarette. 'What did you do last night?' It sounded like pointless small talk to James.

'Hassan came round. Discussed the Old Testament. Eve's name came up,' he replied.

She sighed. 'What did he want?'

'Who cares what he wanted? What the hell is going on? First you're going to Paris, then you're not. Now you're going tonight.'

'Calm down. It was just a change of plan, that's all. Why don't you tell me about your evening.'

'Like I said, Hassan came round. Had a beer. He told me the usual.'

'The usual?'

'You can't trust women. You can't trust *you*.'

'Over here not all women's actions are done through choice.'

'What does that mean?' James said, trying to find the

thread of Maya's conversation, and just becoming more annoyed in the process.

She shrugged.

James took a deep breath. 'Are you seeing someone else?'

'I don't think "seeing" is the right word.'

Her tone didn't match what she was saying. James wondered if she was joking. She held his look, and he realised she wasn't playing.

'Hassan was right?'

'He wasn't right.'

'You choose the word, then.'

James felt a surge of anger, of humiliation, that she could be sitting in front of him and telling him this so calmly, as if he was somehow in the wrong for asking in the first place, for putting her out.

'There is someone I was seeing before I met you.'

'And you're still seeing him?'

'Yes.'

'Any other men I should know about?'

'That's pathetic.'

'Well, explain, then.' James stood up and paced around the room. His fists were clenched, his teeth locked together.

Maya got up too and stood at the window. 'I want to get out of here,' she said.

'Okay, and . . .'

'And this is the only way I can do it.'

'By having two boyfriends?'

Maya wanted to tell him 'I only had one until you

showed up', but she knew it would make him even angrier. She knew there was no way he would understand that because she saw their time together as temporary she couldn't afford to ruin her one scrap of hope for getting out.

'Do you think this is something I like?' Her voice was growing louder and more desperate. 'I have a stream of suitors being presented to me every damn public holiday. My only route out is to go to America and study, do something legitimate that my parents will understand. They don't have to know that when I get there I have no intention of coming back, that I want to find a job and stay.'

'So why don't you do that?' James could hear his voice echoing around the apartment.

'I can't afford it, okay? I do two people's jobs as it is. Do you have a spare sixty thousand dollars in your wallet? He's my route to an exit.'

'I want you to stop seeing him. It's screwed up.'

'Who the fuck are you to tell me what to do? I just met you and you're making demands on me? What are you offering?'

'Offering? I just wanted to have dinner,' James said, exasperated.

'Well, it's a little more complicated than that. It's not *The Waltons*,' Maya shouted back.

'So what does this guy give you?'

'There are two routes out of here: I can apply to study abroad, or I can marry my way out. Walid is my funding for study.'

'So you whore yourself for his cash.'

'Don't fucking judge me. Who do you think you are? We hardly know each other. Walid gives me a lot. Until you can do that, shut the fuck up.'

Anger built up inside James, fuelled by thoughts of Fran with another man, and now Maya. He recalled the evenings he and Maya had spent together, and wondered if she had ever left his house and then slept with this other man the same night. Had the scent of this man's sweat, his aftershave, ever rubbed off on her? He felt the irrational rush of pumping adrenalin, and rage at her for not apologising to him, for somehow twisting it so it appeared that he had got in the way of her plans. Jealousy had a physical basis, a particular taste in the mouth, and it was something like blood.

'You're fucking another man.'

'He's a better man for me,' she spat back at him.

James's open hand connected with Maya's face and made a dull slap as he took his past out on this stranger. She flinched and looked shocked, although not as shocked as James. She reached down, grabbed a handful of CD cases, and hurled them at him. One of them – New Order's seminal *Technique* album – dug into his face, its hard corner bursting his lower lip. He felt blood trickle down his chin and wiped it away.

Maya slumped in a chair. James looked at her, one hand to his swelling lip, the blood leaking through his fingers and down on to his arm.

'Take care of your lip,' Maya mumbled, her head in her hands, her hair falling over her face, sticking to her skin in thin strands.

James grabbed some tissues and ran cold water over them. He handed them to Maya for her face. She waved them away without looking at him. James crouched down in front of her. He rested his arms on her knees, leaning forward to try to catch her eye.

'You've got no right to make demands on me,' she said, still not looking at him. 'If I gave up Walid I'd be condemned to one of the suitors, then you and I wouldn't be together in any way,' she added quietly, gently running a hand over her face.

'You're telling me that you're going to see two people.'

'Or one person.'

James knew what she meant, but he still said, 'One person?'

'If you make me choose, if you can't offer me anything else, then I'll choose Walid.'

'But we were getting on really well.'

'That doesn't matter. It can't go on like that,' she said, finally looking him in the eye.

'I just want to be with you. Just with you,' James replied.

'Saying things like that is pointless,' she said. 'Those words just float up into the air and disappear.'

James got up and put more tissues under the tap before sticking the wet clump to his face. The tissues turned pink immediately.

'So this Walid gives you cash to go abroad. Does he *want* you to go to America?'

'He doesn't know. He doesn't know that's where his cash goes. When I reach the figure I need, I'm gone.'

James rubbed the back of his head with his hand, waiting for some enlightenment. 'Part of me is waiting for you to tell me how the CIA fits into this plan.'

'You think this is what I want? That this is ideal for me?'

'Maya, I can't be with you if you're seeing someone else.'

'Well, I'm not in the mood to make you feel better about this,' she said, getting up and walking to the door.

'So then it's over,' he called after her. She didn't answer. 'Do you know how humiliating this is for me?' James said. 'I can't believe you think this prick is a better man than I am.'

'I don't know what kind of man you are,' she said. 'And believe me, it's a lot more humiliating for me.'

She left the door open and walked to the lift. James followed her into the corridor. He stood behind her, in the low light of the hallway. He didn't know what to say. Maya knew he was right behind her, but she didn't turn around. The two of them stood there in silence, a couple of feet apart, James looking at the back of her head.

'I'm sorry I hit you,' James whispered. 'Someone cheated on me before and now I feel that—'

'I'm not interested in your back story,' Maya said without turning around. The lift arrived and she opened the door.

'Where are you going?' James asked.

'Paris,' she replied.

Mrs Hayek's boutique was tiny, but full of beautiful

clothes. Three steps led into the single room – a small passageway with skirts, dresses and blouses on racks either side and a till at the back. The smallness denoted quality. The shoes sparkled and the dresses were backless. The total value of the clothes easily equalled that of half a department store.

Mrs Hayek went through the day's takings with the phone tucked in her neck as she listened to Mrs Jihad in full flow.

'Did you heard about Mrs Samaha? She was caught with an Italian! It wasn't the first time he'd visited, either. I saw him come over several times during the day when her husband was out. *Haram* Mr Samaha. Poor man. And so soon after his operation. She said the Italian was from the embassy, come to help her son with his immigration papers, but I knew he wasn't. He drove a Daewoo, for God's sake! And he was young – maybe twenty-five years old. Apparently Mr Samaha caught them in the act! That young man, muscular and healthy, full of energy, strong jawline, with his wife! Do you know what he did then? He put a travel restriction on her at the airport! Quite right too. He thought she was going to leave him and go to Rome with her lover. Now she's not going anywhere.'

The phone beeped, signalling a call waiting.

'I have another call,' Mrs Hayek interrupted.

'I'll speak to you later,' Mrs Jihad promised, hanging up.

Mrs Hayek hit the star button. ''*Allo?*' she said. She heard the buzz of a long-distance line, then a familiar

voice. 'This is nice, *habibi*. You never call me at work.'
She smiled. 'I miss you.'

'Who the hell is Maroun Abdullah?' Dr Hayek shouted
down the phone line from Abu Dhabi.

'Is that how you greet your wife?'

'I've been in theatre all morning and I just got an e-mail
about Maya from this man. Who is he?'

Mrs Hayek held the phone away from her ear as she
mouthed goodbye to her last customer of the day. She
knew her husband usually took some calming down when
it came to Maya.

'Why don't you ask her?' she said. 'When was the last
time you spoke to her?'

'Where is she now?'

'Calm down and tell me what happened,' she said. Dr
Najib Hayek could save several lives in one day, but
sometimes his wife had to treat him like a child.

'I have this e-mail right in front of me,' Najib said. He
looked at his screen. 'Listen to this.'

> To: najibhayek@emiratemed.net
> From: Maroun@mfaasolutions.com

> Dear Dr Hayek,
>   Thankyou for permissing me for going
> out with your daughter, Maya. Dr Hayek,
> you know that I respect you too much and
> although that I am successful in my business
> financially (Thanks God), I can'not wait
> to return back to Lebanon and see Maya.
> Please I can have her phone number so I

can speak with her. Thank you for your corporation.

Personal Best Regards,
Maroun F. Abu Abdullah

Najib closed down his e-mail program. 'Don't you think I should have known about this man?'

Mrs Hayek repeated his name to herself: Maroun, Maroun, *Maroun*. 'Yes, I remember him,' she said. '*You* met him when you were back for a weekend. Remember, Najib? Once you used to come back for weekends.' She heard her husband exhale. She knew what overwork sounded like.

'Move to Abu Dhabi, *habibte*,' he said, softly. 'Then we won't have to do this. I don't like leaving you alone.'

'But in six months you'll be finished,' she replied.

'What's for us in Lebanon now? You can open a boutique here instead.'

Mrs Hayek changed the subject. 'This Maroun, I think he's a nice boy. An engineer in Kuwait. We met his parents at the Khourys' wedding. You should give him her number.'

'Okay, I will,' Najib said, finishing his U-turn and now totally in her hands. 'Please . . . just think about moving. I miss you.'

'Abu Dhabi . . . What about my family?'

'We'll bring them with us.'

'I don't know.'

'For the same money we can have a beautiful house, out of the pollution. At least think about it.'

'I'll think about it,' Mrs Hayek said, softly.

'If we don't make the move soon, we'll never do it. We'll be too old,' he reasoned.

Mrs Hayek walked around the shop, locking up as she spoke on the portable. She wondered whether she had spent so long in Lebanon she could no longer function anywhere else.

'Where is Maya now?' he asked.

'She's with Nadia.'

'Where?'

'They've gone away for the weekend, up to the mountains.'

14

Walid thought he would surprise Maya with the glamorous hotel he had booked them into, but on the plane she showed a total lack of interest in the brochures – her only concern was that they have separate rooms. For most people leaving home usually meant some kind of freedom, some kind of release. But Maya felt as if all of her Lebanese life was just being transferred to a hotel in Paris for the weekend. She imagined for a moment what it would feel like if she were with James and not Walid. Her guilt would still be there, guilt that she was letting her parents down. In the same way her mother feared the neighbours, she feared her parents.

Maya had disagreed with everything Walid had said since they had left Beirut. She knew if she didn't disagree with *everything* – his opinion on the weather, the flight so far, the meals, the comparative softness of towels in various five-star hotels – then she would lose even the parts of herself that she still respected. For the rest of the four-and-a-half-hour flight to Paris, she wore the headphones with her eyes closed. When her ears started popping on descent, she looked out of the window and tried not to cry. Paris wasn't made for this sinking, hollow feeling.

As they entered the hotel, Walid approached the reception

desk. He did all the talking, all the organising. In Beirut, he had taken Maya's passport and ticket from her and put them in his wallet bag. Walid always had good-quality watches, bags and shoes. Swiss, Italian, Italian. His pure-grain cowhide bag was permanently slung over his shoulder, and when he opened it to take out their passports for the hotel receptionist Maya caught sight of his Visconti limited-edition titanium fountain pen sitting there like royalty. She hated it that he had to hold on to everything. It made her feel like a child. The receptionist took the passports and disappeared for a moment.

'What rooms would you like?' she asked when she returned. 'We have de luxe, executive and premier.'

'De luxe,' Walid jabbed back before she had a chance to ask any more questions.

'Walid, you know those aren't the best rooms?' Maya said, antagonising him.

'Yes they are. They're de luxe.'

'But the *executive* rooms are more expensive,' Maya said, pointing to the room prices.

Walid looked confused. 'But de luxe is the best, isn't it?'

There then followed two minutes of Walid and the receptionist discussing the nature of the word 'de luxe' and what these rooms were lacking that the executive rooms boasted. Maya watched in silence. It amused her for a moment, but then she felt depressed, thinking about James's little flat, which was also supposed to be de luxe. The word had become so overused it meant nothing any more. She was bored with her game, and was glad when Walid finally paid for two rooms – over two thousand dollars per night, for three nights – in cash. She didn't know anyone from Lebanon who used credit cards.

The floors were polished marble, the chandeliers were Baccarat crystal. That was as far as Maya got reading the brochure in her room before her phone started ringing. Walid would want to go for a walk down Avenue George V and buy her something from Louis Vuitton or Givenchy. Then they would take a cab to Galeries Lafayette and become submerged in the lower-level perfumery, losing all sense of smell as the endless eau de toilette shops sprayed their products at passers-by. Maya had grown very bored with Westerners telling her that Beirut used to be the Paris of the Middle East. She had heard it so many times it made her angry, just as she had been told that Lebanon was a very liberal country. She knew it *was* liberal if you were a foreigner. And foreigners looked around them and were fooled by the clothes and the young people with American accents, and the lifestyles of the wealthy few. A foreigner could easily live their whole life in Beirut and not know what it was really like to live there. She had seen it. She just wondered whether any Arabs had visited Paris in the 1960s and remarked: 'You know what? It's just like the Beirut of western Europe.'

The phone was starting to sound angry, so she picked up.

'Where were you?' Walid sounded gruff.

'Where do you think?'

'Oh.' He sounded embarrassed. '*Habibte*. I have a meeting right now, then I'll be back and we'll have dinner. I'm sorry we won't be able to go to the shops until tomorrow.'

'Shame,' Maya said. She hung up and went into the bathroom. It was a substantial walk from one side to another.

The over-over-sized bathtub looked as if it would take two hours to fill up, so she switched on the shower and slipped out of her clothes. When she emerged a few minutes later, the room had steamed up. Wearing the complimentary slippers and bathrobe, she walked back into the bedroom and fell into the upholstered armchair. She could feel silk and velvet against her skin. She looked modern against the Louis XV surroundings – her haircut, her well-moisturised skin, her lip gloss. But she knew that as soon as she stepped out on to the street by herself she would feel small and unprotected; she would feel old fashioned in this world where girls lived different lives. Even though Maya lived in a city that put the fear of God into most Westerners – there was nothing unusual about her uncles dropping by during the war, leaving their machine guns outside the kitchen door, or a shell taking off the side of their building while their neighbours' flat collapsed – what was outside the Paris hotel, which was what was outside any hotel in any city in the world, was the unknown, and it scared her. The unknown was terrifying, no matter how many languages you spoke, no matter how many dirty militia wars you had lived through. Maya remembered her mother, the fashion designer, running through military checkpoints during the war, holding piles of extravagant dresses and fabrics, a flash of colour against the military grey-and-green background, to deliver to shops on Hamra Street. She wasn't able to drive the car though the check-points, so she was forced to park and run. Life went on.

Maya lit a cigarette and pulled at the heavy brocade curtains that hung to the floor. Beyond the window, she could see the giant fountain, spouting water from every orifice, and the well-manicured hedgerows. She was not supposed to feel miserable in Paris. She remembered what had happened to Nadia's brother when he came to the French capital for the first time. He was a lonely Lebanese, wandering in the big, frightening city. He couldn't work out the Métro; he couldn't understand the map. The only good thing that happened to him was getting mugged on his last night. A group had approached on mountain bikes and swarmed around him. His jacket was almost pulled off as he was spun around. As if falling under a breaking wave, he was disoriented, not sure which way was up. He swore at his muggers in Arabic; he told them to eat shit and said, 'My cock up your sister's pussy! I'm gonna make you fuck a floor tile!'

They stopped instantly.

The dizziness left him and he was able to focus on the attackers. He swore at them once more as he dusted himself down. His wallet was given back to him.

'*Habibi, min wayn?*' The leader of the gang wanted to know where he was from.

'*Lubnan,*' Nadia's brother replied. They liked his Lebanese accent. And after a series of handshakes the teenage Algerian muggers cycled off into the Paris night with no reward except having learned some new swear words. There *was* some unity in the Arab world.

Walid's room was right next to Maya's and he had left his key with her while he went out on business. She crept along the corridor, still wearing her towel, unlocked his door and entered his empty room. His laptop was set up on the large oak desk, plugged into the wall socket. The screensaver was swirling around, and when she pressed the space bar the machine asked for a password. She made a guess at 'Maya' and was then presented with his desktop. She went on-line and opened her chat program, hoping James might be logged on. They had taken to e-mailing each other in the last couple of weeks before they had argued, and she missed their exchanges and the freedom they had given her.

She sat for a moment, transfixed by the screen, the little icons flashing, then, remembering James's face as she had walked away from him, she panicked, not knowing what she would say to him, praying he *wouldn't* log on. She shut the program down and flicked through her new e-mails.

To: MayaHayek@qserv.net
From: Maroun3@mfaasolutions.com

Dear Mayoush,

Why your'e not answering your phone? I was trying to called you from two days ago. Nevermind Mayoush, you can know that its' me calling. Also I tell to my sisters not to answer for a phonenumber they don't know it. I'am sure that a butiful girl like you gets too many calls so I won't be so upset!! lol. Next time I will call don't worry I will send you SMS text first so you know its me.

Personal Best Regards,
Maroun F. Abu Abdullah

NB. Tell to your mother and father that I say hello very much.

Maya's hair was dripping over her bathrobe so she tied it with a band. She blocked Maroun's address, then looked around Walid's room. He rarely brought much luggage; he liked to buy when he arrived. There was just a leather briefcase and his wallet bag with the tickets poking out of the top. Walid's two-hundred-dollar little bag with *her* passport, *her* tickets, *her* mobile phone, representing so much of her that he owned. She wanted to take it back. She was going to steal back what was hers. She crouched on the ground by the bag and took out her passport. She opened it and looked at the first page: Maya Najib Hayek. Her middle name was her father's first name. Only a third of her entire name was really hers.

She heard a sound in the corridor – a man's voice – and realised she hadn't shut Walid's door properly. She instinctively zipped the bag up and ran out of the room with it, slipping into her room next door unnoticed. Still flashing on Walid's computer screen, below Maroun's e-mail, was her unopened university acceptance letter.

The voices she had heard belonged to two men who were now standing outside Walid's room. Maya opened her door a millimetre and peered through the gap. She watched the shorter man knock on Walid's door. No answer. Both men were smartly dressed in suits. The taller one was balding, his remaining hair buzz-cut; the shorter had a side parting and held a mobile phone in one hand. The two men said little to each other; there was an efficiency even in their body language.

Maya moved away from her door and quickly got dressed. She was putting her shoes on when she heard

Walid arrive. She knew his walk like she knew his scent.
She had memorised his walking pattern just as she had
memorised the smell of his cigarette brand, like an early-
warning system. She opened her door a crack and watched
Walid playing with his digital organiser as he walked
towards his room. She saw the surprise on his face when
he looked up and noticed the two men standing there. One
of them said something quietly to him, and Walid nodded.
Maya opened her door wider to get a better look, but it
creaked, alerting the three men to her presence, so she
pretended she was just leaving her room and hadn't even
seen them. Walid spoke to her straight away.

'Hi, *habibte*,' he said. He seemed too cheerful. 'This
won't take a minute. I'm just helping these gentlemen
with something. When I get back we'll go for dinner.
Here . . .' He looked at one of the men, who nodded,
giving Walid approval to move. 'Have this and go and
buy yourself something nice to wear tonight.' He handed
her a thousand dollars.

Maya took the money silently, then watched as Walid
and the two men walked along the corridor together. The
taller of the two men was gripping Walid's upper arm, as
if escorting him away. Maya stood for a moment alone in
the corridor, not sure what to do.

When she got back into her room, it was getting dark.
The flashing lights from the police car parked down below
found their way through her window. She watched as
Walid and the men got into an unmarked car. The police
car escorted it down the road, and out of sight.

Walid called the hotel half an hour later. '*Habibte*, they

just want to speak to me about a few things. I need to stay here until we can clear this up.' He didn't say who 'they' were, and it sounded like he was clearing up a drink he had spilt. 'It's just a misunderstanding. Anyway,' he said, his tone brightening, 'think of it as an extended holiday. Do you have enough money?'

Maya nodded, then realised she needed to say something. 'Yes,' she said, softly.

'Good.'

'When will you be back?'

'I have to go now. I will call tomorrow. In the morning. Okay?'

'Okay.'

Maya hung up and looked around her room. She walked to the wardrobe in a trance, then swiftly started pulling her clothes off hangers and packing them into a bag. She grabbed Walid's wallet bag containing all her possessions and put it over her shoulder. She dropped her key off at reception, took a deep breath and slipped out of the hotel, leaving Walid, and with him her hopes for university, behind her.

When Walid called the next day, the phone rang unanswered in the empty room. Maya was on her way back to Beirut.

April had started with the Islamic New Year, followed by the *Shi'a* day of *Ashoura*, the mourning of the death of Imam Hussein. In between, the fighting in the south had become so fierce that James was sure he could hear it from Beirut, the booms and crashes riding the wind up to the city. The papers had been full of stories about Hizbollah blowing up an SLA outpost in the south. That morning Aisha had told him that the Israeli prime minister had confirmed in a letter to the UN that he would pull his troops out by the end of July, but she said she wouldn't believe it until it actually happened. She gave James the highlights each day: what she had seen on the TV, as well as what she had heard in the camp.

Jerry had a nasty habit of appearing behind people like Dracula, and he seemed to materialise behind James's left shoulder from nowhere as he left the language school after working late.

'Hey, James.'

'Hi.'

'I hear you're doing some kind of music video.'

'Yeah,' James replied.

'That's so awesome,' Jerry said.

'Yeah, it is pretty good.'

'Listen, man. I have a confession.'

Here it was, James thought. A confession. He was right, his students were right: there was always a plot. This man *was* a missionary, after all.

'What's that?' James tried to keep his voice level.

'I kind of thought you were . . . when I first met you . . . I thought you wouldn't . . . uh, *approve* of what my friends and I were doing.'

'Oh,' James said, his throat tightening.

'Yeah. I mean, some people who don't smoke weed get real weird about it. You know?' Jerry said.

'You what?'

'If you don't know if someone . . . *does* or *doesn't*, you don't want to make it public.'

'Jerry.'

'Uh-huh.'

'What do you do with your guitar?'

'Play early Dylan, stuff like that.'

It was dark outside by the time James walked into the dimly lit Arabian Sands and hauled his daily order of three large bottles of water on to the counter. Abu Khalil took the money, his eyes glued to an old episode of *Dallas*. He looked over briefly at James, who wondered whether the small scar on his lip was still visible. His fight with Maya hadn't faded in his mind, even though it had been three weeks since he had seen her.

As he left the shop, there was a huge explosion a few blocks away. He dropped the water, which exploded at his feet on the hard pavement. He looked around, then ran quickly to the café on the corner where he often ate his dinner. Instead of just taking refuge, he found himself paying the man behind the register for a chicken salad, then sitting down at a table and nervously watching through the window. The television screens in the café were displaying a Mexican soap opera and a Nawal el-Zoughbi video, while the Red Hot Chilli Peppers were on the stereo. Even the weird mix of popular culture couldn't take James's mind off the explosions.

As he left the salad bar the bangs grew louder and deeper, the echoes from walls and metal gates became more hollow, urging him to run faster. He changed direction a few times in his confusion, then settled on seeking shelter back in Arabian Sands.

'What are these explosions?'

Abu Khalil looked grave. He seemed to be trying to find a way to tell James the news. These explosions were *not* the sonic booms of jets overhead.

'*El Eid el kbir*,' Abu Khalil answered in Arabic.

James didn't understand, so Abu Khalil tried in French. '*C'est . . . uh . . . c'est . . . Pâques.*'

James wondered whether '*Pâques*' was the name of a bomb or a rocket, perhaps the French word for Katyusha or Scud.

Abu Khalil shouted something and a helper appeared from behind the shelves of rice. As the booms continued, James felt the muscles in his neck tense up, bringing on a headache. A discussion ensued between Abu Khalil and the helper. Abu Khalil's eyes lit up when they made their breakthrough. James had never seen him so animated. He pointed to his diary, which had the public holidays written in English, and James followed his finger to the date.

James had nearly been caught in Lebanon mid-bombardment.

But it just turned out to be Easter.

Catholic Easter. Orthodox wasn't for another seven days. And kids would surely let off a cacophony of illegal-in-Europe-strength bangers then as well.

James had no idea where Maya was or what she was doing, and their time apart hadn't given him a chance to think more clearly, because what he wanted hadn't changed. There was a feeling in his stomach, a sickening sensation that brought back regret every time he thought about their fight; when he recalled the image of the back of Maya's head as she waited for the lift that had taken her downstairs, then to Paris, then out of his life for good, he felt as if he had been punched repeatedly.

The best idea he could come up with in this fractured, unsure state was to try to see Maya once more and say goodbye to her properly. He was preparing to shoot the rest of the video in two days' time, and once that was in the can, he could go back to London. He would find Maya and let her know he was leaving. Then, if she wanted to shout at him, he would stand there and take it.

The *servis* taxi-driver who took him to Maya's house had only two teeth. He turned round and offered James a Marlboro and a coffee-flavoured sweet. James took them both.

'Dinner,' the driver explained, as he pulled up outside the Hayeks' house. James paid him then got out and walked slowly to the front door. Under his arm he had an English textbook; in his head he had his story for when her mother answered the door: 'I'm Nadia's English teacher. I don't have her address, and this book is very important for her exams.'

Meanwhile, Dilki and three other maids were gathered on Mrs Jihad's balcony, drinking coffee. Mrs Hayek's maid, a Filipina called Imelda, sat next to Dilki, and the other two, an Ethiopian who said very little and an Indian with her hair pulled up in a bun, sat opposite. They all wore their chequered pinafores and shared broken English as their universal language. The ladies of the entire street, the entire borough, were out for the day, and the 157th Monthly Maid Conference was in full swing.

'Madame Jihad very bad,' Dilki said. 'Man comes for fix the kitchen. They diggy-diggy. Husband not home, she diggy-diggy. Always diggy-diggy. She is big *sharmouta*. Always diggy-diggy.'

The Indian maid put her coffee down and looked at her friends. 'My madame, she never with childs. I always with her childs. All she do play cards. Her childs speak Hindi good with me. Madame say: "Why childs not speak Arabic? Bad Chandra!"'

All four of them jumped with fright when they heard someone knocking on Mrs Hayek's door. Four worried faces all bent over the balcony in unison to see who was making the noise.

Dilki took the initiative. 'They no here,' she said in a sing-song voice. James turned around and looked up at the balcony to try to find where the voice was coming from.

'Hi, I'm Nadia's English teacher,' he said, craning his neck to look up at the maids. 'I have a book for Maya to give to her.'

No one answered.

'Is Maya here?' James asked.

'Not here,' Dilki trilled.

'Will she be back late?'

'Not here. Wedding.'

'Do you know when she will be back? It's very important,' James said, then rewound to Dilki's last word. *Wedding*. He asked her again, but the more she repeated that Maya wasn't there, the more desperate he became to find out *where* she was and who was getting married. The Indian maid took over.

'Family go wedding. All go wedding.'

'Which family?' James asked.

'All family.'

'Who is getting married?' he asked nervously.

'Daughter.'

The maids' directions, scribbled gleefully on one of Mrs Jihad's expensive white napkins, were perfect, and full of references to cafés and shops close by. No street names or numbers.

Thirty minutes later, James entered the cavernous wedding room, his heart thumping. He looked around, his mouth dry, blinking nervously in the bright lights. The walls were covered in balloons; a lighting rig straight out of a Pink Floyd concert held spotlights and strobe lights. Some flashed, some were coloured. A confetti machine spewed coloured magic all over the guests. Close to the stage was a smoke machine that was being tested before the dance-floor action started. James counted five disco balls hanging from different parts of the ceiling. The overall effect was of an epileptic fit waiting to happen.

James weaved in and out of the many tables, which quaked under the weight of candles and extravagant flower arrangements bunched around the napkins, cutlery and plates.

A bald man in his fifties with a bushy moustache kept his eye on James as he searched for Maya.

'Who are you looking for?' he asked.

'For Maya. Or Nadia.'

The man nodded.

'Do you know where they are?'

'I don't even know *who* they are.' He smiled. 'There's a thousand people here. Most of them don't know each other. Who is Nadia?'

'She is the best friend of the family that live next to the house . . .' James gave up.

The man nodded again, taking it all in. 'I'm sure you'll find what you're looking for,' he said. 'Good luck.'

Then James spotted Maya. She was talking to a group of girls who all seemed to go down in age and height, in two-year or two-inch increments. Everyone in the hall seemed determined to put themselves in his way as he tried to approach her. All the sounds of the wedding disappeared; his peripheral vision shut down, until Maya was all that he could see.

'Maya, who is getting married?' James said, grabbing her.

She looked shocked initially. 'What the hell are you doing here?' she shot back, then noticed the terrified look on his face, as if there was some awful news he was about to impart. 'What happened?' she asked.

'What do you mean, "What happened?"'

'What?'

Silence. Confusion.

'Our next-door neighbour . . .' Maya began. 'Mrs Jihad's daughter.' When James didn't seem to register what she was saying, she spelt it out. 'Is. Getting. Married.'

'*Oh!*' James exhaled every bit of air in his lungs. If there had been a stretcher close by he would have collapsed on to it.

'What are you doing here?'

'Maya, I'm so sorry about what happened, I've been trying to understand about Walid, and I know I can't . . . if I'm honest with myself I can't . . . but look, we're shooting in a couple of days, so I thought, you know, I'll be leaving then and I wanted us to at least say goodbye properly.'

'So now it's not me getting married you're leaving?' Maya said quietly.

James ran her line back in his head twice to check she had said what he thought she had. Then he saw the faintest glimmer of a smile, which he returned. He suddenly noticed, as if for the first time, the group of girls Maya had been talking to, who were now all staring at him.

'This is James, he's Nadia's English teacher,' Maya said to them. She could have been a politician, her cover was so smooth.

James shook the relative hands.

'Yeah, Nadia has an exam and she forgot some important papers.' He waved the evidence in his hand.

'We'll go and find her,' Maya said, just before their little play lost steam.

As soon as they were clear of the group her voice changed pitch and she spoke more urgently, checking who was around them. 'How did you get here?'

'I went to your house. The maid told me you were at a wedding.'

'In Tagalog?'

'She speaks English,' James said.

'I *knew* it.' She laughed.

James was taken aback by the lightness of her mood. 'Part of me was waiting for Simon and Garfunkel to start playing in the background,' he said, trying to sound upbeat himself.

'You wanted to break up Mrs Jihad's daughter's wedding?'

'I don't care about Mrs Jihad's daughter. I care about you.' Only the sound of the band warming up stopped there being a true silence between them. Maya broke it with a smile.

'I'm so glad you came,' she said. 'I wanted to call, but . . .' She tailed off.

'I know . . .' James began, then fell head first into his own silence. 'Well . . . I suppose I'll see you around . . . except that I won't.' He swallowed the last part of his sentence awkwardly.

Maya nodded solemnly. In the background, the drummer worked through his sound check.

James managed half a smile, the smile of a runner-up, then turned to leave.

'Walid is still in France.'

The words cut through the air and the music and the chatter in the background, stopping James in his tracks. He turned around to face Maya again. '*Still* in France? When did he *go* to France?'

'I went with him to Paris. I lied to you.' She spoke evenly, but there was an apology loaded in her soft tone.

James didn't know what to deal with first. 'Is he staying there?'

'His business overran,' she started, then stopped, looking angry with herself when James's expression told her he didn't believe what she was saying. He waited and watched as she searched for the words she wanted. 'His business caught up with him . . . I left him there.'

'What about your college?'

'I'm not going any more.'

'What? *Why?*' James asked, then realised that while coming from most people this would mean that they had made a decision that college wasn't for them, Maya's choices were based on taking the least worst option.

Just as she was about to answer, a woman with an impressive chest and a gold brooch which could have been a sheriff's badge parked her bosoms in front of them.

'Mrs Jihad, this is James. He is Nadia's teacher,' Maya rolled out.

'I'm sorry to arrive unannounced,' James said, quickly jumping into character, shaking Mrs Jihad's hand. 'The bride looks . . . very beautiful. *Ktir helwi*,' he said, wondering who and where the bride was.

He thought the delight painted on Mrs Jihad's face was because of his attempt at Arabic, but it was seeing Maya with an Englishman which was making her day so special. It was as if her daughter was getting married twice.

'You are welcome,' Mrs Jihad said. 'Come, come, we will find you a seat.'

'*Islamu*,' James said, feeling pleased with himself and

wanting to continue with his Arabic. Mrs Jihad's eyes widened and Maya stared at him.

'What?' James said to Maya. 'I was just saying thank you.'

'*Yislamu* means thank you,' Maya whispered.

'What does *Islamu* mean, then?'

'It means "they converted to Islam".' Maya put her hand in front of her mouth to stop herself from laughing.

James had made a rocky start to the Lebanese wedding of the decade, but Mrs Jihad's mind was elsewhere, and she busily carted him off to a table. He watched Maya grow smaller and smaller in the distance. The staging area for the wedding would have made a good football field. James was seated in the relatives-that-no-one-likes terrace.

'Where are the bride and groom?' he whispered to the teenager sitting next to him. There wasn't time for an answer. Suddenly traditional Lebanese music started booming from the Marshall stacks that were positioned either side of the stage. James kept waiting for a roadie with his arse crack showing, a long-ashed Silk Cut in his mouth, to come on and turn them all up to eleven.

The bride and groom made quite an entrance. First came the *zaffa*: a group of fourteen men, all stomping and dancing the *dabke*. This then turned into a perfectly orchestrated sword fight. James caught Mrs Jihad's expression – it was one of pride and exhilaration in her own creation, the director of *The Lion King* on its opening night on Broadway.

Once the bride and groom were safely inside and the sword fight had finished with no casualties, it was time for the first dance. James stood up to watch as 'The Blue Danube' played over the speakers and the happy couple danced a waltz. He spotted Maya, and through elaborate hand signals agreed to meet her after the next song. Just as he got up to leave the teenager he had spoken to earlier stopped him.

'This is the first *slow*,' he said as Celine Dion started wailing and the wedding party smooched to the *Titanic* soundtrack. James waited the song out, then extricated himself from the table and found Maya in the lobby.

'What are you thinking?' Maya asked.

'That I would rather spend my last few days here with you.'

'Me too,' Maya replied.

James smiled, and relaxed for the first time that evening. 'You're sure you're not going to do your MBA?'

'No money.'

'What are you going to do?'

'Be patient. That's all I can do.'

James spotted a woman who bore a strong resemblance to Maya surveying them from a table as Celine Dion was replaced by a mariachi band.

'Romanians in sombreros,' Maya deadpanned, watching the East Europeans take the stage in black *charro* suits, one strumming a *guitarron*, the other a *vihuela*. Then she spotted her mother migrating to the lobby to try to eavesdrop on the conversation. Mrs Jihad had also drifted in the same direction. When Nadia left the dance floor, James made a big deal of giving her the book for the sake of their new audience. Nadia stood with them to provide some cover.

'Your first wedding? What did you think?' she asked.

'Nadia, when you get married, will you have something like this?'

She laughed. 'Maybe bigger!'

James turned to Maya. 'Can we go somewhere? How long will this last?'

'It's been going on for four hours,' she said, looking at her watch, 'so we have about another four left. Depends when they cut the cake.'

Five hours later, the wedding finally came to a climax with the traditional finale of doves being released, to signify the love between the couple. As James walked out, he thanked Mrs Jihad profusely. She was talking to Mrs Hayek, who eyed James suspiciously, but continued her conversation.

'So, the pigeons were a lovely touch,' Mrs Hayek said, knowing that doves were harder and harder to come by, especially the trained ones that would return to their owner so he could use them again.

'They were *doves*.'

'Of course they were. Silly me.'

'Wasn't the *poulet grillé* divine?' Mrs Jihad said.

'It was! You never get tired of fried chicken.'

The two of them paused while James and Maya walked out together. Mrs Hayek tried to contain her shock with a shrug.

'You're so open minded, I really admire it,' Mrs Jihad said, knowing she was going to have the last word. 'I'm so old fashioned, I know.'

'He's Nadia's teacher,' Mrs Hayek insisted, running out of the door. When she reached the pavement, James and Maya were long gone.

*   *   *

'There were a lot of women with blonde hair at the wedding,' James said, as the cab bumped along the road, the wedding party no longer visible out of the back window.

'Usually in a war people's hair turns white,' Maya said. 'Here it turned blonde.'

The driver's dashboard had no lights, so he held up his lighter to illuminate the petrol gauge as he drove. He pulled into a garage. While he filled up, James held Maya's hand.

'Your mother didn't look very happy at us walking out together,' he said.

'She's probably having a heart attack as we speak.'

'Why is that *exactly*? I mean, I know the basics but . . .'

'She thinks the British are imperialist son of a bitch bastard dogs.'

'Did she specify which breed?'

'And really devious and sneaky.'

'Oh.'

'*Habibi*,' she intoned, softly, leaning over to kiss him. 'I think you're a very *nice* imperialist dog.'

James thought about this for a moment. 'She blames the problems of Lebanon on the British helping to create Israel with the Balfour Declaration. She probably thinks that had no Palestinians been driven into Lebanon then—'

'No, it's because a British company stole her brother's idea for computer-controlled parking meters,' Maya replied. 'And besides, what would the neighbours say? It would be a scandal that would last her whole life.' The driver twisted around and interrupted her, asking for a cigarette, which she handed to him before turning back to James. 'She doesn't give a shit about Israel or the Palestinians,' she continued. 'Why do you always think that everything here is about politics? Most people don't wake up every morning and think about these things. Most people are just concerned about their own lives. Same things you're concerned about. These things are never just about religion, or huge ideas coming into conflict.' The driver got back into the car, smoking her cigarette. He hadn't switched the engine off while he had filled up the tank. 'It's like the war here,' Maya went on, trying to find a cigarette for herself but then realising she had given the driver her last one. 'It's always described as Muslim versus Christian. But it was a war about so many other things: power, money, greed, revenge. It was a mafioso-style war. There were no good or bad guys. People changed sides so many times during it. I mean, no ideology can survive that many years of conflict.'

'But I've heard again and again that there *were* good guys and bad guys.'

'What do you expect? Look at this,' she said, leaning out of the open window and feeling the warm evening air on her face. 'Church, mosque, church, mosque,' she counted as they sped past. 'Catholics build a church on one side of the road, so Greek Orthodox build a bigger one on the other side. Muslims build a mosque, so Christians build a church. *Shi'a* build a mosque, so *Sunni* build a mosque. And so on.'

'What about the Druze?'

'Just remember not everything that happens is because

of some divine religious belief. People *do* do things because of religion, but also because of tradition, culture, individual experiences.'

'So why wouldn't your parents approve of me?'

'It's not a case of not approving. They would disown me if they knew about you.'

'But your mother saw us leaving.'

'I have some leverage with her today. I'm meeting a suitor tomorrow. Besides, Nadia's English is improving,' she said. 'I can keep her at bay for a couple of days.'

They walked into James's building, taking the key from the concierge. Inside the apartment, James could smell Maya's perfume as he kissed her. They didn't put the light on in his room, and the atmosphere was charged as James felt memories of their fight come back to him, and knew that the same was happening to Maya. She had tiny sparkles on her chest, and James imagined them sticking to his lips, little pieces of plastic stardust. They made her smell of candy. As she was taking her clothes off her phone rang. She slipped out of her bra as she told her mother she was at Nadia's house, and that she and Nadia had given the *Ingleezi* a lift home.

James sat on the edge of the bed, and Maya straddled him, sitting on his lap.

'I don't want to say goodbye yet,' she said.

'Neither do I. A few more days?'

'A few more days.'

She had her arms loosely around his neck; James had his hands on the small of her back. He kissed her. Being close to each other banished their problems, and for these moments they could forget everything outside the front door. But when they lay together later, the world had not changed. It was more the same than it had ever been.

As usual Maya got up at around midnight and collected her things ready to go back home.

'I hate it that we can't spend the night together.'

'You know, even if you were Lebanese and we were engaged we wouldn't be able to,' she said.

'Maya, if your parents would disown you if they knew you were with me, what would Walid do?'

'You don't want to know, *habibi*. Forget about him.'

James walked out with Maya to flag down a taxi. She kept scanning the street, checking people walking towards them.

'It would always be like this, wouldn't it?' James said.

'What?'

'Looking over our shoulders.'

'That depends. I don't want to spend my life in Lebanon, do you?'

Outside Arabian Sands, Maya said goodbye to him. Even though he knew they were going to see each other again before he left, he still felt upset just letting her go, out of his reach.

A boy in his late teens standing outside the shop looked at Maya and then at James before saying, 'What a waste,' in Arabic. Maya didn't bother to translate the comment into English, but when she got into the taxi she mouthed a kiss at James as it drove off, hoping the boy had seen her. She realised how much James missed in everyday life: once, when a little boy had approached the two of them asking them for money, he had said to James, 'May God keep this beautiful one for you.' James had given the boy some change, and Maya had, without really thinking, incorrectly presumed he had understood what the boy had said. She felt envious of him: she wished she could wake up one day and discover that she and her mother now spoke different languages, and were no longer able to communicate.

Fifteen minutes later they pulled up outside her house in Ashrafieh. Maya's mobile phone rang as she walked to her front door, making her jump – she had been on edge every time it had rung since she had left Paris. But it was just Maroun leaving his fourth message of the day.

James had the phone in one hand and was playing with the earrings Maya had forgotten in the other. He wondered whether she deliberately left something behind as a piece of evidence – something for James to find, and Maya to miss, a little bit of proof behind closed doors that something existed between them.

'It's near Cyprus,' James said. He was on his third country. Turkey and Israel hadn't registered with Del Pico. James sipped his drink; he needed a little anaesthetic when he talked to his ex-boss. Del Pico's raspy voice seemed out of place in James's apartment, even if it was only at the other end of the phone.

'I was hired to do a major breakthrough artist. Listen, Bobby, I want to send this to you when it's finished,' James said. He listened as Del Pico blustered in between puffs of his cigarette. It still made James feel sick having to deal with him, but he continued, 'You can tell everyone I'm in the Middle East. They'll love it. I heard that when the whole Latin thing dies, it'll be Arabic influence that takes over. And I'm right here for it.'

Del Pico ummed and ahhed for a few minutes.

'Bobby, you know when the Latin thing started, suddenly Christina Aguilera cashes in, so does everyone. Well, I promise you, when this hits, Britney will be telling Carson Daly that she's one-fifth Syrian.'

Del Pico bought it.

'How long till I have a copy? I can't get you work until I have the tapes . . . *if* it's as good as you say it is.'

'It is. And you'll have it very soon.'

'Get it to me in a couple of weeks. *Finished*,' Del Pico said, and hung up.

15

James was experiencing culture after-shock – at least, that was what it felt like. He had felt shock when he had first seen the destroyed downtown, and then again when he had first tried to work out the dating rules in Beirut. But there was something about the three-month mark – perhaps it was just an artificial marker of time that his fast-expiring visa kept reminding him of – and again he found himself feeling slightly displaced. It wasn't to do with pollution or language or strange business hours, or people laughing at his ridiculous English notion of walking being fun. And his shower ritual – taking shampoo, conditioner and a torch in case of power cuts – now seemed anything but strange. The shock wasn't to do with the boys letting off bangers in the streets for Easter, both Catholic and Orthodox, although that had given him a jolt; it hadn't come from one student referring to Hizbollah as resistance fighters, then another saying they were 'Iranians' with no business in Lebanon, although the infinite different opinions on history, politics – *everything* – had made his head spin. This feeling James was experiencing was to do with living in a city of mobile phones and Chevrolet SUVs where people lived by rules different to the ones those objects suggested. Beirut whispered to you that it was European, but the only people who heard it were those who weren't listening properly. Again and again, James had fallen for it. Beirut may have got under his skin, on to his clothes, under his fingernails, in his hair, under his eyelids, but it only revealed its true self periodically, before hiding again. After three months, the after-shock was simply the realisation that despite the many things he and Maya shared and enjoyed together, they were living by different rules in the same city.

He had one job to do before they finished the video. His three-month visa had run out and he had to get it extended to cover him for the last few days, and so he found himself queuing up at General Security alongside the Slavic hookers who provided the entertainment at the Super Nightclubs along the highway. They had to get their work visas renewed just like everyone else, but while they had their passports stamped with 'artist', James watched in horror as an Ethiopian maid standing in front of him, flanked by her rich employer, was forced to give her thumbprint. The shock of this potential human rights violation soon subsided when James's thumb was duly grabbed, stuck into the ink, then pressed on to his visa document. A hooker gave him a 'We're all in it together' look. One of James's favourite things about the British was that there were street protests any time national ID cards were even mentioned. In America, a state ID or driving licence was needed to do anything, but the British had visions of bar codes on wrists whenever the subject of ID cards was brought up, and James was a healthy product of his country, with an irrational dislike of giving his signature, let alone his thumbprint. But this time he had no choice. Ten minutes later, the Slavic prostitute, the Ethiopian maid and the English music video director were all standing outside on the pavement, holding slips that they would exchange for their new visas in a few days.

Julien had taken some footage of the Israeli Defence Force dismantling their outposts in south Lebanon during the break in the video shoot. He didn't understand why they were doing this if they weren't going to pull out for two more months. They seemed to be handing them over to the Lebanese SLA militia, which itself was looking shaky. The rumour this week – and it changed regularly – was that the SLA members would flee if the Israeli army left.

James sat in the passenger seat of Julien's car, peering into the viewfinder, watching the shots of camouflaged men leaving outposts, sometimes blowing them up to hide evidence. Nasser was sitting in the back and leaned forward to watch.

Hot air blasted in through the open windows as they started their journey to the Bekaa Valley. Julien drove with his usual enthusiasm for speed and disregard for life. He wasn't religious, and didn't believe that if he crashed he was destined for a better life, so James decided that driving like a crackhead must be a French thing.

Julien laughed. 'It's not French. The less time we are on the road, the safer it is,' he reasoned. This made some sense to James.

The steep, winding road that took them out of Beirut offered views of the hills and the small villages that were perched precariously on them. As Julien drove, James typed messages into his mobile phone and sent them to Maya. During the few seconds it took to type and send he felt happier than he ever recalled being: there was something so unremarkable and uncomplicated about what they were doing, how they were communicating, that for a brief moment they were free of their problems. It was almost an act of defiance, as Maya was having lunch with Suitor Twenty-five and his family, but still replied swiftly, giving him regular updates. This back-and-forth continued until the signal cut out and James looked up from his phone to find that they were in midair.

The car landed with a crash, the suspension crunching. Julien held on to the steering wheel, stopping them from skidding. Once he had levelled them out, they continued down the half-finished road. Giant potholes were dotted along the tarmac as if meteors had rained down; other parts were raised, looking like post-earthquake damage. It was one of these raised areas which had catapulted their car into the air. Julien hadn't flinched for even a second.

A new world opened up when they arrived in the Bekaa: open space, never-ending plains, Bedouin tents by the roadside – the anti-Beirut. The Bekaa was fertile and flat with mountains in the distance, the home of the hashish-growing trade which had prospered during the war and would soon return with a vengeance.

James held the wheel while Julien looked at the map. James had brought with him a postcard of the single Roman pillar that stood in the valley, perhaps left there by a lone Roman who had taken a wrong turning and dropped it there. He held the picture up to his eye, then the real thing appeared in the window. He spotted Joelle, Hassan and a small crew, who were already there.

'Are we trespassing?' James asked Hassan, as he got out of the car.

'Depends on who you know,' Hassan said, keeping an eye on a farmer who was already walking towards them. He was wearing a *keffieh* – it made James think of Yasser Arafat – and an old jacket, ripped to pieces. He had dark, gnarled skin on his hands. James, wearing only a T-shirt, wondered whether they were operating in the same climate. Hassan explained to the farmer what they wanted to do, and the farmer asked why.

'Well . . . it's a sort of mainstream video, this one, it's a romantic setting, so I suppose we're just trying to—'

'I don't think he was asking about your framing, Hitch,' Hassan said as an aside, before continuing with his fast-talking and finally winning the farmer over. They were invited to have coffee before they shot anything.

'We need to get on,' James said, impatiently.

'No, we *need* to do this,' Hassan explained.

They walked up to the farmhouse, through a small orchard of cherry trees, past some tobacco plants growing in a nearby field. James and the crew were introduced to the farmer's family, but the farmer himself disappeared while his wife brought in coffee on a tray. The house was tiled, cool and comfortable. Several different brands of cigarettes were arranged in a bowl on the coffee table like a lucky dip. An elegantly dressed man entered, obviously on his way out to dinner. It took James a moment to realise it was the farmer, having changed clothes. Through his son, the farmer told them about the difficulty of growing crops in the Bekaa, while never admitting that he had personally grown hashish before. Hashish took little water, he told them, which was perfect as water was not in abundance in the valley.

'He's worried, it might take five years before other crops bring in a decent harvest,' his son said. 'It could be years before he can earn a decent revenue from them. He is subsidised by the government, but he needs more. He needs to feed the family.'

Other farmers started turning up as news of the visitors got around. Or maybe they were simply coming round as they did every day. James was starting to understand Hassan's strategy: a couple of hours of coffee-drinking and chatting bought them the *wasta* for whatever they wanted to film or wherever they wanted to go.

James asked the farmer's son to translate for him. 'The climate you live in,' he began, the farmer's son following him in Arabic, 'is the exact atmosphere hundreds of illegal dope growers try to re-create in basements across Britain. It's so common that the British police use helicopters with heat sensors to track down marijuana-growing households from the air.'

The farmers laughed, then one of them asked the farmer's son to translate something for James.

'During the war, a lot of farmers set up anti-aircraft guns in case anyone tried to spray poison on the fields of hashish from the air,' the farmer said, his words echoed in English by the translator. The farmer was still laughing as he finished, imagining hash growers in Britain shooting down helicopters to protect their little hydroponic systems. He sipped his coffee as if he were considering something. Then he said, 'Hashish, *Hamdilla*.' *Thanks to God*.

Before they said their goodbyes, James and Julien considered their finances and decided to buy some fruit and hire a jeep from the farmer. A couple of minutes later, having changed the shot, James climbed into the boot of Julien's car. The hatchback was wide open, and the wheels threw up dust from the road, creating a nice diffusion as Julien drove. James held the camera to his eye and pressed record. Little by little, Joelle edged into the frame. She was driving the farmer's red jeep, and James scrambled to his knees, into a half-lying, half-crouching position, so he could film her. The two cars shot along the road, one with the boot open and an Englishman with a camera inside, the other with a Lebanese pop star. The light in the Bekaa was perfect behind her, the greens and browns of the hills in the distance, snow-capped mountains high above. As he filmed, James's foot got caught up in his students' exam papers, which he had only just finished marking and had stuffed away in the boot to hand back that evening. The back of the car smelt wonderful – either the girls wore so much perfume on their wrists that it rubbed off on their papers or they just sprayed the damn things with Chanel. James was so pleased that Nadia had done well; it looked good for her upcoming TOEFL exam. She had messed up only one question, her stylishly incorrect answer to 'What is the supernatural?' being 'The power of the woman'. Michel had completed only half the exam as he had spent the morning at the police station. All his essays ended with 'Lebanon for the Lebanese!' Omar had written a letter returning a faulty watch, repeating: 'Do you know who I am?! Do you know who I am?! I will use all my connections against you!' He had put in brackets at the bottom of his paper: 'Mr James, if you want to get anything done in this country, you must write like this.'

James moved the papers safely into a bag, just as Joelle's fiancé Tony – playing the love interest who had jilted her, causing her to drive off in the first place – pulled into frame right on cue. This was vintage Lebanese pop, and it would remain firmly in the not-for-London version. James couldn't stop smiling, one eye attached to the viewfinder. Lying in the boot of a car, exam papers fluttering in the corner, a Frenchman behind the wheel, a portable CD player strapped to the roof, a soon-to-be Lebanese diva driving a jeep: James was home. Tony looked suitably moody as he drove, chasing his girl, begging her to go back to him. Then a wasp flew into his face and he started waving his hand wildly and spitting, as if he might have swallowed it.

James kept shooting.

He had Joelle in the frame. She was mouthing the words to her song, the wind in her hair, holding the jeep steady, only a few feet away from the boot of James's vehicle. Just as James started climbing all over the car, grabbing shots from different angles, the three vehicles screeched to a halt.

A group of Interior Security soldiers dressed in light blue-and-white camouflage stood in the middle of the road, blocking the cars' passage. One approached and started asking questions. They wanted to know what was going on. Hassan was still at the farmer's house and was not there to work his magic. Tony did his best while Julien tried to call Hassan, but he couldn't get a signal in the valley. When James next saw Hassan, they were all down at the Bekaa police HQ being asked why they were filming without permission. Hassan did a good job apologising, but the boss didn't seem interested.

'What's the problem?' James asked.

'They think you're drug smugglers,' Hassan said.

'Are you kidding? This is our livelihood. If I don't have this video . . . *this* is my career.' James was desperate.

'Apparently you were saying something about growing hashish in England?' Hassan said.

'What?'

'Well, did you?'

'No!'

'James?'

'*Yes*, but I didn't mean that *I* grew it. You were there – didn't you hear? I was having a joke with the farmers. Helicopters. I was just saying—'

Hassan sighed. He had a lot of work to do. 'They want to watch the tapes, see what you were doing.'

'Why would we be taping our drug smuggling?' James said, looking at the thick metal bars on the cell doors.

The security boss squinted at James. Perhaps he spoke good English. James was starting to sound guilty himself – his last sentence wouldn't hold up in court as the statement of an innocent man. The boss confiscated the bag of tapes. It was the entire shoot.

Outside the HQ, the crew mooched around, without

tapes, without a video. Joelle and Tony were still inside, trying to persuade the security men to change their minds. Nasser was the only one unmoved by the situation, busying himself with removing dust from the different lenses that had been kept safely in his pocket, before putting them back into their bags.

'I thought *wasta* could take care of anything,' James said to Hassan.

'We just had some bad luck.'

'Do they know who we are?' James had frustration all over his face. 'We have connections!' He didn't notice Hassan allowing himself a small grin at a bit of Lebanon rubbing off on his English friend.

'Ask him if he knows our tape-stealer guys,' James said, as a man in combat fatigues walked past. Before Hassan had the chance to say anything, the soldier started speaking in English.

'You are the people with the video?'

'Yes,' James said. 'Do you know about it?'

'Of course. Why you film in a military area?'

'It's a military area? We didn't know.'

'Who is that?' he said, pointing at Joelle, still in her complete diva make-up as she and Tony left the building empty handed and walked into the car park to join the others, their faces telling their own story.

'This is Joelle. The next Samira Saeed,' James said.

'*Walla?*' The soldier was intrigued. 'One minute,' he said, then disappeared, leaving the crew in the car park, waiting, as the sky blackened and it began to get cold.

The soldier reappeared.

'Can we have them, then?' James demanded.

Hassan glared at him, wishing he would calm down and play the game.

'No. Is not possible,' the soldier said.

'Can we have *any* of them?' James pleaded.

'No. For security reasons.'

'What security reas—' James was about to explode again.

'*Mish mushkila*,' Hassan interrupted.

'What did you tell him?' James asked.

'I said *no problem*.'

'Why? It's a big problem!'

James noticed that the soldier had wandered off. 'How are we going to get them back?'

'They're gone. We tried everything,' Tony said, then added, 'That was pretty close, wasn't it? Did you see the prison cells?'

James and Julien gave him a look that said 'shut up'.

Tony tried to redeem himself. 'Look, Baalbeck isn't far away. I know someone who does security there. Maybe we could talk to him.'

'Or we could reshoot the stuff in Tyre, the beach stuff, and just go with the cool version,' Julien offered.

'We need both,' Joelle said, making sure everyone remembered the deal. James nodded. He didn't want to go back on what he had agreed – he knew he would lose Joelle if he didn't deliver the two versions.

'We're not going south – I'm not going to Tyre again. It's too dangerous now,' Tony said.

Hassan's eyes darkened. He hadn't said anything for

a while, and he was now standing with his hands deep in his jacket pockets as the outside temperature dropped quickly.

'Okay, we won't go to the south if it's so bad,' Julien said.

'What the fuck do you know about the south?' Hassan glared at Tony.

Tony misread Hassan badly, thinking he was joking. 'That it's fucked. It's going to burn. And I don't want to be there when it does.'

'How can you say that?' Hassan asked, his tone the polar opposite of Tony's, as if they were having completely different conversations.

'Very easily. Relax.'

'Don't tell me to relax.' Hassan took his hands out of his pockets and moved slowly towards Tony, who seemed to shrink instantly. Tony had a spindly frame, but Joelle was next to him, which gave him confidence – or arrogance.

'Hassan, forget it. He didn't mean anything.' James attempted to intervene, putting himself in Hassan's path.

'Shut up,' Hassan said, moving around James, getting closer to Tony.

'What do you care? All I'm saying,' Tony said, trying to keep his voice even so as to make his point without angering Hassan even more, 'is that if Israel are going to leave, I don't want to be there when the whole thing blows up.'

'It's not going to blow up,' Hassan replied coldly, now face to face with Tony.

James sighed. 'Hassan, why are we having this conversation? I think Tony is right. Anyway, I read yesterday that the SLA is going to kill all the prisoners when they go.'

'And you're concerned how that affects your little video.' Hassan's voice was ice. 'You don't know my country at all.'

'*Fine.*' James shrugged. 'So I didn't handle them stealing the tapes so well – what am I supposed to do? We worked so hard for it.'

From the second floor of the HQ, the soldiers watched the group of unlikely drug smugglers fight among themselves.

Down on the ground, Hassan didn't answer James. He just shook his head, looked around the group then back at James, before turning around and walking away. James let him go a little way, expecting him to stop.

'Where're you going? What about the tapes?'

'I'm finished with this,' Hassan said, without turning around.

283

16

Heat and humidity strangled the city. It was only May but already the pollution was increasing with the temperature. After he had been walking along the street for half an hour, James's throat felt sore – oil and petrol fumes hung between buildings, unable to escape. In the evenings, car headlights lit up what appeared to be fog – but it was the thick city air. Beirut was surrounded by water on two sides, and the city sucked up the moisture before diffusing it into the air. When it did rain, it didn't clear the pollution, it just redistributed the dust, coating cars with a fine brown residue. The arrival of the *Khamseeniyya* – a swirl of sand blown up from the Egyptian desert – had covered everything in a light smattering of yellow-brown summer snow. It had brought visibility down to a few feet and created so much dust that James felt it on his teeth.

In an awful way, in a way that James could never truly admit to himself, having his tapes confiscated had provided him with a certain *I don't care what happens now, so do your worst* energy, while posing the question: Was he subconsciously pleased the tapes had been taken, because now he would spend longer in Beirut, and therefore with Maya, while he worked out what to do next? He shook the question out of his head and decided it was easy enough to be simultaneously disappointed about the tapes while being glad to see more of Maya. He was going to find a way to finish the video, he wasn't giving up, and in the meantime why not try to continue the relationship, as long as they both kept their thoughts about the future firmly in denial.

James and Maya had been sitting in the café together for only ten minutes when he had flung himself behind the counter, as if the place were about to erupt into gunfire and he was diving for cover. Maya had given him the signal. The danger was coming from a friend of Maya's aunt, who happened to be walking past. From the friend to the aunt to Mrs Hayek. Those three degrees of separation would take one day to connect. You didn't have to be famous to be talked about in Beirut. It was the world's largest village and it was starting to suffocate James. He had loved the fact that if he had a problem someone knew someone who could help him. Now it felt like living in a pressure cooker. James and Maya were living in a spy movie where everyone – the street cleaner, the shop owner, the barber, the mechanic – was a potential double agent. They had to sneak around the city, and the hotter the weather became the harder it was for them both to breathe. James's neck hurt from looking over his shoulder. All Beirut's hotels and apartment complexes made copies of their guests' passports, but that was the least effective method of keeping track of people. After one week in Beirut someone, somewhere, would know everything about you. Gossip circulated through the city like the *servis* taxis.

James had woken up that morning to find himself standing

by the end of his bed. He checked his clock: it was 3 a.m.
He looked around in the darkness, wondering whether an
explanation would present itself. He tried to figure out
how he had gone from sleeping soundly to standing in
the middle of the room. Usually it was the cockerels which
woke him up. The urban chickens crowed for hours, and
just as they ran out of breath the call to prayer from the
mosque started. At other times of the day it was a beautiful
and elevating sound. *Allahu Akbar.* The second 'a' of Allah
stretched out for ten seconds as the *mu'azzen*'s voice rose
and fell in a lilt before the short, clipped *Akbar*. But at four
in the morning it fell into the same category as car alarms.
One pair of earplugs later and the problem was solved. In
part, at least. The mosques had good speakers – and there
were always one or two echoes from other *mu'azzenin*
farther away, some on a delay as the *Sunni* and *Shi'a*
mosques started at slightly different times. Beirutis got
the call to prayer in surround sound.

There was a loud bang. James didn't know which direction it came from, but he now recognised it as the same
noise that had woken him up. It sounded like a giant slamming an enormous door to a castle. Then there was silence
for ten minutes. When it seemed that there weren't going to
be any more sounds coming from Beirut that night, James
got back into bed, scratching his head, worrying that the
best his brain could come up with to explain loud noises
was fictional superhumans.

'The Damascus road,' Maya told him, once he had climbed
from behind the counter and reseated himself. 'Now with

a crater in it. And a power station as well. Just for good measure.'

'Are there any power stations left to bomb?'

'It's calculated,' Maya replied. 'Like a show of strength. A reminder of what will happen if they pull out and bombs start dropping on Israel.'

James sipped his coffee and lit one of Maya's cigarettes. As he looked at her beautiful face, he realised he had no photographs of them together – photos were not memories, but incriminating evidence.

'What's the matter?' Maya asked.

James paused for a moment, then said, 'The tapes were confiscated and Hassan walked out on us. He's not going to help us for the rest of the shoot.'

'What *happened*?'

James didn't want to answer. The waiter, wearing a tuxedo but managing to look very comfortable despite the heat, approached and asked whether they wanted anything else. James made the gesture for requesting the bill, scribbling on his hand with an imaginary pencil. 'I had a fight with Hassan,' he said to Maya, finally.

'What did you say?'

'*I* didn't say anything. Tony did. It was getting out of hand, so I told Hassan to calm down and he flipped out.' The waiter placed the bill on the table and James fished around in his pocket for some change.

'What did Tony say?'

'That the south was going to burn.'

Maya thought about this. 'Where is Hassan from?'

'He's from Beirut.'

'*Habibi*, no one is *from* Beirut,' she said. 'Everyone is from somewhere else.' They walked to the door, and back out into the hot sun. 'With or without Hassan, you need those tapes.'

'I need those tapes,' James agreed.

'Well, what would you do if something happened to them in London?' she asked.

James wasn't sure why he was driving so fast. He wasn't sure why he was driving at all. He careened out of Beirut in a hire car and pointed it in the direction of Baalbeck. Cars cut in front of and behind him, and he quickly started to admire Julien's driving technique as he screeched around a tight bend with cement blocks creating a makeshift central reservation. He was also starting to wish he had hired something that wouldn't show up the scratches as much.

He paid his money to get into the Baalbeck site. In front of him was a tour group, all craning their necks to look up at the ancient buildings. James jogged around the site trying to find the security guard that Tony said he knew. He entered a small metal hut where two guides were relaxing, and described who he was looking for, dropping Tony's name. Once they had located the guard, James explained who he was, and they exchanged introductions. The guard was a thin man, with a head slightly too big for his body. James accepted his offer of coffee and they sat down and discussed the guard's children, Lebanon's best hospitals and the recent fighting in the south. James drank so much coffee his left hand began to shake slightly, but he happily continued to accept the offers of refills. He shared his cigarettes out. After nearly three hours of James not getting to the point, of not being English, the guard had to start his shift.

'Meet me at Restaurant Baalbeck in two hours,' he said, as he got up to leave.

James feigned surprise and said he would love to meet for lunch. Back in his rental car in the car park, he tried to suck down two litres of water to disperse the caffeine that was attacking his nervous system. He turned the CD player up and closed his eyes, as the sun blasted through the windscreen. He dozed fitfully, the coffee never quite letting him sleep, until there was a knock at his window.

'*Yalla*, let's eat,' the guard said.

As they finished their miniature banquet, and were sparking up the *nargileh*, James told the guard how he was trying to restart his career after leaving London. Without specifically mentioning the tapes, he explained his situation. When the guard had finished smoking, he produced a cloth sack and put it on the table in front of James.

'For you.' It was the kind of sack a hunter stuffs his catch inside. James opened it, expecting to see a dead badger.

There were three of his tapes.

'This is very kind,' James said.

'No problem. They keep two tapes only. Two tapes are problem. Please say hello to Tony.'

Maya had gone out to dinner with Maroun only once. Two hours into the extravagant meal – the kind of Lebanese feast that took six hours to get through – she made an excuse and left early. She told him she had forgotten it was her cousin's wedding that evening. As she was walking out of the restaurant she looked behind her and saw his eyes, gazing longingly at her. It wasn't a lecherous look, and it wasn't a look that said he was in love with her. It was the kind of look that surfaces when a little bit of hope has been taken away from a person. Everyone is a child in that moment. Maroun looked as if he was just watching a missed opportunity for some kind of connection disappear on him, before he had even finished his dinner.

All Maroun had talked about was his work. He wanted to be able to provide anything for his future family – he talked about this family as though it were already in existence, and it was just a matter of locating where they were hiding. When Maya thought back, she felt guilty: the image in her mind was of him still eating as she walked out. He hadn't done or said anything wrong, she had just wanted to go, and she didn't want to meet anyone else who measured up to certain criteria and came with the stamp of 'approved'. Every meeting and introduction – whether at Maya's house or at a wedding or someone else's apartment – had begun to weigh on her until she couldn't take any more. She now regretted that she had run out on him like that, that she had lied to a decent person. Maroun hadn't challenged her or judged her. He didn't ask for details of her cousin's wedding, or how she could possibly forget something like that then remember it at eight in the evening.

A few weeks had passed after their dinner before she received Maroun's first e-mail. She never replied to any of them. He kept sending them as if she *were* replying, as if they were engaged in a dialogue, but he was just writing to a ghost. Every time she blocked his address he just added a number to his name to avoid ending up in the junk mail folder. He was up to fifteen. In each mail he updated her on his life and his work and what his plans were. He spoke perfect Arabic and French, but insisted on writing to her in English, thinking she didn't speak French, and unable to write Arabic on his computer. The e-mails had irritated her to begin with, then she started almost to look forward to them. Maroun's messages were full of excuses for her behaviour and the fact that she never replied to him. Now she understood they were probably for his own benefit, to reassure himself that there *was* a chance of him finding someone. He had given her the benefit of the doubt, right from the time she had left him at dinner.

To: MayaHayek@qserv.net
From: Maroun15@mfaasolutions.com

Dear Mayoush,

Your'e not answer your phone. I get too worried. I called much times and send text message also. However, I've got good news to tell for you. My company is too successful businesswise (Thanks God) so I'm gonna expand to computers. I love everything called hi-tech and inshallah this is a big market. I will have many business trip in another countries and coming to Lebanon soon. So boring of Kuwait! (lol) I loved the time that I spent it with you. See you soon.

Personal Best Regards,
Maroun F. Abu Abdullah

The smile on Maya's face disappeared when she caught her mother reading the e-mail over her shoulder. She turned around sharply.

'What?' Mrs Hayek went straight on the defensive.

'Stop reading my e-mails.' Maya quickly closed down all the programs that were open on the desktop. Her acceptance e-mail from university was safely stored. She had picked it up when she got back from Paris. On first reading it she had been excited, then it just made her feel depressed and she decided she wouldn't tell anyone about it. She left it there, still unanswered.

'Your father received a phone call from this Maroun.'

'That's why I've got fifty missed calls from him,' Maya said, shutting the computer down completely and standing up.

'We want to invite him and his family around to dinner when he is next here.'

'Let's not bother.'

'Maya, listen to me. You're not getting younger. This is not good.'

'What is not good?'

'You know what I'm talking about. Your father and I have spoken about it. Why can't you meet this Maroun? Maybe you will like him.'

'I *have* met him.'

Mrs Hayek was briefly distracted by someone walking past the house, then she turned her attention back to her daughter. 'What is wrong with wanting my daughter to be secure in her future?' She put her hand to her forehead in exasperation, then ran it through her hair. She had recently had her hair cut, but repeated confrontations were taking away the chic look that her hairdresser had been so proud of creating.

Maya walked into the kitchen, taking a bottle of water from the fridge. Her mother followed.

'Your father and I want to see you settled,' Mrs Hayek said.

'The pressure must really be on now Mrs Jihad's daughter is married,' Maya said, sipping her water. Her mouth was dry; she knew that eventually her excuses were going to be exhausted, her resistance was going to run out of energy. She could feel it seeping out of her during every conversation they had. *From a good family*. The words echoed around her head every day. He would be wealthy too, money that would be spread horizontally across the family tree as well as vertically – once the ring was securely on the finger.

'Who were you with in the café yesterday?' Mrs Hayek asked, her voice rising in pitch as if she were barely interested in the answer.

'It's none of your business,' Maya replied, walking towards the front door.

'It's the man from the wedding, isn't it? Nadia's teacher.'

Maya stopped. 'I wasn't in a café yesterday.'

'Yes you were.'

'I was?' Maya was going to force her mother to confess. She could see her working out her tactics.

'Someone saw you.'

'I know they did. That bitch friend of Aunt Mona.'

Mrs Hayek looked as if she was going to cry, but she was too angry, every muscle in her face was tensed. 'How dare you talk to your own mother like that? Shame on you.'

'Shame on *you*. You know what my friends say? "*Minimum*: good car. *Minimum*: cell phone." It's like a mantra. They're talking about men. I don't see that what you're doing is any different. Why don't you marry Maroun? He has a house in France as well – did you know *that*?' Maya flung the door open and stormed out of the house.

'Where are you going?' Mrs Hayek followed her, lowering her voice now they were outside.

'To Nadia's!' Maya defiantly kept her reply at the same volume. To hell with anyone who was listening, she thought, as she spotted Mrs Jihad on the balcony, observing the situation. '*What are you looking at?*' Maya shouted up to her. 'How about I tell your husband that it doesn't take six months to fit a new kitchen. Maybe he'd like to know why that designer comes over every day?'

Mrs Jihad scurried off her balcony and back into her house.

17

It was a bright, sunny day in late May, and in the Armenian suburbs north of Beirut a dog chased its tail on a flat roof. At the petrol station next door, people filled up their cars. The bells from a nearby church announced the service.

In west Beirut, Josef stood outside his salon. He pulled down the metal shutters then was distracted by a man walking past in a dressing gown, holding an umbrella to protect himself from the sun. Josef watched the man for a moment, then continued to shut up shop. He padlocked the front, then made his way home.

In Jack's living room, his wife searched around for the lock to her suitcase. She had finished packing her bags. She told her husband that she wasn't leaving *him*; she was just leaving the country. When he came to his senses, she told him, she would be waiting for him: at home, with the children, in England. Jack stood in stunned silence. First his friend Malcolm getting engaged to his secretary, and now this.

In a car park near Bliss Street, Mahmoud – now with the coolest home-made head shave in town – was marking the celebrations by speeding around on his moped, letting off bangers and waving thin firework tubes which shot their spray out of one end like fire tinsel. Haj Ahmad had been silent from the early morning, glued to the television and speaking to his brother on the phone. When Hassan had seen the pictures on the television he had left the house without telling anyone where he was going.

And in the south, Israeli troops destroyed their old outposts before leaving, after twenty years of occupation. The Israeli soldiers made the victory sign as their tanks rolled towards the Lebanon–Israel border. Hizbollah guerrillas made the victory sign as they took over the outposts. Palestinian guerrillas had once made victory signs as they left Beirut for exile during the war.

A loud banging woke James again. This time it was someone knocking on his door. His clothes were piled neatly on a chair – he had put them out the night before, ready for the final day's shoot. With only two tapes missing, he had worked out and storyboarded what pick-ups he needed to finish the video. It was still early, but he was full of energy as he opened the door to find Aisha standing there.

'Have you seen?' she asked. She was wearing a pastel-green *hejab*, her eyes wide, as if she had been up all night. She squeezed past James and switched on the television. There were images of the pull-out on all the channels.

'Have you been watching?'

James shook his head, and tried to move the storyboards which Aisha was sitting on.

'They are leaving the south,' Aisha said.

James was momentarily mesmerised by the pictures, but then checked his watch and continued getting ready for the shoot. He had bought four extra blank tapes which he would hide as soon as they were full to avoid confiscation. He stuffed them in a bag along with a director's viewfinder and his notepads. Aisha flicked from channel to channel, as if to check that what she was watching was real. The flickering screen answered her question: the pull-out that had been set for July was happening two months early. It was happening *now*. The planned slowly-slowly retreat was now a rush. The South Lebanon Army had collapsed as soon as the Israeli army had started leaving, all the members of the SLA fleeing to Israel or giving themselves up to Hizbollah.

James caught the phone after one ring. 'Julien, where are you? We have to catch the light.'

'James, it's Hassan.'

'Oh.'

'Are you watching TV?' Hassan's voice was fragile, about to crack.

'What do you want?' James said, hearing the anger in his own voice.

Hassan didn't say anything.

Aisha had finished with the television and had now started a conversation with the creepy concierge which was rebounding up and down the stairs. She told him she wanted to take the day off. James put one hand over his ear so he could make out what Hassan was saying. But Hassan wasn't saying anything for James to hear.

'What do you *want*?' James repeated.

'I need you to help me with something.'

'I'm going to finish the shoot with Julien. He'll be here

in a minute.' James tucked the phone into his neck as he tied up his shoelaces.

'None of my friends even knows what's happening in the south,' Hassan said quietly. 'One told me he heard something was happening in the north. I can't handle this alone.'

James stopped what he was doing and stood up. 'Hassan, what's going on?'

'Once the Israeli forces have left the south, Khiam will be back in Lebanese control. They're going to storm the prison.'

'And?' James said, impatiently.

'My brother is in Khiam.'

Hassan had left Beirut in the early morning by himself and had got as far as Sidon, a coastal city twenty miles south of Beirut, before stopping, unable to go farther. He sat there paralysed for an hour before calling some of his friends. Then he called James. The unsteady tectonic plates of Middle East politics were shifting again, throwing people around like a tiny ship on a huge, angry ocean. It was how Lebanon trapped people. They wanted to leave, but they never allowed themselves to, in case they missed what happened next. James was entangled. Beirut had grabbed him and dared him to break free of its hold. Westerners were warned about the dangers of the Middle East; but they were never warned of the dangers of forming friendships.

When James reached reception, the creepy concierge was

threatening to sack Aisha if she took the day off. James quickly got Mr Toufic involved and Aisha was cleared.

Half an hour later, they were climbing into Aisha's car in Sabra-Shatila, her husband Marwan behind the wheel. Then they stopped at the hospital, Aisha bursting through the doors and dressing her mother, not listening to the doctors when they told her that she shouldn't be moved. Fatima was manoeuvred into the back seat of the car. She sat next to Safaa, who sat next to James. Marwan and Aisha were in the front.

They drove southwards.

Fatima had her hand over her mouth. Her eyes were as bright as a child's, her skin as old as the land. In her pocket was the thick, rusted key to her parents' house in a country that didn't exist. It looked as if it had been rescued from a shipwreck. The elderly lady was confused. The pneumonia had left her in a severely weakened state and she saw only the outlines of her family members; she had the sensation of movement, but didn't know she was in a car. Any moment of lucidity was immediately crushed by confusion. Then Safaa took her hand and she knew it was her granddaughter. Fatima said nothing; the fear of not being able to form coherent sentences frightened her. She could hear the words in her head, but as she readied herself to speak them out loud she felt them disappear. Light flashed past her eyes, sunlight reflecting through the car window. She believed that her sister would take the key and magically open the house up, ready for them to inhabit again. She believed it was that easy.

In the southern suburbs, Marwan slowed down to ten

miles an hour. He was a quiet man with short dark hair, and long eyelashes which his daughter had inherited. The only movement he made was to rub the back of his neck in the heat. Aisha watched boys hanging from passing cars, waving flags with hastily written Arabic slogans. She had left her boy at home – he was happy to stay with Kathy and the broken computers. In the heat haze, policemen in blue uniforms and white helmets stuck out like lighthouses as they pretended to direct the traffic; the cars decided which way they were going, then the policeman encouraged them in that direction. One policeman stood in the middle of an intersection chatting to a driver who was blocking the rest of the traffic. Soon there was a chorus of car horns. People were impatient, in a hurry to see a part of their country many had never set foot in.

Once Marwan had broken free of the south Beirut gridlock, cars and trucks started overtaking them, people hanging off the sides of vehicles and cheering. Soldiers waved at the checkpoints. One soldier had his hand down by his side, his fingers in a quiet victory sign. Safaa was busy leafing through a pile of photographs, pictures of children who lived in the camp in Bethlehem. She hoped she would recognise them in person.

Hassan was waiting in Sidon when they arrived. He looked nervous but exchanged greetings with Marwan. James jumped out of one car and into another. He got into the passenger seat next to Hassan and they watched Marwan and Aisha drive off. Hassan shook James's hand, then, without saying anything, rammed the car into first and accelerated out of Sidon. The BMW emerged from the exhaust fumes of Marwan's car as if in a wind tunnel experiment. They waved as they passed them. Then they were gone, each in search of their past.

Hassan shot along the coast road down to a roundabout with a large martyrs' statue, then took a left into a new world. As they drove farther south, there were more Hizbollah flags and pictures of leaders on lamp-posts. The pictures started getting bigger – until James saw fifteen-foot-high faces at every crossroads. Like everyone in London, James had learned, almost instinctively, the different colours of the Tube lines on the Underground map. He had never set out consciously to learn them. When he changed lines, he just caught the colours out of the corner of his eye as he navigated around the maze. In Lebanon it wasn't Tube line colours, it was pictures of political figures. In Beirut they were among the muddle of 'Belly Button Piercing Inside!' and 'Big Sale!' fly posters. Outside the city, they were pasted on to walls, propped up at checkpoints, hanging from bridges. They had sunk in subconsciously: James knew Moussa Sadr from Sayyed Hassan Nasrallah; he knew Emile Lahoud from Salim al-Hoss – although the Lebanese president and prime minister's pictures were conspicuous by their absence; he knew Ayatollah Ali Khamene'i from Ayatollah Khomeini. There was an enormous painting of the late Iranian leader as they approached the first roundabout in Nabatiyeh. His revolution in Iran had provided almost spiritual encouragement to the dispossessed *Shi'a* of south Lebanon, the area James and Hassan were now entering. The style of the paintings reflected this, James thought, showing him as an almost superhuman figure.

'In Iran you see thousands of those pictures,' Hassan said, following James's eyeline. 'As well as David Beckham posters.'

'They ban pop star pictures but they allow footballers?'

'Of course,' Hassan answered, visibly relaxing when talking about something other than his brother. 'Isn't it great that you can get pictures of England footballers in Tehran? Don't you think Michael Owen scoring a goal represents England abroad better than the royal family or your prime minister?'

James laughed.

'I'm serious. You should thank Paul Scholes and the rest of them. They're the only good bit of foreign policy you have.'

James looked at Hassan, whose face had finally lost its tension and had dissolved into a wicked grin. '*Habibi*, thanks for coming,' he said.

Hassan's car clung to the road like a magnet to metal. He powered around bends, never checking a map, only occasionally asking directions if their route was blocked. A man selling Pepsi by the side of the road said, 'You are welcome in Lebanon,' before advising them on a short cut. A few miles past Nabatiyeh, while speeding around a sharp horseshoe bend, the car made a grinding sound, then the exhaust started vibrating.

'What the fuck is that?' Hassan shouted.

'I think we're breaking down.'

Hassan pulled over to the side of the road. He switched

the engine off and opened his door. Before he got out, he looked over at James.

'BMWs don't break down,' he said. 'It just needs a tune-up.'

'A tune-up with a welding iron.'

Hassan got on his knees and looked under the car. A large Khomeini stared down at the vehicle from above. Immediately two men from across the street were also on their knees, peering at the chassis, offering opinions. One directed Hassan to a garage, a small metal door that opened on to a room with a few tools. The mechanic that greeted them on arrival had a short dark beard and moved briskly around the car, before jacking it up from the front, Hassan's eyes widening as his baby rose into a static wheelie.

'There's a jacking point back there . . .' Hassan said, trailing off and giving up. The mechanic was now underneath the car, welding iron in one hand, no goggles, cigarette in mouth. As Hassan watched his precious car undergo surgery, James looked around him. The electricity pylons were perfect; they didn't seem to match the mess of Beirut's lines. It was a sign of the occupation, Hassan told him: the Israeli army had put them in.

Close to the garage a man was asleep, sitting on a piece of rock. Exhaustion. Two kids were playing in the street next to him, but he was too tired to be disturbed. The rattle of Israeli tanks leaving was now just a memory from a few hours earlier. The occupiers had been chased out by Hizbollah, or had decided to leave of their own accord – depending on who you believed. A man with a red *keffieh* wrapped around his head and under his chin hobbled down to the car and offered James his plastic seat. The man was in his eighties, and it took James a long time to persuade him to accept his own chair. He split the difference and accepted one of his cigarettes instead. Hassan kept anxiously looking at his watch. He opened the car doors – making it look as if it were about to take off, wings outstretched – and turned up the radio.

'They've worked out an agreement for the prison guards to leave unharmed if they don't hurt the prisoners,' Hassan translated the report.

'We'll get there.' James rested his hand on Hassan's shoulder. The welder finished his work and the car's front wheels were lowered back down to the ground. Hassan paid him three dollars, which he wouldn't accept at first, saying there was no charge. Eventually Hassan gave him five and got in the car.

When the radio played a clip of a Western politician congratulating Israel on its pull-out, Hassan said, '*Ma t'rabih jmeeleh*,' then turned to James and explained, 'It means "Don't expect me to reward you for doing what you were supposed to do. Don't award debt".'

'Do you think the Israeli leadership will change now?' James asked.

Hassan shrugged. 'Maybe. Depends how smoothly all this goes. Anyway, politicians never go away. Not in Israel, not in Lebanon.'

The recurring political pictures on every wall proved his point – leaders in the Middle East didn't get put out to pasture after their tenure, they merely came back in a different guise, in a different party, or sometimes just a different suit.

At the top of a steep incline was a large checkpoint where cars and buses were being searched. Hassan was silent as they approached. At the crest of the hill, James could see down into the south for the first time. Row after row of hills were covered in mist, like a series of green waves stacked one behind another. Behind them were mountains, snow-capped tsunamis watching over the hills. It was hard to imagine the horror such a beautiful place had witnessed.

'*Ajnabi*,' Hassan replied when the soldier asked him to identify his passenger. James would always be the *foreigner*. Hassan handed over his Lebanese ID card and James's passport. The soldier examined them.

'*Ingiliterra*,' Hassan answered, when asked for James's country. 'They're being very strict on any Palestinians, Syrians, Iraqis, *English*,' Hassan told James, before talking the soldier into letting them pass. His status as a relative of a Khiam detainee made it impossible for the soldier to say no.

From the checkpoint onwards, as Hassan steered around S-bend after S-bend cut deeply into hills where sharp rocks protruded through the grass like bare knuckles, James saw the effect that this day was having on his friend. As they got closer to their destination, the nervous jokes about football stopped; Hassan's eyes kept filling up, only for the tears to be impatiently wiped away. His face told the story of someone who finally knew what being on the edge was like, in a way few people would ever experience. The look in his eyes was intense and complex, showing toughness, as if bracing for impact, while at the same time also being soft and forgiving.

The border fence. Within the same few hundred square metres were Palestinian refugees from Lebanon, Israeli soldiers, Palestinians from Israel, and, watching through binoculars from the well-irrigated gardens above the dust, some Israeli settlers.

Aisha and her family got out of the car and climbed up the steep bank that led up to the wire fence separating the two countries. Aisha held Safaa's hand tightly while Marwan helped Fatima, putting one arm around her and holding her hand as they slowly crept up the incline. A group of Palestinians on the other side of the fence were shouting over to them, calling out family names, hoping for recognition; others were just watching. Safaa broke free of her mother's hand when she spotted her penpals on the other side. She ran up the bank to greet them, swapping names of villages that none of them had ever seen. Israeli soldiers patrolling the border fence tried to clear the Palestinians away on the Israeli side, but they resisted. Hands found hands through the barrier. The soldiers looked on as if they were witnessing a group of Martians perform a bizarre ritual, and decided to leave them to it. Some told stories of groups of Palestinians who had been stopped before they could reach the fence, and were reduced to blasting their foghorns from a distance. Razor wire and barbed wire got caught on people's clothes as they reached across to exchange gifts. Safaa took off her necklace and gave it to a girl of the same age on the other side. The girl filled up a small plastic cup of sand and passed it through to Safaa, who ran along the fence with it until she got to Marwan, who was standing with Fatima, shouting her sister's name. Safaa handed her grandmother the cup of soil, but the elderly lady was too distressed to realise what it was. She was waving her hands in the air, and knocked the sand out of Safaa's hands. The cup fell to the ground and the sand spilt on to Lebanese soil. Marwan was silent, offering no opinion, simply standing there supporting his mother-in-law. He knew Fatima would stand there as long as she physically could – it was all she had. He was right next to her, but she was alone in the crowd.

At the bottom of the bank a few people were dancing the *dabke*, others were waving flags. One read: 'Lebanon today, Palestine tomorrow'. It seemed so naive to Aisha. She wondered whether she was the only one who could see that, while hope danced around, an old woman was crying, now with no more energy to call out her sister's name.

Marwan decided he had seen enough and gently brought Fatima back down to the car and gave her some water. She sat in the back seat with the door open, watching the young people dance and Safaa run around exchanging messages with people on the other side. Even from the car, Fatima could see a woman holding a picture of her son, shouting out his name, asking if anyone had seen him. Fatima felt around in her pocket, clutching the key to her house, grasping it tightly as if it were the most precious diamond. Marwan could see the hope drain from her eyes.

'We'll leave in five minutes,' he said to Aisha.

Aisha agreed, then turned to Safaa. '*Hayate*, I want you to go along the fence asking if anyone knows your grandmother. Tell them her name and her village. Okay?'

Marwan gave his wife a look that said this was a bad idea.

'Just give us five minutes,' Aisha told him. Safaa had already rushed off, excited by the prospect of a new project. Aisha started fifty metres along the fence from her daughter. The elation of their arrival, the exhilaration of the first minutes of speaking to people on the other side, started to disappear as evening drew in and it got dark. As Aisha moved slowly along the fence, people started throwing stones at the Israeli soldiers. When she found no one who could help her, she scrambled back down the bank, happy to be leaving a situation that was now simmering with hostility. As she approached the car and got in the back with her mother, she tried not to let her face show the disappointment. Marwan started the car as Safaa bounced up right on time and got in the front seat.

'Are we going?' Safaa asked.

'Yes.'

Safaa handed a crumpled piece of paper to her grandmother. '*Teta*,' she said, leaning over the back of her seat. 'There is a man. The son of a man from your village. He will come tomorrow to talk to you.'

Fatima gave a weak smile and patted the little girl. The news would mean nothing to her until the next morning when she would wake up, her head clear, her thoughts uncluttered for just long enough to process the events of the previous day.

Safaa rode in the front seat all the way home, the little hero.

The car in front of James and Hassan was one foot away, as was the car behind. These cars were flanked by more cars, until the train in both directions stretched farther than the eye could see. The Lebanese and Syrian checkpoints had become UN checkpoints as the roads turned to tracks. *Flak jackets must be worn beyond this point.* Hassan put the windows down and James could hear the sounds of the UN: Italian, Irish accents, African languages.

Hassan held on to the steering wheel tightly, even though they were advancing very slowly. At the side of the road people were throwing rice and sugar-almond candies in the air in celebration. They were returning to their villages. The energy was visible, but it was as if Hassan somehow couldn't see them, he was so disconnected from it all. He put the windows back up and turned on the air conditioning.

'Where are your parents?' James asked, breaking the silence.

'Waiting at home.'

'For what?'

'For me to bring Majed back to them.'

There was just the sound of the air con whooshing around the vehicle, and the radio playing in the background, when suddenly the ground shuddered, and the car rocked hard on its suspension. James craned his neck around; Hassan jumped out of the car. There was shouting in Arabic, then Hassan jumped back in the car.

'Fuck! This is mined!'

'Someone went over a mine?' James asked.

'I think so.'

'Can you see it?'

'No, it's miles back. Someone swerved off the track.'

All around them, people jumped in and out of cars, spoke on mobile phones, tried to work out what was going on. There was chaos outside, yet James, inside Hassan's plush car, felt calm as they passed a Pink Panther ice-cream van with *Allah* written in large letters on the side, 'We Wish You a Merry Christmas' tinkling from its speakers. Some children were playing on an abandoned tank, spinning around the gun barrel like little gymnasts.

'If you want to go back,' Hassan said, fixing his gaze on the steering wheel, speaking quietly, 'then I understand. We can easily find someone to take you back.'

James looked at Hassan, then out over the rough terrain of dry grass, dust and rock as the train of vehicles started moving again.

'No, it's okay. Let's keep going,' he replied, as they passed two armed Hizbollah men sitting by the entrance to a village, a large banner slung over the entrance celebrating independence. The car radio crackled then lost its signal completely, before coming back strongly with a Hebrew-language station from Israel.

James saw the prison in the distance, alone on the hilltop. As they approached, they saw forty or fifty men from the village running up the road – it looked like the start of a marathon, but the men had anger in their eyes. More and more people joined them, the numbers growing quickly. Coming in the other direction, going against the angry tide, James saw the prison guards in their cars. The group of village men kicked the doors of the vehicles and banged on the windows. Inside the cars it must have felt like thunder, punctuated only by the shouts of 'Traitor'. Luckily for the guards, the men were in too much of a hurry to stop them and drag them from their cars.

Hassan pulled the car awkwardly on to the side of the road, then jumped out and, without locking it, started running towards the prison gates, James close behind him. Once they were inside, they followed the flow of men through the courtyard, past a small square of concrete with a caged roof which looked like an exercise yard, and into one of the prison buildings. There was row after row of tiny cells, one pace by two paces, with damp floors and no light. The crowd's shouts were being echoed by the prisoners. The men followed the echoes into another building, passing the guards' abandoned rooms, then a medical office with supplies that looked to be from the Second World War. Then they found them: groups of men locked in rectangular cells. The frenzy was intense; the crowd wanted to break the place apart.

Hassan started grabbing people from the village and asking if they knew where Majed was being held. No one had any information – the outside world hadn't touched the prison. There was a fork, two corridors breaking off with cells along each of them. They were thin and painted a sickly light yellow. It was dark, and only the occasional cruel bare light bulb splattered light into the dimness. James and Hassan looked at each other, then shot down the right-hand corridor. There was a series of red-brown metal doors, each with a gap the size of a letter box. Arms and hands were reaching out through the tiny holes. '*Allahu Akbar*,' the crowd cried. The prisoners shouted it back.

The men from the village started kicking the doors while the prisoners inside looked out through the grilles, grabbing a friendly human hand while the brutal human foot tried to end their captivity. Hassan tried to get a glimpse inside, shouting, 'Majed, *waynak*?' *Where are you?* His voice was becoming hoarse. Sweat was running down his forehead. His expensive clothes were covered in perspiration and dust. The airless corridor generated its own humidity from the number of people packed into the tiny space. The sound of the doors being kicked from the outside grew louder and louder.

'Hassan!' a voice replied. James heard it first. It was coming from the other corridor. He raced around the corner, shouting Majed's name. When he saw a man's eyes peering out of the tiny hole in the door, he knew he had found Majed. He grabbed a stunned Hassan – the stench of the decaying prison, of the rotting lives of the detainees, the horror of what he was living through in these few moments, knowing his brother had lived through it for ten years, was hitting him. Hassan strained to see his brother through the small rectangular window. Majed looked just like an older Mahmoud. Hassan couldn't smile; he didn't laugh or cry. He started kicking the door frantically. Other men came to help. James could see a series of tiny metal bunk beds inside the cell, the men all crammed in like battery chickens. James and Hassan kicked the door; the noise was so overpowering they could barely hear each other's instructions. Hassan was shouting and gesturing to Majed and the other inmates to get away from the door as he grabbed a thick metal crowbar and rammed it into the lock again and again. When he had dented it, he put the crowbar in the weak spot and kicked it. They both started kicking it, in time. The door creaked and groaned. Then it burst open.

His brother was now a grown man with a beard – not the boy that Hassan had last seen ten years ago, the boy that Mahmoud had always reminded him of. Mahmoud could never have known how he upset Hassan just by sharing the looks of his lost brother.

Hassan helped Majed to his feet and carried him towards the exit. James went ahead, clearing a path for them out into the sunlight. Majed was gasping for air, as if he had been holding his breath all these years. Outside, they slumped into a heap on the steps, crying. James moved his eyes away out of respect, and watched history take its course inside the prison.

18

Aisha didn't like the border. She had felt the atmosphere change during her first visit. Now she didn't want to see it again, to think about it, or to talk about it. She had shared the moment of jubilation when she saw the pull-out, when she could talk to people on the other side. But it quickly became a stale reminder of her impotence. She had gone back on her promise to herself not to get involved in politics and she had got hurt because of it. She had watched her mother return to hospital after their day in the south, emotionally and physically worn out, and wondered what could be worth that. The doctors again strongly advised against Fatima doing anything that took her outside, so this time Aisha travelled to the border with just Marwan. They found the man Safaa had met and absorbed as much information as possible, and gave as much as possible. As people overheard them talking through the fence, they offered assistance and little pieces of knowledge that completed the puzzle. Marwan and Aisha wrote hundreds of notes, asked for a lot of favours, and passed their hopes through the wire on small pieces of paper so that the next day, finally, Fatima could stand, stooped, at the border fence, kissing her sister on the cheek, her lips finding part skin, part metal wire.

Dalia wore a long flowing black coat and a white *hejab*. They weren't able to hug each other, but their fingers entwined through the fence, and when Fatima closed her eyes it felt like a hug. Fatima was the elder sister, and after the emotion of first seeing her sibling she became businesslike, telling Dalia to unlock the front door of their house and leave it open – so it would be ready for when they returned. Dalia didn't say anything as her sister spoke; she had tears in her eyes, was still in shock, and didn't even understand the words Fatima was saying.

Fatima passed the key through the fence in a tiny private ceremony shared just between the two of them, Aisha and Marwan waiting silently behind her while she spoke to her sister. Later, when Fatima was resting in the car, Dalia quietly told Aisha that she had visited their old village on a couple of occasions, and that it was now just a pile of old stones and overgrown shrubs next to an Israeli town with a different name. She explained that Fatima hadn't understood what she had told her – she *also* lived in a refugee camp. She wasn't at home keeping the door open for her guests as Fatima imagined.

'She has been very ill,' Aisha whispered, while a few metres along the fence a small boy threw rocks, using a slingshot. 'She is very confused.'

Dalia cried gently. 'Thank God for bringing us together.' They were so far apart.

In the months that followed, Aisha and her family would watch as the prime minister of Israel who had taken the move to pull out of south Lebanon was replaced with the once-disgraced defence minister, Ariel Sharon. A Palestinian state, something Yasser Arafat had been threatening all year, was never announced. No one had yet sold out their right of return. These would be the last pieces of information that Aisha would take in before switching off her television for good. But as they drove home from the border, the memory of Dalia's face imprinted forever in all of them, Aisha already knew she would never speak about politics or the refugee situation ever again. She would think only of her children. At the border, other families would continue to exchange information and news about the second *Intifada*, the al-Aqsa *Intifada*, named after the mosque that was painted on the walls of Palestinian refugee camps across the Arab world. One of these pictures was visible from Aisha's kitchen window. That night, having returned from the border after the longest day of her life, she stared at it as she went back to the comforting ritual of preparing food for her family in her little temporary house, deep in the heart of Sabra-Shatila.

Nadia's new room-mate made a grab for the remote control – she didn't want to watch any more of 'that crap' on television – but after a brief struggle Nadia retrieved it and handed it to Maya, who flicked back to the news. On the coffee table, Nadia's TOEFL certificate was proudly displayed, but although it had brought her promotion at work and the chance to move out of her father's house and into a small two-bedroom place, she and her new room-mate were having teething problems after two days of living together.

Maya and Nadia hadn't grown bored of watching the pull-out on television, even though the images were now a few days old.

'Did you have another fight with your mum?' Nadia asked Maya, not taking her eyes off the television.

'Put *The Real World* back on. You guys suck!' Nadia's room-mate cut in. They ignored her. A Valley girl who had never been to America, she had an American accent learned from sitcoms, and would surely be disappointed to discover that very few Americans sounded anything like her.

'I stormed out again,' Maya said. 'She still hasn't forgiven me for some things I said to Mrs Jihad.'

'How is James?' Nadia asked.

'I don't know.' Maya exhaled her answer, shaking her head.

'You're still seeing each other . . .'

'His video has been delayed, so we kind of . . . until he leaves, we're carrying on.'

Whenever Maya thought about the secrecy, the practicalities of their relationship, she forgot the things that had made it worthwhile, so she turned the conversation on to Nadia. 'How's Hakim?'

'He tried to call Dr Dre from my cell phone. I had a bill for two hundred dollars. I dumped him. He said it was *wack*.' Nadia shrugged. 'Listen, Maya. It's a public holiday, let's do something. I feel like celebrating.' She picked up her TOEFL qualification and waved it around excitedly.

'I don't know.'

'*Come on*,' Nadia said, pulling a reluctant Maya out of

her chair. Finally, Maya allowed herself a smile and followed her friend outside, where they climbed into Nadia's
new, but very second-hand, car.

'Where is James doing his video?' Nadia asked, starting
up the engine.

'I don't know, somewhere in the south.'

'Is that a good idea at the moment?' Nadia said, pulling
out, looking at the 425 flags hanging from the buildings
on her street. 'Why don't you call him?'

'I've tried but his phone is out of range.'

Nadia drove along the empty streets. Most of the shops
were still shut, but as on all extended public holidays a
few had stayed open. They ducked into Arabian Sands to
buy an ice cream but Abu Khalil had sold out. Something
was smouldering at the back of his shop, but he seemed
uninterested, so the girls left, not knowing that later that
day Arabian Sands would narrowly escape another potential inferno.

Maya's phone rang. Nadia couldn't help smiling as
Maya's face lit up as she grabbed it out of her bag and
checked the number. It kept ringing.

'Why aren't you answering it?' Nadia asked.

Maya let it ring. The feeling of dread that eight numbers
in a certain order could give her was permeating her body.
She didn't answer and she didn't switch it off; either would
have been like admitting she was there.

'What's the matter?' Nadia asked, as Maya stared at her
phone display. '*What?*' Nadia raised her voice.

'It's Walid's number.'

Nadia slowed down and leaned over to check Maya's

phone, like an irritated parent investigating their off-spring's wild claim about having lost their money. Nadia saw the numbers – Maya's automatic redial was displaying his name. *Walid*.

'Do you think he's back?' Maya's face had lost its colour. She was breathing irregularly, appealing to Nadia to give her the answer.

'Okay, let's think here . . .' Nadia said, trying to be calm. 'I thought he was in jail in Paris.'

'So did I.'

'Look, he's probably still there. Maybe someone else is messing around with his phone.'

Maya agreed half-heartedly. 'I don't feel like doing anything now. Can we just go back to your apartment and sit around there?'

'*Shu*, you don't want to go and get ice cream?'

'Ice cream then back to your place,' Maya agreed.

Nadia stopped outside an ice-cream parlour and shouted their order from the pavement. A man delivered two cones to them in their car. Maya raised a smile at Nadia's drive-by technique.

Nadia turned the car around and headed back to her apartment, balancing her ice cream in one hand while steering with the other.

'It always looks so easy when you do this and drive at the same time,' Nadia said, trying to lighten the mood.

Nadia pulled up behind Maya's car, which was parked right outside her new apartment building. Across the road, the light bounced off the dark blue shine of a new Mercedes. It was one of those vehicles that seemed to pass through the streets without making a noise, the silent shark that cruised along, knowing everything would get out of its way. Nadia switched the engine off and was about to get out of the car when Maya grabbed her arm, stopping her from moving.

'The Mercedes over there.' Maya's voice was a whisper.

Nadia gasped. 'Oh, *shit*.' She started her car back up and took off down the street. The sighting of a dark blue Mercedes was nothing special in Beirut. They were everywhere. But it was a sight that made Maya's pulse race. Walid was looking for her.

'Maybe you can speak to him,' Nadia suggested. 'We'll talk to him together.'

'That won't work.'

'I think you should confront him.'

'How? I'm not going back to him, and he'll just go and have a little word in my mother's ear if I do anything he doesn't like,' Maya said as she dialled James's number, cursing when the Libancell automated voice told her it was out of range.

'Maya, listen to me. You have to calm down.'

'Walid is at your apartment,' Maya said, as if she needed to hear herself say it out loud to confirm it was true.

'Tell me what you want to do.'

'I want to go to my house.'

No one was at home at Maya's, and Mrs Hayek wouldn't be back for a couple of hours. As they walked in, Imelda leapt off the couch and started looking busy.

'It's okay, Imelda.' Maya indicated that the maid didn't have to put on a show for them. Imelda beamed at her and sat back down.

In the bedroom, Nadia watched as her best friend grabbed piles of clothes, still on hangers, and threw them into a suitcase. 'What the hell are you doing?'

'I'm leaving,' Maya said.

'Leaving where?'

'I'm going to university.'

'You're going to America? Now?'

Maya closed up the suitcase and hauled it out of her bedroom. She pushed past Nadia on her way to the living room, then froze in the hallway when she heard the doorbell.

It rang again.

Maya didn't move. She thought she could smell Walid's brand of cigarette permeate the house. She could feel his rough hands on her skin when he fastened a new necklace around her neck. She lunged to stop Imelda from answering it. Then, as it rang a third time, her thoughts switched. What if it was James? He could have finished his shoot and be back in Beirut.

There was nothing she could do when Imelda answered the door on the next ring. She and Nadia stood out of sight, while Imelda calmly told Mrs Jihad that the whole family was out.

'What about money?' Nadia whispered.

'I have enough to start,' Maya replied, pushing herself up against a wall to keep out of Mrs Jihad's eyeline.

'But I thought—'

'I have enough to start,' Maya repeated as Imelda shut the front door and locked it. 'It'll have to do.'

'What do I tell James?'

Hassan kept watch by his brother's hospital bed as the hours slipped by. James sat a little farther away, keeping watch on Hassan. Hassan's mother had hugged both brothers when she saw her lost son for the first time in ten years. It surprised Hassan that she could, even then, show love to both her boys at the same time. Hassan was welcomed back.

'You should get some sleep,' James said to him quietly.

'I'm okay,' he replied. Outside the window, it was first light. 'My mother will be here in an hour. I'll sleep then.'

As the first dull rays crept through the window, Majed slept, the light on his face illuminating the details of his scars. In Majed's half-sleep, he heard the hollow sounds of prison – the guards shouting, detainees whispering to each other. While he lay there, some of his fellow detainees were taking part in a parade through Beirut, people cheering as the truck moved slowly through the streets. The men on board were weak and ill, but they were all smiling. Majed was not the only one who couldn't take part – others were also suffering from panic attacks and weren't able to get out of bed. These people, Majed's fellow detainees, were lying in the other beds on the ward. At least one of them wouldn't make it to the end of the week. After Majed's initial euphoria at seeing his family again, the dark thoughts of what had happened to him crept back and wouldn't let him sleep. These were the first minutes of peace he'd had for ten years, as he lay there with his brother's hand holding his. He was suffering from trauma to the head, arms and genitals. The doctors said it was unlikely he would ever be able to have children, but Hassan had kept this to himself. The family would deal with one thing at a time. For the moment, Hassan tried to make the situation as easy as he could for his parents.

James and Hassan looked at Majed as they spoke to each other. 'Do you think things will be better now the pull-out has happened?' James asked softly.

'Nothing in Lebanon ever finishes that quickly. We have to wait and see,' Hassan said, taking his eyes away from Majed for a brief moment. 'We already have one day of independence for the end of French rule. The Israelis leaving was number two. And when the Syrians leave I suppose we'll have number three.'

Majed would recover. A few months later, close to the end of the year – and after surgery on four separate occasions – he was moving well considering the injuries he had sustained. The mental injuries would take longer to heal. Perhaps they never would. As the months passed, as his body slowly mended, it craved exercise. But his mind trapped him, wanting only darkness and solitude in his bedroom. It was all it knew.

Returning to the prison was what finally drew Majed out of his small room at his parents' house. And as the sun beat down on Khiam prison it no longer stung Majed's eyes. He looked around the room that he had been tortured in; he saw where the guards had gassed detainees during a riot; he ran his hand along his old bunk bed, and remembered the men that had also lived in there. The man who had shared his bunk had been strong enough to resist the guards' torture and would not give them the information they wanted, and Majed remembered how they had kidnapped the man's wife and tortured her in the next room while he listened.

Majed picked his way slowly down the narrow corridor as the line of people behind him obediently followed. He led the group outside, passing another ex-detainee who was at the head of a group of Canadians and Norwegians, a man whose stories of life in prison were so appalling that his audience could barely process such horror. They simply had no frame of reference.

Khiam was now a tourist site, a very open prison.

Majed didn't have Westerners in his group of tourists, they weren't even strangers, but as they emerged back into the winter sunlight from the dark corridors their faces were solemn from what they had witnessed. In the courtyard, Majed squeezed his mother's hand – this woman who for ten years had laid an extra place at every mealtime for her lost son. Majed's father was a few feet away, his head hung low, just repeating, 'How could they? *How could they?*' Haj Ahmad and Mahmoud also stood close by – Mahmoud had been just an infant when Majed was kidnapped, and had greeted his new cousin with excitement, and promises to introduce him to the pleasures of Counterstrike.

Majed felt an arm over his shoulder, he felt the warmth. He and Hassan had the same eyes. The whole family had that unbreakable link between them. They didn't say anything to each other as they continued the tour. The pull-out was now a memory, but as they drove home through the south, they heard explosions in Shebaa farms. Hizbollah and the Israeli army were fighting over this last piece of territory. The UN claimed that Shebaa farms were Syrian, therefore the pull-out was finished. So did Israel. Syria and Lebanon claimed they were Lebanese. Hassan knew that nothing in the Middle East ever finished.

Majed's route back to the prison, and his new job as a guide, was still in the future, but now his future was at last beginning, and with the first flicker of his eyelids in the morning sunlight that was now pouring through the hospital windows, he started his journey home.

Hassan looked at James. 'You go back to Beirut,' he whispered. 'You've been here for days.'

'When will your mother get here?' James asked.

'Ten, fifteen minutes.'

'Okay,' James said, standing up, looking at Majed in the narrow bed, then back at Hassan sitting next to him. 'He's going to get better, Hassan. He just needs to rest.'

Hassan nodded in agreement as he brushed Majed's hair away from his eyes.

Maya's hand was clenched into a fist, crumpling the ticket she was holding. She told the taxi-driver to hurry, and he did as he was told, slowing down only for her to run into the travel agent's, and then once more at the checkpoint outside Beirut airport where the young

Lebanese soldiers waved them on. Maya paid the taxi-driver and lugged her bags into Departures. This time she was going to leave the country and leave it behind properly. She wasn't taking Lebanon with her on this trip. She looked up and down the long hallway, half expecting to see James there, waiting for her. Years of watching movies have created this expectation in people when they arrive at airports. She imagined him coming up behind her and putting his arms around her, leaning in and kissing her. She put her bags on to the scanner and walked through the detector. There was no beep. Her hand luggage was Walid's wallet bag, still with her passport inside, together with a small amount of cash, a mobile phone, her cashpoint card which would work once she got to America, and a pair of earrings that James had bought her. She couldn't remember which clothes she had thrown in her suitcase; she had done it in such a rush she could have put in ten pairs of socks and nothing else. As she reached for her passport her hand found something unfamiliar in the bag. She pulled it out – it was Walid's mini-Filofax. She dumped it in the rubbish bin.

'Did you pack this yourself?' the girl at the check-in asked. Maya answered her and lifted the suitcase on to the weighing machine. The girl punched in some numbers then attached a tag to it. Maya watched as her suitcase disappeared along the conveyor belt, took her ticket back, then walked over to Immigration.

The immigration officer wore a dark green uniform and didn't look any older than she was. His pale face was clean shaven and he smiled as he took her passport and typed the number into his computer. Maya looked at the corridor that led from the immigration booths; at the end of it were the departure gates. A missing passenger's name was announced over the hollow Tannoy as the people waiting in line behind Maya filled in their pink departure forms.

'There is a problem,' the pale officer mumbled. Maya knew her passport had years left on it before it expired, but she said nothing as the officer called over to a superior. The superior grandly introduced himself as Mr Ramzi before examining Maya's passport. He had kind eyes and a thick moustache flecked with grey, and spoke brusquely to the pale officer.

'There is nothing wrong with this.'

The officer pointed to his screen, so Mr Ramzi impatiently leaned over to look at it for himself. Maya relaxed slightly – the officer was just a rookie who didn't know what he was doing. Mr Ramzi then typed her passport number into the machine himself and looked at Maya, as if to comment on his inferior, *These kids don't know anything*. He nodded when the display was updated, and turned it at an angle so Maya couldn't see.

'Please,' he said, motioning for Maya to walk through. He led her into a small room with two chairs and a full ashtray on the table. 'You would like coffee?' he asked. Maya shook her head. 'Please,' he said, motioning for her to take a seat. She resisted, but then gave in when she realised the conversation wasn't going to start until she did as he wished. 'Mademoiselle . . . Hayek,' he said, looking at her passport. 'I am sorry, there is a travel restriction on your name.'

Maya didn't answer straight away. She had once been accused of shoplifting in a clothes store on Hamra Street. After the accusation, she had briefly felt as if she were watching herself from somewhere else in the room, monitoring events on a closed circuit television screen. For a split second she had questioned whether she *had* in fact stolen something. When she allowed the security guard to check her bag, he found that she did have an item that the store sold, but she had purchased it somewhere else. The guard had apologised profusely when he found another store's price ticket attached to it. Now she was waiting for Mr Ramzi to do the same. Perhaps she had filled out a form incorrectly; perhaps there was another Maya Hayek.

'You are not allowed to leave without permission,' Mr Ramzi told her. Maya watched him pour her a small plastic cup of coffee. It seemed absurd for him to think she would want to drink anything.

'What are you talking about?' Maya asked.

'Women are not allowed to travel without permission from either their husband or father.'

Maya didn't know why he was talking around the subject – everyone knew the rule existed but was never enforced. Women travelled freely. Unless a father or husband had exercised his right specifically to register his daughter or wife's name at the airport because he feared they were going to run away.

'I promise you, my father did not put on a restriction.'

'I will not make any calls, but I suggest you go home,' Mr Ramzi said. He sipped his coffee, then wiped his moustache. Maya could see from his eyes that he thought he was doing her a favour by not calling her family.

'Tell me at least when this restriction was put on.'

Mr Ramzi sighed. When he saw the large tear fall down Maya's cheek, then land on her top, making a tiny damp impression on it, he gave in. 'Two days ago.'

'Impossible. My father is in Abu Dhabi.'

Mr Ramzi shrugged and stood up, then motioned for Maya to do the same. She was certain this was not her father's style. But only a husband or father could do this. Or someone who could pass for a fiancé, with the kind of money to make it happen. Walid had trapped her.

'I'm asking you,' Maya pleaded. 'Let me through. I'm not married. My father didn't do this.'

'It's not my business who put the restriction on. I do not meddle in people's lives.'

'Thank you *so* much for respecting my privacy,' Maya spat back at him.

Mr Ramzi escorted her back through the departure lounge, and arranged for her baggage to be taken off the aircraft and returned to her. Then he left her, alone with her tears, outside the airport. Maya looked around at other travellers as they arrived: families, businessmen, students. They would soon be busy with those mundane distractions: watching the movie, eating the processed food, all the things which somehow cleverly disguised the fact that aircraft not only transported salesmen around but also took people to and from great moments in their lives. The ease with which they passed through the airport ridiculed Maya's failed efforts.

Across the road, the taxi-driver who had brought her to the airport was watching closely. He was smoking a cigarette, tipping the ash out of the window, beckoning for her to walk over to him. His radio played *'Ya ghazaly'* – a summer hit that boomed out of cars throughout the city. Maya could hear the same song, but at different stages, emanating from at least two other vehicles. It was so cheery she wanted to rip the tapes out and stamp on them in the street.

'Where do you want to go?' he asked, turning down the radio as Maya walked towards him. Her phone rang and she snatched at it, dropping her bags on the ground.

'Maya, it's me,' James said. 'Where are you?' Maya didn't know what to say to him. She couldn't form a sentence. 'Tell me where you are and I'll come and get you,' he said.

'Where've you *been*?' Maya said accusingly.

'I'm on my way back from the south. I just got a call from Nadia.' James could hear airport announcements in the background. 'Where are you?'

'Walid is back,' Maya said. 'I'm leaving.'

'Leaving for where?'

'I'm going.'

James softened his voice. 'Maya, just tell me where you are, okay?'

'I don't think the French authorities could hold him any longer,' Maya said. Her sentences were coming out in random order. 'I went to the airport. They wouldn't let me leave.'

'I'm an hour away from Beirut. Come to my flat and we'll sort it out.'

'I can't. There's nothing you can do,' Maya said, wiping her eyes with her free hand.

'Just get into a taxi and come to my house,' James said, as if he were talking a suicidal jumper down from a bridge.

'I'm going to Damascus.'

'Listen to me. You don't have to do that. Who stopped you leaving?'

'There's a restriction on me.'

'*What?* Who can do that?'

'Walid knew I would try this. He'll find me if I don't go now.' Maya's voice was cold, there was no feeling left in it. 'If I take a taxi to Damascus I can be there in three hours. No one can stop me flying out of Syria.'

'Damascus no problem,' the taxi-driver interrupted, seeing dollar signs.

'You're not going to Syria,' James said.

The taxi-driver was becoming impatient, but Maya gestured for him to stay, so he lit up another cigarette and turned his music back up.

'It's the only way to clear this up. It's too complicated,' she said.

'Get in the taxi and come to my house,' James pleaded as his bus wound its way north, the tracks becoming roads, the checkpoints now less frequent. As soon as he had finished the call to Maya he rang Hassan. On the outskirts of Beirut he jumped into a taxi and gave the driver his address: the apartment block on Bliss Street, close to Arabian Sands, opposite the dry-cleaning place.

As they approached his apartment, water started spraying up from the road. A drain had burst and flooded the street, already hot and slick with a film of petrol and oil residue. James's taxi found a new elegance spinning 270 degrees in the middle of the road. When they came to rest – having miraculously missed everyone and everything – the driver crossed himself. Other taxis skidded in similar patterns, creating a kind of synchronised swimming for cars.

James paid the driver and ran the rest of the way, water splashing up from his shoes. When he got to his apartment, Maya was sitting in front of his door, her arms folded across her knees, her hair falling over her face, covering her eyes. She looked up when she heard his footsteps.

'Here's what we're doing,' James stated bluntly as he unlocked the door and they entered the apartment. 'You're staying the night here. Walid doesn't know this place. If he speaks to Nadia she's not going to tell him. You're safe here. Tomorrow we're going to pay off the bribe and you can leave.'

'How?' Maya asked. She was exhausted and lay back on the bed with her arm over her eyes.

'Hassan can help us. I called him and he's coming to Beirut tomorrow to tell me how to do it. Then I'm taking you to the airport and you're leaving.'

'*Habibi*,' Maya intoned softly. Her face was streaked with red. She walked over to James and moulded herself into him. He wrapped his arms around her slender body;

she buried her head in his shirt. Tied tightly together, they stood there for a moment.

Ending the silence, Maya said something James wasn't expecting. 'Do you miss home?'

'I miss the privacy. And no one ever has any change here,' James answered, not letting her go.

'I would miss privacy if I'd had it.'

'Why do you ask?'

'I wonder if there's anything I'll miss about this country.'

James didn't like watching Maya dwell on what she was about to do, it wouldn't help her, so he took two beers from the fridge and said, 'You know the transvestite beach up the coast where they all dance around and have a great time? I wonder what their neighbours say?'

'They don't give a fuck about their neighbours,' Maya said, sipping her drink, and allowing herself to laugh for a moment. 'That's why they've got it made.'

The clock ticked as James and Maya lay in bed on their last night together. When Maya spoke to him, she whispered, that strange natural reaction people have to darkness. James could hear the words 'I love you' on his breath, so quietly only his subconscious could make them out. But Maya squeezed his arm gently as he thought the words. He was sure she had heard them. Perhaps there was a way you could hold someone that would be impossible to do if you didn't love them. Fran had leaned on James's shoulder and slept on the train back from Paris, but that had injected only enough life into him to continue the relationship until their next problem. With Maya he felt he had everything he would ever need, and although there would always be problems, the solution seemed to be in matching two people with an equal will to keep going.

Behind the sound of the clock ticking was the barely audible whirr of the mechanism that pushed the hands around. It was the sound of time being pushed forward, cruelly, always forward. It was ending their last night together, and starting a day when some people would end up in hospital, others would lose their jobs, others might lose someone they loved. James would watch Maya leave. Nothing could reverse the rising light that had already woken India and Pakistan and Iran, and would soon bring morning to their little apartment on the edge of the Middle East. Even if James and Maya kept talking, even if Maya spun tales to prolong the night and keep the realities of the next day at bay, they would eventually have to give in. As the first light of dawn came through the windows, James could feel himself let go of her; he held her tightly as she slept but a part of him let her go. She had to leave the country and he would get her out.

They were ready to leave when Hassan arrived.

'In Lebanon lots of things are done under the table,' he said, as if he were instructing James on how to play blackjack. 'Sometimes they're done over the table. *Under, over* – sometimes there *is* no table because someone took it.'

'Stop talking about tables,' James said.

'You have the money, right?'

James nodded. Inside an envelope was two thousand dollars saved from his teaching. Apart from what he had spent on rent and hiring film equipment, it was his entire earnings, and it was looking decidedly unimpressive: twenty hundred-dollar bills stuffed in a brown envelope. He had kept just enough back to pay off his final rent, and hadn't even considered how he would pay for the rest of the video.

'So you've got your envelope, and that's what you're going to give this guy to show "good trust" and your "confidence" in him. You have to make him feel important.'

'Do you think it will work?' Maya asked.

'It will work,' Hassan replied. He paused for a moment and looked at Maya. 'Are you okay?'

She smiled. 'Thanks, Hassan.'

Waz-waz concierge helped Maya take her bags downstairs, leaving James and Hassan in the room together.

'You know it would never have been okay for you and Maya, not as long as you were here,' Hassan said. As James paced around his room, Hassan could sense he was running through different ideas, ways to stop what had started. Finally, sighing, he bowed to the inevitable. 'Look, if it's the video you're worried about, I'm *chief* assistant director – Julien and I can finish it off and send it to England next week. Del Pico can have his tape.'

James didn't know what to say. He thought for a moment. 'You'll explain to Julien?'

'Of course.'

'I don't know . . .' James said, weighing it up in his mind while his body, having already made its decision, was throwing clothes into his bag, grabbing them violently and stuffing them inside. He handed Hassan his

rent money, keeping enough back for a ticket for himself.

'Will you settle with the concierge for me? Tell him I'll
post the rest.'

'No problem.'

James got downstairs and ran towards the car. Maya
was already in the passenger seat. Before James got in, he
turned around to Hassan and smiled.

'What's Del Pico's address?' Hassan shouted after him.
'So we can send it.'

'Send it directly to me,' James replied. 'I'm going to
produce myself from now on.'

'What were you and Hassan talking about?' Maya asked
as James pulled up on the pavement outside the airline
office on Hamra Street. 'Why're you stopping?' Her voice
was fragile and nervous.

James looked at her.

'What are you doing?' Maya said.

'When does your semester start?'

'Two months.'

'I don't want this to be over because you're scrambling
to get away from Walid.'

'I have to leave right away, you *know* that. Don't bail
out on me now,' Maya said, her voice desperate, her hands
trembling.

'How about a stopover in England?' James asked. He
watched Maya process the idea.

'For how long?'

'As long as you like. Five minutes. For ever.'

She hesitated for a moment, then smiled her answer back at him. That was James's cue to run into the airline office, returning quickly with a ticket, then slamming his foot on the accelerator without looking behind him. The car skipped off the pavement and shot down the middle of the road. The stereo was old, tinny and so loud it made Maya's ears hurt. She switched it off.

'Don't turn that off. Fairuz helps me drive,' James said. He pulled up to an intersection, stuck the nose of the car firmly out in the middle. An SUV, coming in the other direction, sneaked past, blocking him in.

'What are you doing? Get out of the way!' James's hand was on the horn for twenty seconds. The man in the SUV backed up, waved James through with a smile. James nodded 'thanks' to him, as if they were both friends again. Maya wished she could love Lebanon as much as James did.

'What happens if they don't take the bribe?' Maya asked, as James drove down the highway to the airport, slaloming around the huge potholes in the road. Some were two foot deep and could rip off a car wheel in a second; others were covered with car tyres. One got caught on the chassis of Maya's car and they dragged it for a few yards before it broke itself loose. Going in the opposite direction on the highway, as if part of a relay race, were minibuses and taxis taking people from the airport and feeding them into the city.

* * *

'I'll be back in a minute,' James said, as they entered the airport. Maya waited in a small corridor next to the cleaners' room, out of sight. James located Mr Ramzi and asked to speak to him privately.

'This travel restriction was a mistake,' he said. 'Surely you can understand that sometimes these errors are made. I wanted to speak to you directly because being a very important man you would understand that sometimes your subordinates cause these problems when they are left in charge. A busy man like yourself doesn't have time to check every single thing they do.' *Make him feel he is important.*

'I understand your concern, but I believe the restriction was legitimate.' Mr Ramzi wasn't budging.

James's mouth was dry, his hands damp with perspiration. He wondered whether his opponent could tell. He accepted the offer of coffee, and while Mr Ramzi poured him a cup he took the envelope from his pocket. He passed his one and only shot over to Mr Ramzi, who kept his poker face, but couldn't stop his moustache twitching.

'I want to show my good trust,' James said as he let go of the envelope. 'To show my confidence that you will be able to rectify this situation. I'm sure some *new* employee caused this mess.'

'We have had a lot of young people working here recently,' Mr Ramzi agreed. 'I will be back in a few minutes,' he added, leaving to inspect the envelope more closely in private.

James found Maya in the same place, sitting on her suitcase. 'I don't think this is going to work,' she said, her hand nervously over her mouth.

'It's going to work.'

They waited in silence for Mr Ramzi, listening to the calls for passengers, watching people say hello and good-bye. When he appeared in the distance he looked sour faced. James and Maya walked quickly towards him. Suddenly a hand grabbed Maya's arm, a strong male hand that halted her abruptly. He was stocky and wore jeans and a black T-shirt.

'Are you Maya? Maya Hayek?'

It was Walid's cousin. Maya recalled meeting him once, very briefly, but she was now thinking so quickly, the adrenalin pumping so hard, that he wouldn't have been able to sense the slightest pause, the tiniest hesitation, before she replied, 'No. No I'm not.'

'Mademoiselle, if you would like to follow me,' Mr Ramzi interrupted. James thought Mr Ramzi was smiling at that moment, but it may just have been his imagination. Mr Ramzi personally escorted Maya swiftly through security, then Immigration, and she was soon walking down the corridor towards the departure gate, eyes sparkling, clutching her freshly stamped passport as if it were a trophy.

James checked in and let his bags go through. He hadn't had time to pack all his things. He didn't need them. He cruised through Immigration, having his exit marked on the cedar tree in his passport. Then he raced up the corridor to catch up with Maya.

epilogue

The man in the neat suit one size too small for him left his car hitched up on the pavement, a short walk from the battered elegance of the Hayeks' Ashrafieh house. He carried the gifts that had sat on his passenger seat during the drive: some perfume for Mrs Hayek and a bracelet for Maya. He hoped she would like it; he hated picking out jewellery, always unsure whether it would be to the recipient's taste. There didn't seem to be any lights on in the house as he approached, trying to contain his breaking smile and the urge to run to the door in excitement. There was a rotund woman in her fifties sitting on the balcony opposite. He caught her eye and she looked away, pretending not to be interested. He waved at her anyway; he would have waved at anybody. He worked through what he was going to say then rang the doorbell. When the maid answered the door – Imelda was her name if he remembered correctly, and he remembered *every* detail about the Hayeks – he spoke to her in Arabic.

'I am here to see Maya. Please tell her I have arrived.'

'What is your name?' Imelda asked. The man paused for a second, to infer that she should know who he was.

When she said nothing, squinting at him as if she thought

he had forgotten his own name, he announced, 'Maroun Fouad Abu Abdullah.'

Imelda shut the door, and when it opened again Mrs Hayek was standing in the doorway. It was playing out just as Maroun had hoped.

'Hello,' she said. There was a naturally friendly lilt to her voice.

'Hello, Mrs Hayek,' Maroun continued in Arabic. 'It is wonderful to see you again. I am Maroun. We met briefly when I took Maya out to dinner last year.'

'Maroun, of course,' Mrs Hayek said. She motioned for him to enter the house.

'It was quite a long time ago,' Maroun said, making small talk as he followed her inside.

'Yes, it was. How is your work?'

'It's going very well. Thanks to God.'

'Please, sit down,' Mrs Hayek said, instantly producing coffee and some cakes arranged neatly on a plate. Maroun tucked into them gladly, and Mrs Hayek was too polite to mention that some of the icing sugar had become lodged in the corners of his mouth, giving him a clownish smile.

'So you have kept in touch with Maya?' Mrs Hayek asked.

'Oh yes. We have exchanged many e-mails while I was working in Kuwait. I tried to call her but she has been very busy.'

'What brings you back?'

'I am here for work and of course to pay your family a visit.'

'You are very welcome,' Mrs Hayek said.

Maroun looked through the open door into an adjoining room, where five or six large cardboard boxes were stacked on top of each other. The room had been cleared of furniture. He brought his focus back to Mrs Hayek. 'I brought you a gift.'

'That is so kind,' she replied, opening the beautifully wrapped box and taking out the perfume. 'It's lovely. Thank you.'

'I brought this one for Maya,' Maroun added, showing her the other parcel. He could feel excitement speed through his body – he could already envisage Maya walking down the stairs to greet him, making the entrance of a 1940s Italian film star. It had been so long since their dinner; he had so much he wanted to say to her. Finally, they would be able to speak properly, in Arabic, and he could tell her how he felt.

'You are very kind, Maroun,' Mrs Hayek said. He noticed the tone of her voice change; she was more careful in her choice of words, and she wasn't as relaxed. 'Did you speak to Maya before you came back?'

'No, I wanted it to be a surprise,' he replied, putting another cake into his mouth. He stood up. 'Will you call her?' he said, looking towards the stairs and the imaginary future wife that he thought was up there, waiting to receive his present.

'Maroun, I'm afraid she isn't here.'

Maroun thought this through, then spoke carefully. 'Mrs Hayek, I should have called first. It is no problem, I know she works very hard. I can arrange to visit perhaps at a weekend when it is more convenient.'

'She's not in Lebanon.'

Again, Maroun wanted his words to be well chosen, but this time 'Where is she?' came out before he could stop it.

'She's in England,' Mrs Hayek said. Maroun sat back down as if someone had punctured him and he no longer could support his own weight. As the couch swallowed him, he studied his knees, like a child who had been scolded. 'I thought you knew,' Mrs Hayek added. She thought she saw Maroun wipe a tear from his eye, but it may have been irritation from the dust that taking down old curtains and moving furniture around had created.

'Would you like some more coffee?' she asked, giving Maroun a chance to say no and make his exit.

'Yes please,' he said. She was surprised, but walked into the kitchen to get the long-handled pot, then refilled Maroun's cup.

'So . . . are you spring cleaning?' he asked, trying to pull himself together, pointing to the cardboard boxes.

The last male visitor to Mrs Hayek's house had not been given cakes. He had got his timing very wrong; he had lasted a fraction of the time that Maroun did. Walid had visited on the day that Mrs Hayek found out her daughter had left. And she blamed Walid, who was standing in *her* house, telling her lies about *her* daughter. It didn't matter how she would have reacted had Maya told her in advance, that she would have tried to stop her, that she would have listened to Walid. It was too late for that. Maya was gone, and she just wanted Walid out of her home.

'We're moving house, Maroun,' Mrs Hayek said. 'I've decided to join my husband in Abu Dhabi.'

'I see,' Maroun replied, looking at his feet. Everywhere around him couples were making sacrifices for each other. It was as if they were doing it just to spite him, showing off their intimacy.

'It must have been hard to be apart,' he mumbled.

'I missed him very much. But he had to be there for his work,' she explained.

'I'm sure you will be happy there.'

'I think so,' Mrs Hayek replied, looking through the window at Mrs Jihad on her balcony. Maroun fell silent, and Mrs Hayek didn't know what to do apart from bring more cakes. He thanked her but said he had to go. He stood up, the icing sugar still on his lips.

'Mrs Hayek. Will you please give Maya a message for me. Please tell her that I wish her luck and God bless her,' he said. 'I hope good things happen for her. She deserves it.'

Mrs Hayek smiled. Maroun shook her hand as he left, then from the doorway she watched as he walked away, down the street, one present still unopened under his arm. Then she closed the door softly and went back to packing up her old life into boxes.

Maroun was alone in the street. Emotions were rushing through him, blocking the little pieces of information he needed, such as where he had parked his car. He stooped, his head hung low. When he tried to cross the road he was beaten back by a pizza delivery moped which buzzed past him, going the wrong way up the one-way street. Maroun remained on the pavement until he judged it was safe. He crossed over and realised he didn't want to get back into his car.

Imelda, Dilki and two other maids walked past him, chatting away to each other as they hauled their houses' overflowing bin bags towards the large green rubbish bins at the end of the street. They helped each other lift the bags into the bin, then ambled back to their separate houses, ending their short social break for the day.

The smell coming from the bin was overpowering as Maroun approached. He leaned over it, and among the rotten bananas, pieces of car tyre and soggy unidentifiable remains of people's households he gently placed Maya's present. A skinny cat toured the perimeter of the rubbish bin, eyeing its next meal inside. Maroun turned around and stood in the middle of the street, first looking to the left and then to the right. The city was busy, everyone was overtaking him. Cars and people and shops. Music boomed from a nearby record shop that had its doors open. The cat made its dive into the rubbish bin. Maroun wasn't sure which way to walk, so he just followed the streets, into whatever Beirut held for him.

THANK YOU:

As always, to my parents for their never-ending support. To Patrick Walsh and Helen Garnons-Williams for all their work. And to Ziad Doueiri, Ayssar Arida, Makram and Sumaya Kubeisy, Tom Bromley, Lisa Hoftijzer and Annika Hampson. Also a big thank you to Nicholas Blincoe.

And to the hundreds of people who answered questions in person or via e-mail especially Mai, Leila, Raja, Sarah, Anna, Marilyn and Nigel.

And for their hospitality, thanks to Kathy, Robert and MC; Hussni, Alex and Kristin; Nadeem. And to Hanan for the encouragement.

Any mistakes or inaccuracies are all my own work.